Angry Andie

Spoils of Vengeance

A Novel by E.S. Bennett

A 2025 Megaverse City Publication

ISBN: 979-8-218-99970-4

Library of Congress #2025912344

Cover Design: Exlus S. Bennett
Interior Formatting: Megaverse City L.L.C.
Printed in the United States of America
First Edition

DEDICATION PAGE

To every unheard voice, every survivor who fought silently,
and every soul who rose from ruin—
This is for you.

Also dedicated to

Victoria 'Tori' Shropshire

and

James 'The Flash' Phillips

TABLE OF CONTENTS

Just a Girl

(Ode for Andrea Montgomery)

They called her names no child should hear,
With every glare, they made it clear.
Too quiet, too plain, too strange to save—
They handed her silence, then dug her a grave.

"Smile more."
"Wear this."
"Don't be so tough."
But when she broke, it still wasn't enough.
Words became razors—sharp, unseen,
Cutting through armor she'd never been given.

They said, *"Boys will be boys,"* with a laugh in their eyes.
She screamed in her soul, but no one heard cries.
The house held no warmth, just the clatter of rage,
A father's fist, a mother's cage.

They whispered *slut,* though she'd never kissed.
They branded her wrong for simply *exist-*
ing. A girl with no say, no shield, no guide,
Just pain that grew louder the more she'd hide.

She bled in silence, stitched wounds with shame,
Learned how to vanish, then shoulder the blame.
Until rage took root, quiet and deep,
Waking the vengeance that wouldn't sleep.

Now they stare in fear at the girl they forgot—
Too broken to mourn, too scarred to be caught.
No halo remains, no soft-hearted plea—
Only fire and fury where a child used to be.

Chapter One

Year of 2023

The Montgomery house was the last one on a dead-end street, tucked behind a rusting chain-link fence and a yard that hadn't been mowed in three summers. The mailbox leaned to the side like it had given up trying to stand straight, and the porch light had long since blown out. Inside, the air smelled of stale beer, old wood, and something sour that clung to the curtains.

Andrea "Andie" Montgomery had learned early how to move through the house without making a sound. It wasn't a trick — it was a survival instinct. She could sidestep creaking floorboards like a trained acrobat and knew exactly how far to turn a doorknob before it clicked. Every sound risked waking her father when he was passed out — and when Patrick Montgomery woke up angry, someone paid the price.

Patrick hadn't always been a monster. Or maybe he had and just hadn't shown it yet. He used to work at the steel mill before the layoffs, back when he still came home with sweat in his hair and grit under his nails. But after losing the job, something inside him curdled. He found a new routine: drinking from noon till blackout and blaming everything on someone else.

His wife Liz bore the brunt of it.

Most nights started the same. Dinner would be on the table — something simple Liz had made from whatever she could scrape together with EBT and coupons. Andie always helped, chopping onions or peeling potatoes while Billy babbled in his high chair. They'd plate up quietly, trying not to set him off.

If Patrick liked the meal, he grunted. If he didn't, the plate hit the wall. Sometimes Liz got slapped just for the way she looked at him when it happened.

Andie remembered one such night with painful clarity. She'd overcooked the rice. Patrick had tasted it, spat it out, and then hurled the ceramic bowl across the kitchen. It shattered near the sink. Billy started to cry. Liz apologized — not for the food, but for existing in that moment.

Patrick stood slowly. His belt was already off.

Liz tried to move between him and the kids, her hands raised like she could stop a train.

"Please, Pat," she whispered, eyes wide. "Don't—"

The first blow landed across her back. She dropped to her knees, shielding Billy's high chair with her body. Andie stood frozen near the table, a knife still in her hand from cutting carrots. Her chest throbbed, not from pain, but helplessness.

Afterward, when Patrick retreated to the couch and passed out with his mouth open and the TV still blaring, Andie crept to her mother's side.

Liz sat on the floor, silent tears rolling down her cheeks. Her hair clung to her damp skin. A thin cut ran along her temple where the belt buckle had nicked her.

Andie knelt beside her and pressed a cold cloth to the wound.

"You should go," Andie whispered. "He'll kill you."

Liz shook her head. "And go where? With what money?"

"We could hide," Andie said. "At the church. At Ms. Romero's house. She always said—"

Liz reached out, her hand trembling, and touched her daughter's cheek. "I won't leave you here alone with him. I can take it. I've always taken it."

Andie didn't know what to say. She wanted to scream, to drag her mother to the door, to shove her into the night and beg her to run. But she didn't. She sat there, still, and wiped the blood from her mother's face.

When Andie was ten, she started going to daily mass. Liz had taught her how to pray when she was little — how to light candles and bow her head and ask for protection. Andie started asking for something different.

Not for safety. Not even for rescue.

She asked God to kill her father.

And when the prayer went unanswered, she asked for the strength to kill him herself.

By the time she was fifteen, Andie had become the house's second mother. Kayan had married young and moved to France with her new husband, and Jarrod was stationed with the Army in Texas. That left Andie to raise Billy, manage the kitchen, help her mother with the bills, and maintain straight A's.

It wasn't out of obligation. It was out of fear. If she slipped — if any part of the fragile order cracked — someone would bleed.

Liz tried to shield her daughter from it all. On good days, they would bake something together, just the two of them, and pretend for half an hour that they lived in a world without fear. Liz would sing hymns softly under her breath, and Andie would roll dough with her elbows tucked in tight, mimicking everything her mother did. For a fleeting moment, the world was quiet.

Then Patrick would wake, or stumble in from the bar, and that moment would shatter.

One autumn evening, a week before Andie's seventeenth birthday, Liz came home with a split lip and bruised eye. She'd gone to the gas station to buy milk and had returned late. Patrick had assumed she'd been flirting. His words, not hers.

When Andie saw her mother's face, she didn't say anything. She just took her mother's hand, led her into the bathroom, and helped her sit on the toilet seat lid. She cleaned the blood off gently, working with the care of a nurse dressing a sacred wound.

"He's getting worse," Andie said.

"I know."

"You always say you'll leave one day."

Liz didn't answer. Instead, she reached up and brushed a lock of Andie's hair behind her ear.

"You're the best part of me, baby," Liz said quietly. "I pray you never become me."

Andie tried to smile, but her lips trembled. That night, when she knelt beside her bed, she didn't pray for rescue. She prayed for patience. For the ability to hold it all together. For the strength to endure one more day.

But she didn't know how many more days she had left before everything broke.

Jarrod Montgomery had been the first to understand that their father's rage wasn't just a phase.

He was nine years old the first time Patrick knocked him off his feet for spilling orange juice on the carpet. Patrick had been in one of his moods — seething from some layoff rumor or money argument — and when Jarrod apologized too quickly, too meekly, it only made the man angrier.

The backhand came so fast that Jarrod didn't even register the pain until he was on the floor with a ringing in his ears. That was the day he stopped being a child.

He began sleeping with his door locked. Started lifting weights in the backyard with a set of rusted dumbbells from a garage sale. He grew quiet and watchful. Jarrod wasn't afraid to fight back, but he knew fighting wouldn't win. It would only escalate. He needed to outlast the house.

And when he turned eighteen, he left.

No goodbye. No long letters.

He enlisted in the Army because it was the only way out with a roof, a paycheck, and a reason. He didn't love the idea of wearing a uniform or being deployed, but it was the only plan that didn't require permission or an application fee.

He sent money home at first — small amounts to help Liz — but over time, even that stopped. He answered Andie's first few texts. Then came the slow fade: longer reply gaps, fewer calls, and eventually silence. His absence was a wound Andie didn't talk about. He had been her protector once. Now he was just a ghost with dog tags.

Kayan, the oldest, had always been different. Sensitive. Private. She read books obsessively, wrote in notebooks that she never let anyone see, and kept to herself more often than not. She wasn't cold — just distant.

Patrick didn't hit her often. She made herself invisible. That was her shield.

Kayan would hide in closets or behind locked bathroom doors when he drank too much. She rarely intervened when Liz got slapped or when Jarrod shouted back and earned a black eye. But Andie remembered the way Kayan's hands trembled after — the way she sat in her room and tore the corners off her notebook pages in silence.

When Kayan turned nineteen, she met Gerard, a quiet French exchange student who worked part-time at the college library. He wasn't rich. He wasn't handsome. But he offered her one thing that no one else ever had: a ticket out.

They got married fast. No ceremony. No honeymoon. Just a courthouse license and a flight out of the country. Gerard's family lived in Marseille, and within a month, Kayan was gone.

Her final words to Andie had been, "You'll be okay. You're strong."

It wasn't a promise. It was a prayer of resignation.

Andie never blamed them — not at first.

She told herself Jarrod had to leave. That Kayan had to protect herself. That it was better for someone to get free.

But as time went on and the walls of the house seemed to lean inward, pressing tighter with each month, the forgiveness grew brittle.

There were nights when she cried in the closet with Billy asleep on her lap, and she imagined what it might be like to just disappear. To be in France, eating fresh bread and sipping coffee at a sunlit café. Or deployed somewhere far away, learning how to fire a weapon, answering to someone who wasn't her father.

But she didn't leave.

She stayed because Liz stayed. And Liz stayed for Billy.

The beatings got worse after Jarrod and Kayan were gone. Patrick's drinking intensified. There were fewer people to witness the abuse, fewer excuses to behave. Andie became the new target, and Liz — always trying to protect her daughter — absorbed what she could. Some nights Liz walked with a limp. Other times she used makeup thick enough to cake.

Andie had mastered the art of hiding a bruise. She wore hoodies year-round, grew her hair long to cover the marks on her neck, and learned how to lie with a smile.

But every lie made her feel more hollow.

One Thursday night, Patrick came home early. He'd been fired from another construction job for showing up drunk. The back door slammed so hard it made the fridge rattle.

Andie and Liz were in the living room watching a TV drama rerun while Billy colored on the carpet. Liz flinched at the sound.

Patrick was already yelling from the kitchen.

"I ain't gonna sit here while you two watch your trash. Where the hell's my dinner?"

"We already ate," Liz said, standing slowly. Her voice was calm, practiced. "We saved you a plate. It's in the oven."

"Saved me a plate," he mocked. "What, the leftovers? Like I'm some goddamn dog?"

"No, Pat. It's still warm."

"Don't lie to me."

He grabbed the plate from the oven and threw it on the floor. The casserole splattered against the linoleum.

Billy began to cry.

Andie stood quickly, moving toward her brother. Liz stepped between them, placing herself in the crosshairs.

Patrick was on her before Andie could blink — grabbing Liz by the arm and yanking her forward. "You treat me like I'm nothing in my own house!" he screamed.

"Patrick, please," Liz gasped.

He shoved her against the counter.

Andie screamed.

In a blur, she grabbed a wooden spoon from the table and struck Patrick's back. He turned with fire in his eyes, raised his hand—and froze.

Just for a moment. Just long enough.

Liz stood, shaking, and put herself in front of Andie again.

Patrick spat on the floor. "Next time, I won't stop," he said coldly.

Then he stumbled to the recliner and cracked open a beer from his jacket pocket.

The next morning, Liz woke Andie gently with a whisper.

"Don't speak," she said. "Just help me pack a bag."

The first time Liz tried to leave Patrick, Andie was thirteen. It was July, and the heat in the house pressed down like a wet towel over a flame. Andie had come home early from school orientation to find her mother sitting on the edge of her bed with a duffel bag in her lap.

"I'm going," Liz said. Her voice was flat, exhausted. She had a split lip and one arm tucked against her ribs where a bruise was blooming.

Andie didn't speak. She dropped her bag on the floor and sat beside her mother, knees touching. The fan in the corner rattled as it turned its tired head.

"I packed a few things for Billy," Liz continued. "Enough diapers and wipes for a couple of days. The shelter downtown said they might have space if I get there early. They don't usually take kids under five, but the woman sounded kind."

Andie looked at the bag, then at her mother's swollen face. "Why not go now?"

"I'm waiting for him to leave."

Patrick was passed out on the couch, a bottle resting on his stomach like a trophy. The midday news droned from the living room. Liz watched the clock like it might break her free.

But then the phone rang.

Liz picked it up on instinct — old habits. It was Patrick's brother, Gary, calling from two states over. He said he had a lead on work for Patrick — union gig, decent pay, if he could get clean. He wanted to talk to Liz. Wanted to see if Patrick was serious.

And just like that, the resolve drained from her eyes.

"I'll wait and talk to him," Liz said, setting the duffel down by her feet.

She never picked it up again.

The second time was months later, after a particularly brutal winter night. Patrick had come home covered in snow and fury, muttering about lost money and stolen tools. He blamed Liz for everything. Called her a "jinx" with venom in his voice.

He slammed her head against the kitchen cabinet.

She didn't scream. She didn't cry.

She locked herself in the bathroom while blood ran from her scalp, and she whispered to the reflection in the mirror, "You don't get to win."

Andie waited outside the door, whispering prayers through the wood.

The next morning, Liz called her cousin in Dayton and asked if she could stay for a few weeks.

"Of course," the cousin said. "You get here and we'll figure it out."

That afternoon, Liz took $40 out of the emergency envelope in the cabinet and packed two small bags. She told Andie to grab Billy and get in the car.

But when they got to the driveway, the front tire was slashed. A nail — deliberate and unmistakable — stuck out of the rubber like a signature.

Patrick sat on the porch, smoking.

"You going somewhere?" he asked without turning his head.

Liz didn't reply.

They went back inside. Andie watched her mother carry the bags back to the bedroom like they weighed three times what they did the first time.

Andie stopped believing in escape after the third time.

It had rained that night. Liz had managed to hide some money over a few weeks from Andie's café tips. She kept it in the flour canister, thinking Patrick would never look there.

She'd gotten a burner phone. Called the church. Pastor Maynard offered the rectory's guest room. It was small, he said, but warm and safe.

Andie helped her mother gather their things in the dark, speaking only in whispers. Billy was already asleep in the carrier. Liz's hair was still wet from the shower she'd taken to hide the bruises under her blouse.

They were ten feet from the car when the porch light snapped on.

Patrick stood in the doorway.

He didn't speak. Just held the hammer in his hand, not swinging it, just showing it.

"I said I was sorry, didn't I?" he asked.

Liz froze.

"You wanna walk away after everything I done for you?" he continued. "You think anyone's gonna take in some used-up girl with a baby and a whore for a daughter?"

That word made Andie step forward, but Liz held her back.

"It's not worth it," her mother whispered. "He's drunk."

"Always drunk," Andie said, barely restraining the tears.

Liz turned and walked Billy back inside. Andie followed, numb, the duffel sagging on her shoulder like dead weight.

The next morning, Patrick brought flowers. Plastic ones. From the gas station.

Liz put them in a cracked vase anyway.

Each failed escape left Liz more hollow, more resigned. She stopped making real plans. Stopped speaking of tomorrow. She only talked in half-phrases and tiny lies — "maybe someday," "we'll see," "not now, baby."

Andie learned not to ask.

She still tried, sometimes. She would make suggestions. Quietly. Cautiously.

"We could save some cash again."

Liz would nod and say, "That'd be good."

"We could go to Ms. Romero's."

Liz would say, "Maybe if it gets worse."

"How much worse can it get?"

Liz never answered that.

Andie watched her mother unravel slowly, strand by strand, like thread from a worn-out sweater. She still smiled sometimes. Still hummed in the kitchen. Still brushed Billy's hair and told Andie she was beautiful.

But she was leaving them in other ways. Internally. Spiritually. Hope had begun to feel like a dangerous thing. It led to slashed tires and cracked ribs.

So she stopped hoping.

Andie didn't.

Not yet.

But something inside her was changing.

The way she looked at her father was changing.

The way she looked at herself was changing.

And sometimes, when the lights flickered for no reason or when the wind pushed against her window with sudden, unnatural force, Andie felt like something *else* was watching. Waiting.

Not God.

Something older.

And it was waiting for her to break.

Patrick Montgomery hadn't always been like this.

There were photos—long buried in shoe boxes and dresser drawers—of a lean, smiling man with grease on his hands and a socket wrench in his pocket, grinning beside an old Chevrolet engine he'd rebuilt from scrap. In those years, people said he had "gold in his fingers" and a head for mechanics that could've taken him far. But Patrick didn't go far. He stayed.

He got Liz pregnant at twenty and married her without much ceremony. He said it was what a man was supposed to do. Then came work—real work—on the line, in the pits, under cars and trucks and tractors. At first, it was enough. His hands stayed busy, his shirts stained, his wallet decent. They had two kids—Jarrod, then Kayan. They bought a small house with chipped paint and rusted gutters, but it was theirs.

But then came the closings.

The factory shut down when imports got cheaper. The union dried up. The next garage job paid less. The one after that, even less. Eventually, no one wanted the older guy with the chipped knuckles and short temper. Patrick tried for a while. He made phone calls. Picked up odd jobs. But every "no" chipped away at something vital.

Then came the bottle.

And with it, the shame. And with shame, came rage.

He began blaming everyone but himself. The government. The foreigners. His bosses. His coworkers. The banks. His wife. His kids.

They became reminders of the man he used to be and the man he wasn't anymore.

Especially Andie.

Andie reminded Patrick of something he'd lost—the future.

She was smart. Confident. People liked her. She had dreams, energy, options. And he hated her for it.

"She thinks she's better than us," he told Liz one night, after Andie had gone to her room. "Walking around like she's some princess. Like we didn't bleed to get her this far."

Liz didn't answer. She just wiped down the counter.

Patrick drank more. He spoke to old friends on the phone with sour tones. He went to the VFW and got into arguments. Once, he picked a fight at a gas station with a man who cut in front of him in line. Came home with a split lip and a bruised hand.

But at home, it was worse.

He would pace the living room at night, muttering under his breath. When Billy cried, he roared at Liz. When Andie came home late from work, he accused her of "whoring" and slammed doors. His voice became a weapon. So did his fists.

He punched walls. Broke a chair. Kicked over the kitchen table one Sunday when the eggs were cold.

Once, he ripped the phone off the wall because it rang too long.

"He's just frustrated," Liz would whisper to Andie, pressing ice to her cheek. "He wasn't always like this."

But Andie couldn't remember that man. All she saw was the rot that had eaten through him from the inside.

All she heard was thunder, even when the skies were clear.

Andie learned to move silently, like prey. She anticipated Patrick's moods before they erupted. A twitch in his eye. The way he rubbed his temples. The set of his jaw. These were signs. Warnings.

She'd scoop Billy into her arms and vanish into the bedroom before a shouting match became a punch. She kept her schoolbooks at work in case they got torn up. She slept with shoes on some nights, just in case she needed to run.

There was no comfort anymore. No normal. Even on the good days—when Patrick was quiet and subdued—there was the fear of when it would snap. He was like a dormant fault line, and they lived on top of it.

Jarrod had seen it coming. That's why he'd left.

"He'll kill someone if he stays," Andie remembered her older brother saying before he enlisted. "And I won't be here to see it."

He left the morning after Patrick hit him in the face with a broken plate.

Patrick cried that night. Genuinely. Told Liz he was sorry. Told her the army was good for Jarrod. That he'd understand someday.

But Andie remembered Jarrod's eyes. He wasn't leaving for service. He was escaping a house on fire.

He never came back.

Kayan was different. She disappeared inward long before she left physically. She began shutting doors, keeping secrets, whispering on the phone. She would lock herself in the bathroom for hours, sobbing quietly into towels.

She avoided Patrick like he was diseased. She avoided Liz, too.

"I have to survive," she once told Andie, when they were huddled in the closet during a particularly violent fight. "That means not caring. That means not getting dragged under."

Andie didn't understand then. But she did later.

Kayan got pregnant young. Didn't tell anyone who the father was. Didn't keep the baby.

Six months later, she married a man twice her age and moved to Canada.

Andie never saw her again.

Kayan didn't call. Didn't write. She posted once—on social media, a filtered photo from a ski trip with her new husband. A smile that didn't reach her eyes.

Liz cried when she saw it.

Patrick barely looked. "She was never tough," he said. "That one never had the guts."

That was how he talked. Like he was the only one who stayed. The only one who fought. The only one who mattered.

But every night, he sat on the couch, the TV blaring old war movies, his eyes red-rimmed and hollow.

Andie watched him from the hallway sometimes.

Watched him shrink into himself.

And she knew: this man wasn't just angry—he was lost.

And in his rage, he would take everything he could with him.

The house had its own memory now. Its own pulse.

There were dents in the drywall from Patrick's fists. Stains in the carpet from spilled whiskey and blood. The doorframes were warped from being slammed too many times. The ceiling fan ticked with each rotation like a metronome counting down to the next explosion.

Andie kept a backpack hidden behind her dresser. Just in case. Some cash, a phone charger, a pair of clothes for Billy. She told no one.

Her prayers grew quieter, more hesitant.

She still believed in God, but He seemed so far away. The crucifix on her wall looked tarnished now, like it had absorbed the fear and couldn't reflect the light anymore.

Liz was fading too. She smiled less. Talked less. She moved like her limbs were heavier than they used to be.

Every now and then, Patrick would have a good day. He'd cook pancakes. Joke about the past. Say things like "we're still together, that counts for something."

And for a moment, the house would feel normal again.

But Andie had learned not to trust the eye of the storm.

The silence before the thunder wasn't peace. It was warning.

Patrick didn't see himself as abusive. Not really. He saw himself as a man burdened. A man surrounded by people who didn't understand what he'd sacrificed. When he struck, he claimed it was discipline. When he screamed, it was because no one listened. And when he drank, it was only because the world had stopped offering anything worth staying sober for.

"I work hard," he'd mumble, beer bottle swinging from his fingers, even though no one had paid him a wage in over eight months. "I deserve some goddamn respect in my own house."

Respect. That was the word he latched onto like a leech. As if his children owed it to him, not love or dignity or care. As if Liz's bruises and silence were proof that she respected him enough to stay. And when Andie flinched or lowered her gaze, that too, in his mind, was respect.

Andie had learned the pattern.

When Patrick lost something—his temper, a fight at the bar, another job interview—he came home looking for control. It was always the same: walk through the door like a hurricane in denim, mutter about slights, let the bottle clink on the table, then explode. Sometimes physically. Sometimes just with words sharp enough to draw invisible blood.

She memorized the sounds of his boots on the porch. The metallic clatter of his belt buckle. The exact creak of the floorboard by the sink that preceded one of his rants.

Liz would meet him at the door, trying to intercept the blow.

Liz had her own rhythm to survival.

She cooked when he was angry, as if the smell of fried onions and meat might sedate the beast. She kept the lights low to avoid eye contact. She whispered rather than spoke. When Patrick's eyes grew bloodshot and glazed, she'd touch his arm gently, like one might approach a wild dog.

Sometimes it worked.

Other times, it earned her a slap that cracked across the room like a starter's pistol.

Andie hated how fast her mother would recover—how quickly she'd say, "It's alright, baby," through bleeding lips. How she'd wash the blood from her blouse in the sink and still make tea afterward. How she'd smile, as if pretending could rewrite what had happened.

But Andie knew Liz wasn't delusional. She was tired.

"I can't leave," Liz whispered once, sitting on the edge of Andie's bed, a hand pressed to her ribs. "Not with Billy. We wouldn't make it two weeks before someone called CPS and took him away."

Andie didn't argue.

She just held her mother and let her cry in silence.

It wasn't that Liz didn't want better. She simply couldn't find the exit anymore. Somewhere between Patrick's fists and her own fear of the world outside, she'd lost her roadmap.

And Andie, still a child herself, was being left to memorize the maze alone.

That night, the air in the house was dense. Summer heat clung to the walls, and no amount of open windows could push it out. Patrick had come home later than usual—his breath rank with whiskey, his shirt stained with sweat. He didn't say much. Just dropped onto the couch and stared blankly at the television. The glow flickered against his face like firelight over stone.

Andie watched from the kitchen doorway, heart knocking against her ribs. Billy played on the floor with a chipped plastic fire truck, blissfully unaware of the pressure mounting in the room.

Liz moved carefully, setting a bowl of soup down on the coffee table without speaking.

"You think this is food?" Patrick muttered, eyes not leaving the screen.

Liz said nothing. She started to retreat, but his hand shot out, grabbing her wrist.

"I asked you a question."

Andie stepped forward instinctively, but Liz met her with a look that froze her in place. It was a silent plea—*Don't.*

"I'll make something else," Liz whispered.

Patrick let go, not with mercy, but boredom. His fingers dragged along Liz's skin as he withdrew, leaving red marks in their wake.

Later, as Liz dabbed aloe onto her wrist, she said, "He's just upset. He got turned down again."

Andie didn't respond. She was counting the money tips in her apron pocket. Wondering how much it would cost to disappear.

Patrick's failed job interview had been at a tool and die plant, the only one left within fifty miles. They needed someone younger. Stronger. Willing to work overtime for half the wage Patrick had earned ten years ago.

He didn't make it past the second question.

“They looked at me like I was already broken,” he’d growled into a beer can that night. “Like I was just taking up space.”

He didn’t mention how he forgot his resume. Or how he’d been ten minutes late. Or that his boots were caked in dried mud.

In his mind, the world had betrayed him. His family had betrayed him. Liz was too soft, Andie too proud, Billy too loud. The only thing he had left was the control of the home he thought he built.

So he took it.

With fists. With words. With threats.

He had one rule—don’t talk back.

Andie had broken it once. Told him to “get help” after a particularly violent episode that ended with Liz in the ER and Billy howling into the night.

Patrick had backhanded her so hard she fell against the fridge and chipped a molar.

He didn’t apologize. He didn’t even speak to her for two days.

But when he finally did, it wasn’t anger. It was pride.

“You finally learned,” he said. “That’s what respect looks like.”

Andie didn’t answer.

She’d bitten through her tongue to keep from screaming.

She began to look at her father differently after that night—not with fear alone, but with a forensic gaze. As if studying a specimen already dead but still twitching. The bruises he left were one thing. But the decay inside him was another, and it fascinated her in the way corpses might fascinate morticians.

Andie saw how he retreated after every explosion. Into silence. Into a bottle. Into himself. She noticed the limp in his left leg, the knuckle that never healed right from punching a wall. His belly was soft now. His muscles—once strong from lifting transmissions—had become doughy, flecked with old tattoos blurred by sagging skin.

He was still dangerous. But he was unraveling.

Andie wondered what might be left when there was nothing left to break.

She didn't have a plan yet. But she had intent.

When she came home, Liz was usually waiting in the kitchen, nursing a bruise or a cup of tea. Andie would kiss her on the cheek, check Billy's breathing as he slept, and retreat into her room.

Behind her locked door, she would sit at the edge of her bed, stare at the walls, and try to imagine a world where thunder didn't live under her roof.

But no matter how hard she tried, the storm always returned.

Andie had been rehearsing how to ask for days.

She knew how fragile her mother's nerves were lately, how any question could become a landmine if Patrick was in earshot. But Andie was nearly an adult now—seventeen, a senior with solid grades, a solid future, and a growing hunger to finally take some control of her life.

Her guidance counselor at school had even encouraged her to seek part-time work—"It builds independence," she said, "and looks great on college applications." Andie wanted that. She wanted structure, purpose, her own pocket money, and most of all, a few hours out of that house every day.

So she waited for the right time, a rare moment when Patrick had slumped on the couch with a hangover and the television blaring nonsense he wasn't really watching. She found her mother alone in the kitchen, folding laundry by the sink, the smell of meatloaf burning in the oven.

"Mom," Andie said, softly.

Liz didn't look up, but Andie saw her body flinch. Her mother always braced, even for kind voices.

"I was wondering... I want to get a job. After school. Just part-time. Maybe the café down on Green."

Liz's eyes finally met hers—tired, red-rimmed, and ancient beyond her age.

"You're already doing so much, honey."

"I want to help. For college. For... us."

Liz nodded. "Let's talk about it later. Maybe tomorrow."

But the words hadn't been quiet enough. In the other room, Patrick sat up.

"A job?" he barked. "The hell she need a job for?"

Andie froze.

"I'm not gonna have my daughter whoring herself out for coffee money!"

"It's just a café, Patrick," Liz said quickly, moving toward the door as if to block the impending storm. "She's being responsible. It's good."

"Good? You think it's good for her to run around dressed like some city slut, grinning at every customer for a tip?"

Andie clenched her fists. “It’s not like that.”

Patrick stood up, beer bottle in hand, slurring his fury. “You think you're better than me, huh? Your high school diploma and your part-time apron? You're still under my roof.”

Liz put herself between them, her arms spread. “Stop it, Pat. She just wants to help—”

The slap came so fast Andie didn’t even see it land. Liz stumbled back, clutching her cheek, her laundry basket crashing to the floor.

Billy, at the kitchen table with crayons, began to cry.

Andie’s voice trembled, but she didn't back away. “I’m taking the job.”

She got the job.

The café wasn’t glamorous, but it was clean, quiet, and, best of all, not home. The manager, a middle-aged woman named Cheryl, liked her immediately. She trained fast, moved efficiently, and could handle the usual awkward customer with a smile that didn’t betray the knots in her stomach.

Her shifts were short—just four hours after school—but Andie clung to those hours like a lifeline. She arrived early and stayed late to clean. The café smelled of cinnamon and coffee beans and soft-baked pastries. It became her sanctuary.

She hid her bruises well. The oversized sweatshirt she wore to school helped. So did her habit of brushing her hair forward to shadow her cheekbones. But Cheryl saw more than she let on. She once paused as Andie stocked the sugar packets and gently asked, “Everything okay at home?”

Andie smiled and lied, “Of course.”

After her second week, Cheryl handed her an envelope with her first paycheck—small but hard-earned. Andie's heart swelled with quiet pride. She bought groceries with half of it: eggs, milk, pasta, even a small bouquet of flowers that she tucked into a vase at home. The other half she hid in an envelope under her mattress.

But Patrick found it.

And he was waiting when she came home one night, half-drunk and bitter.

"You think you can keep secrets from me now?" he said, waving the envelope in her face.

"It's my money," she said, jaw tight.

"Not while you live here it ain't."

He grabbed her arm, twisting. She didn't scream, didn't cry. Liz rushed in, pulling Patrick back, her voice cracking with panic. Billy hid behind the couch, sobbing into a stuffed rabbit.

Patrick left that night with the money, his coat, and a promise to "spend it on something worthwhile."

He didn't come home until morning.

That became the pattern.

Andie worked. Patrick drank. Liz apologized. Billy grew quieter.

The house felt colder each week. Empty bottles gathered like ghosts in corners and countertops. Liz stopped cooking most nights. She sat on the edge of the couch, eyes hollow, folding the same pile of laundry again and again.

Andie tried to keep the rhythm going. She paid for school supplies, took Billy for ice cream on Fridays, and even used her tips to replace the broken microwave. But the more she did, the angrier Patrick became.

He didn't like being made obsolete.

"You think you're the man of the house now?" he spat once, shoving her against the wall. "You gonna put food on the table with that little girl money?"

But the truth cut deeper.

Patrick couldn't hold a job. Not for more than a few weeks. Construction sites, delivery vans, even custodial work—he was always too late, too drunk, too proud to listen to anyone. When the layoffs came, he took it as a personal betrayal. When he was fired, he blamed everyone but himself.

And when the letters came—late bills, missed rent, collection notices—he tore them up without opening them.

It was easier to punish his family than admit he had failed them.

Liz tried to talk him down. At first.

She'd sit beside him after a shouting match, her voice low and sweet like a balm. "We can figure this out," she'd say, brushing his greasy hair from his forehead. "Maybe we talk to the pastor. Or your brother, I know he's hiring again—"

But Patrick didn't want solutions.

He wanted silence. Obedience. Reverence.

"You don't get it," he'd sneer, eyes glazed. "I was supposed to be more than this. I had chances. I had goddamn talent. Then you got pregnant and everything changed."

That line stung more than most.

Liz had heard it a hundred times—every time the guilt surfaced and he needed to bury it under blame. Sometimes she'd fight back.

Sometimes she'd take it. And sometimes, she'd leave the room and cry quietly in the hallway, knees tucked to her chest.

Andie often found her there, mascara running down her face, trying to keep her sobs hidden from Billy.

"Mom," Andie would whisper, kneeling beside her.

Liz would smile through the tears. "You're the only thing keeping me sane."

But it wasn't enough.

Not anymore.

Billy had started having nightmares.

He'd wake up screaming, drenched in sweat, clawing at his blankets. Andie would run in, heart racing, and find him curled into a ball on the floor, whispering, "Don't let him yell at me... I didn't mean to spill it..."

She'd scoop him up, hold him in her arms, rock him until his breathing slowed.

Patrick never came in to check.

Sometimes he wasn't even home. And when he was, the sounds didn't bother him. They didn't register.

Andie knew Billy would carry scars from all this, too. They all would.

But what choice did they have?

She got up every day. Went to school. Went to work. Came home. Cooked when Liz couldn't. Cleaned when Billy spilled. Hid her tips in new hiding spots every week. And always, always kept her ears tuned to the sound of tires on gravel—waiting to know which version of Patrick would come home.

The slurring, mean one.

Or the silent, broken one.

And sometimes... they were one and the same.

The first time he walked into the café, Andie noticed him immediately. He was clean-cut, dressed in a snug hoodie and jeans that looked intentionally worn, and he had the kind of effortless posture that made him appear like he belonged anywhere he stood. He was probably nineteen, maybe twenty. His eyes were sharp but kind, scanning the menu like he'd been there a hundred times. When he stepped to the counter and smiled at her, something inside Andie fluttered. His voice—measured, smooth—asked for a black coffee and a blueberry scone, but his gaze lingered just a moment too long.

The next day, he came back. Same order. Same smile. "You again," he said lightly, as if it were a happy coincidence. Andie responded with a small, nervous laugh. By the end of that first week, they'd shared small talk about school, weather, music. His name was Jacob.

Jacob came in every afternoon around 4:00. He never pushed, never flirted overtly. But his presence was comforting, and his attention never felt leering or hungry. It was the first time a boy had looked at Andie like she was a whole person and not just a girl with curves. She started adjusting her hair more before her shift. Lip gloss returned to her pocket. The emotional debris of her home life seemed to settle just slightly when Jacob was near.

Jacob's visits became routine, predictable. He'd ask her about her favorite books, tease her about her taste in coffee, or joke about how she always managed to get blueberry jam on her apron. Once, when a toddler threw a tantrum nearby, Jacob whispered a dramatic line from Shakespeare, and Andie burst into laughter. He had that gift—the ability to make a moment feel like its own small world. And in that world, Andie wasn't the daughter of a drunk or a victim of kitchen-table bruises. She was just a girl talking to a boy.

Liz noticed the change almost immediately. "Someone's smiling more," she said, her voice light but edged. Andie blushed, brushing it off, but one night she sat beside her mother at the kitchen table while Billy napped in the next room and confessed. She told her about Jacob—the way he talked to her, the way he made her feel seen. Liz's expression softened, but only for a moment.

"I know what it's like to fall for a charming boy, baby," Liz said, placing a hand over Andie's. "But charm isn't always kindness. And attention isn't always love. Sometimes, it's a shadow dressed up as light."

Andie was silent. Liz's words lingered in the air, coiling into her thoughts.

Despite her mother's warning, Andie found herself drawn deeper. She looked forward to Jacob's visits. Sometimes she'd catch herself daydreaming—imagining what it might be like to go out with him, to sit across from him without an apron and a name tag between them. She hadn't told him about her life—not about Patrick or the chaos or the things she prayed every night to forget. But there was a hope blooming in her, small and bright.

One evening, after the café had cleared out, the owner, Mrs. Halvorsen, asked Andie to stay behind to help with closing. "You're reliable, Andie," she said, smiling. "The others rush to punch out. You finish what you start."

It felt like praise. Andie said yes. That night, she walked home under the stars alone, her bag slung over her shoulder, the tip money still tucked inside. When she got home, the lights were off. Patrick hadn't returned yet.

The extra hours became more frequent. Mrs. Halvorsen praised Andie's work ethic and began asking her to cover evening shifts more regularly. "You're my closer now," she said, handing her a set of keys. It felt like a promotion.

Jacob noticed the shift in her schedule, too. "Burning the midnight oil?" he asked one afternoon.

"Yeah. Feels good to be trusted," Andie replied, tucking a loose strand of hair behind her ear. She meant it—there was something empowering about being needed. In a life where she was so often invisible, these hours made her feel real.

But she also began to feel tired. Her mornings dragged. She caught herself zoning out during class, writing Jacob's name in the corners of her notebooks.

One night, Liz waited up for her. "It's not safe walking home that late," she said.

Andie offered a tired smile. "I'm careful."

Liz nodded, but her eyes darkened.

Andie's world was becoming divided—school and café, light and shadow. At the café, she smiled. At home, she held her breath. Patrick's outbursts were now more frequent and more random. He didn't ask about her job or her hours, but the money she left on the kitchen table was always gone by morning. She knew where it went. The local bar's backroom had become his confessional.

Jacob remained the only constant. He came even on rainy days, even when the café was empty except for a few older couples sipping tea. One day, he brought her a dog-eared copy of a book they'd talked about. "Thought you'd want to read it," he said, shrugging like it wasn't a big deal.

Andie stared at the book, her fingers brushing the cover. No boy had ever given her anything—not a flower, not a compliment, not a reason to hope.

"Thanks," she whispered.

Jacob just smiled. "I'm around if you want to talk."

Andie didn't know how to say what she wanted. That maybe she didn't need to talk. Maybe she just needed someone to look at her the way he did—like she mattered.

She slid the book into her backpack like it was a secret worth keeping.

The sound of the front screen door banging open and closed was a trigger that froze Andie in place—whether she was studying, cooking, or simply moving through the house. It always meant the same thing: Patrick had returned. If his footsteps were sluggish, there was time to escape upstairs before his drunken gaze settled on her. If they were quick and uneven, danger was already at the threshold. But it was the silence that truly terrified her. Silence meant he was calculating.

Liz had taken to hiding bruises under long sleeves and heavier makeup. The older she grew, the thinner she became, as if shrinking into herself. She moved through the house with a kind of flinching grace, always alert to where Patrick was, always attempting to redirect his attention or anger—toward a missing beer or a broken chair or a fictional slight. Anything to keep him from turning on the kids.

But Andie was seventeen now. Her presence couldn't be ignored or minimized. Boys stared at her in public, and women whispered behind their hands. Patrick noticed. His rage grew in proportion to the recognition his daughter received. He saw her as a reflection of everything he had lost, and a reminder that time was moving forward without him. He didn't trust her smile, her youth, or the way the world responded to her. And Liz noticed this too—with a rising, unspoken dread.

At night, Liz would sit beside Andie's bed in the dark, whispering her fears like secrets too dangerous for daylight. "He looks at you different now," she would say in a trembling voice. "I know that look. I've lived with it for years. But when he drinks, baby... I think it's changing." Andie never responded. She didn't want to speak the terrible thought aloud, but she knew exactly what her mother meant. Her father had begun to blur the lines between fury and something even darker.

"Maybe you should go stay with Kayan," Liz suggested one night, clutching Andie's hand so tightly her knuckles turned white. "Or ask Jarrod if he can find a place for you. I don't trust him anymore. He's—" She stopped herself, unable to finish. "He's thinking things."

Andie lay in bed that night unable to sleep, haunted not just by fear of her father but by the helplessness in her mother's voice. Liz had always been a buffer, a quiet shield, but now she sounded like a woman preparing for war she could not win.

The unwanted attention Andie received in town only made things worse. At the grocery store, a clerk barely older than her winked and leaned across the counter, brushing his hand too close to hers. At the gas station, older men leered from their trucks as she passed by. Even at church, a deacon's handshake lingered too long. It was as if everyone had agreed she had become available, ripe for consumption. Andie didn't know how to hide her body. She had inherited Liz's full figure, but on her, it invited danger instead of admiration.

Liz began sending Andie out with oversized coats, telling her to keep her head down and to walk with a purpose. "Don't let them see you hesitate," she'd say, "and if anyone follows you, come right home. Don't stop. Don't talk."

Andie hated that her very existence felt like bait. She wanted to be seen as smart, kind, capable—but instead she was becoming aware of how others measured her: hips, chest, face. Even the café owner had begun to pause mid-sentence when she was near, his gaze a second too long on her figure before returning to the register.

Andie noticed the change most starkly at school. She used to be invisible—background to the louder, more assertive girls. Now boys bumped into her in the halls on purpose, using the moment to touch her back or arms. Some whispered crude things behind her as she passed. At lunch, she found notes slipped into her locker—some romantic, some vulgar.

The same boys who ignored her in middle school now made her a target of obsession.

And the girls? They noticed. Cold stares and whispered mockery began to follow her. "She thinks she's all that now," they'd mutter, pretending to laugh. Andie stopped eating lunch in the cafeteria and started hiding in the library. Her popularity was not affection—it was pressure. Andie was stuck between admiration and envy, attraction and resentment, and it made every step at school feel like walking a minefield.

Patrick noticed her growing unease and relished it. One afternoon, when she tried to leave for her shift at the café, he stood in the hallway and blocked her way. “You really think you’re something now, don’t you?” he sneered. “You think all those boys want you ‘cause you’re special?” He leered openly, making Liz rush in and physically place herself between them.

Liz’s hands trembled as she held Andie behind her, shielding her daughter with a fierceness born from panic. “Don’t you talk to her like that!” she yelled, her voice cracking. Patrick leaned against the wall and smirked, still drunk. “She’s just like her mama was,” he said darkly. “Wears it like a uniform, struttin’ around like she’s beggin’ for it.”

It was the first time Andie saw her mother cry not from pain—but from pure anger.

Later that night, Liz stood in the kitchen, staring blankly at the floor as she stirred a pot of soup that had long stopped simmering. “You need to leave,” she said quietly when Andie walked in. “We’ll figure it out. But you need to go before he does something we both can’t fix.”

Andie didn’t argue. She just nodded and said nothing, because deep down she already knew. There were things in Patrick’s eyes that no prayer could burn out. Liz had spent her life sacrificing and softening blows. But she couldn’t stop this.

Andie stood by the kitchen doorway for a long time, watching her mother crumble—her back hunched, shoulders shaking in silence. That image would stay with her. So would the scent of scorched soup and the knowledge that no one was coming to save them.

Chapter 2

Jacob didn't ask for her number. He didn't need to. Every afternoon at 4:17, the small brass bell above the café door chimed and in he walked, like he had stepped out of a frame frozen in time. His khakis were always pressed, his polos ironed, and his sneakers looked too clean to have walked the same cracked sidewalks as the rest of town. Andie noticed these things. She noticed *everything* about him.

He never flirted—not in the way the other boys did. No slick jokes, no touching, no try-hard bravado. Just that same calm voice, carefully worded questions, and those oddly old-fashioned manners. He'd ask how her day was. If her brother was doing okay. What book she was reading. Then he'd sip his coffee with both hands and listen—*really* listen. It was like no one had ever done that before.

Andie caught herself lying once. Not a big lie, just something small: she said she didn't mind staying late. Jacob had asked if she ever got nervous walking home after dark, and she'd replied too quickly, trying to sound tough. "No, I like the quiet." But the truth was that the quiet had started to feel like a *trap*, especially now that Patrick had started coming home drunk again.

And the worst part? He wasn't coming home *alone* anymore.

"You should get a ride," Jacob said one evening, watching her through the café window as she wiped down the outside table. "This part of town's changing. People change with it."

It was the closest he'd come to sounding concerned, or even *real*. Andie looked up, startled at the protective edge in his voice. "I'm fine," she said, but she couldn't keep her eyes from searching his face. "I've lived here all my life."

He smiled, that same sideways, too-knowing smirk. “Sometimes that’s the problem.”

She almost asked then—where *he* was from. Why he always wore the same class ring but never talked about school. But the moment passed. He pivoted the conversation like always, gently steering it to something else. Music. The weather. What she thought about fate.

That night, she didn’t go straight home. Instead, she stopped by the library—her safe place since childhood—and checked out three books: *Folklore of the Damned*, *Superstitions and Sightings in Appalachia*, and *The Black Veil: Women and the Wound Beyond Wounds.*

She didn’t know what exactly she was looking for, but a cold part of her—the part that trembled behind her ribs when she locked eyes with Patrick’s bar buddies—thought maybe she’d find something *true* in those pages. Something that *understood* fear.

Andie read at night now. Late. Alone in the corner of her room, with a towel shoved under the door to muffle the light. She took notes like she was prepping for a final. Symbols. Patterns. Shared visions of shadowy women, bleeding eyes, or shrieking wind. Women whose pain manifested as unnatural events—wilting crops, blood weeping from walls, animals fleeing before they died.

Liz noticed her growing quiet but said nothing. Instead, she began to pile change into a mug by the stove, their private signal. “Trip fund,” she whispered once. “You, me, and Billy. We’ll slip away when no one’s watching.”

But someone *was* watching. Patrick’s friend with the knotty beard and oil-stained fingers. The one who smelled like beef jerky and beer. He stared too long. Another one, thinner and louder, had asked Andie if she had a boyfriend yet, laughing like it was a joke. Patrick had grinned like a dog and let it pass.

Andie had never hated someone so efficiently. It wasn't a fiery hate. It was cold. Focused. Like an icicle forming on the edge of a roof—sharp, inevitable, waiting.

She didn't tell Jacob about any of that. Not the men. Not the books. Not the coins by the stove. Instead, she listened to him talk in riddles. He told stories, sometimes—urban legends about mirror rituals or cursed dolls that blinked. Once, he spoke of an entire town that drowned in fog, leaving behind only teeth.

"I think people underestimate the power of belief," he said once, stirring his tea instead of drinking it. "They think something's fake until it touches them."

Andie nodded. "I read something like that," she offered. "About women whose grief changed things. Made things *move.*"

He smiled faintly. "Grief is a kind of gravity. Strong enough to warp reality if you hold it long enough."

After he left, she scribbled that line into her journal, underlining it three times. That night, she dreamed of the men in her living room—drunk, laughing, too loud. But in the dream, they stopped laughing. One by one, their mouths filled with blood, their teeth loosened, and their faces turned toward her like she had summoned something... darker than herself.

The next morning, Andie woke to find one of the drunk men's jackets draped over the kitchen chair. He hadn't come back for it. She picked it up carefully, like it might bite. The stench of old beer and tobacco filled the air.

She thought of fire.

It would be easy. Just one match. She imagined the flames curling upward, taking that part of her life with it.

But she didn't burn it. She stuffed it in a garbage bag and shoved it deep into the alley dumpster behind the café. On her break, she washed her hands five times and then stood outside with Jacob, silent.

"Are you okay?" he asked, his eyes searching hers again.

She almost told him. About the jacket. The dream. The rage like a noose tightening around her breath.

Instead, she said, "Do you believe people can become something... else? Not just bad. *Wrong.*"

Jacob looked at her for a long moment, then said softly, "I think some people are already something else. They just forget the shape they used to be."

Andie didn't know what that meant. But it scared her.

It happened on a Tuesday morning, while the sky still held the color of wet slate and Billy snored in front of the TV.

Liz was folding laundry, humming something tuneless, when Andie asked offhandedly, "Did you ever... feel things? Before?"

Liz froze with a pair of socks balled in her hands. Her knuckles tightened like bones rising beneath paper-thin skin. "What kind of things?"

Andie didn't flinch. "Like... shadows that don't belong. Or... cold air in a warm room. Like the world shifting, but no one else notices."

Liz sat down, hard, on the edge of the couch. Her hands trembled as she rubbed at her jeans. "There was a time," she said slowly, "before you were born. When I worked nights at the clinic. I used to fall asleep in the breakroom. There was this spot under the ceiling vent… no matter what season, it was cold. Like dead skin."

Andie leaned in. Liz's voice had dropped to a whisper.

"Sometimes I'd wake up to find the radio turned on. Full static. And once… once I swear I saw a woman, soaking wet, standing in the mirror behind me."

"You *saw* her?"

"She was gone before I turned around," Liz muttered, eyes darting. "But my scrubs were damp at the hem. Just the hem. Like something brushed past me."

Andie stared. "Why didn't you say anything?"

Liz smiled weakly. "Because I couldn't afford to believe in things I couldn't explain."

But Andie could.

Andie pulled her library books closer that night. Added new search terms to her late-night rabbit holes: *mirrors, water spirits, damp hem symbolism, Appalachian hospital hauntings*.

She discovered recurring figures in folklore—*The Wet Widow, The Watered Wife*, *The Mourning Sinkhole*. Each tale different, but each one a version of a woman torn apart in life, only to rise in waterlogged fury. They didn't scream. They didn't chase. They stood behind glass. They dripped. They waited.

Andie began circling words in pen. Began mapping common traits. The same way she studied her life—quietly, obsessively.

But the more she looked, the more the lines between sleep and wakefulness frayed. Dreams that began as flickers of memory now erupted into sensations—cold fingertips brushing her shoulder, muffled voices under her bed. Once, she jolted upright and found her fingers raw, her nails cracked like she'd been *digging* in her sleep.

She hid that from Liz.

Instead, she made herself presentable, tying her apron a little tighter, pretending the bags under her eyes were just late shifts.

By now, the café owner had stopped asking if she wanted to go home early. He liked that she stayed late. She didn't tell him it was because she didn't want to *go* home anymore.

Jacob walked in that Thursday with someone else. Andie noticed immediately—there was a wrongness in the air, subtle but sharp, like the moment right before a lightning strike.

His name was Mark. Tall. Handsome in that polished way that made the edges feel manufactured. His smile was too quick, too practiced. His laugh too loud for the quiet space.

"This her?" Mark asked, sliding into the seat across from Jacob. He looked her up and down like a menu item, then stuck out his hand. "Jacob told me all about you, Andie."

Jacob didn't meet her eyes.

She shook Mark's hand, trying to keep her fingers from recoiling. His palm was clammy, and he held on half a second too long.

Mark leaned back in the chair like he owned it. "So... when are you off?"

"I'm not," she said flatly.

He laughed again. "That's cute. You know, Jacob said you were smart. Thoughtful. I told him that usually means lonely."

Her jaw tensed. "I'm not interested."

Jacob finally cut in, his voice soft but edged. "Mark."

But Mark didn't back down. "Relax, man. I'm just talking. You don't have to be her big brother."

Andie turned sharply. "You should go."

The moment they left, the air felt lighter, like someone had opened a sealed window. But the residue lingered—Mark's tone, his gaze, Jacob's silence.

She couldn't focus the rest of the shift. Every plate clattered louder. Every whisper in the corner booth felt like a threat.

After closing, she walked home slower than usual. Her body felt off-balance, as if her spine didn't sit quite right inside her skin. Streetlights buzzed louder. Shadows crawled just a fraction too slow. Once, she swore she saw someone—*something*—in the reflection of a store window. A pale hand raised as if to greet her. She didn't stop to look closer.

At home, Patrick was passed out on the couch. One of his friends—Knotty Beard—was awake, swaying slightly by the fridge, holding a can of beer like it was communion.

He looked at her and smiled without teeth.

"You're late."

She didn't respond. Just walked past, head down, muscles tight.

"Got something for you," he said.

She froze.

He held up a lighter. "For your smoke breaks. Thought you might want one of your own."

"I don't smoke."

He winked. "You will."

Andie didn't answer. Just grabbed a water from the cabinet and disappeared into her room, locking the door. She pressed her forehead to the frame, her pulse screaming in her ears.

Behind her, the room was cold.

Too cold.

She turned, heart pounding—and there it was. A puddle of water. Just beneath her desk chair. No source. No leak. Just still, dark water, like it had been waiting.

She didn't scream.

She knelt.

Touched it.

It wasn't cold.

It was *warm.*

The heat bloomed under her skin like something *recognizing* her.

She stood up, shaking. Looked in the mirror—and swore she saw her reflection blink twice, out of sync with her own eyes.

That night, Andie didn't sleep.

She *watched* the mirror instead. Andie lost time.
It started in the stockroom at the café—just another Tuesday, just another box of paper napkins. The fluorescent bulbs above had been buzzing all afternoon, a persistent mechanical whine that clung to the back of her skull. She bent over, hands wrist-deep in packaging, counting sleeves for the inventory log, when everything... stopped.

The sound cut out, not gradually, but like someone had hit *mute* on the world. The fridge motor, the clatter of dishes from the front counter, even her own breath—it all vanished, leaving only a sharp, impossible *stillness*.

Andie blinked once.

And suddenly, she wasn't in the stockroom anymore.

She was outside, in the alley behind the café. The light had shifted. Sunset. Her sleeves were rolled up. Her hands were wet. A cluster of garbage bags lay at her feet, twisted shut like sleeping bodies. One had split at the seam, oozing something reddish-brown onto the cracked pavement.

She staggered back from the bags, heart hammering, brain slow to catch up. The metal backdoor behind her slammed open, and a co-worker poked his head out, frowning.

"I thought you were doing inventory?"

Andie opened her mouth. Closed it again. Her voice felt far away, like trying to talk underwater.

"I was," she said finally, but she didn't believe herself.

That night, she noticed her fingertips were stained a dull crimson. Not paint. Not ink. Something sticky. Faintly metallic. She scrubbed her hands raw before bed, trying not to think.

But the worst part came later, in her journal.

A new entry. In her handwriting.

"I saw her again. She didn't blink this time. She smiled."

Andie didn't remember writing that.

The plate shattered before it hit the floor.

Andie had come into the kitchen that morning expecting the usual—burnt toast, lukewarm coffee, Billy half-awake on the couch—but what she found instead was her mother, standing frozen with wide eyes and trembling hands.

The plate had slipped from Liz's grip as soon as she stepped into the room. She didn't even look down at the broken shards. Her eyes stayed fixed on the far corner of the kitchen, just past the pantry door.

Andie followed her gaze, but saw only an empty stretch of wallpaper peeling slightly near the ceiling.

"Mom?"

Liz's lips were pressed into a tight line. Her face had gone a sickly gray beneath the eyes. She pointed, but her hand shook too much to be steady. "She was there," she whispered. "I saw... I thought I saw a woman. Standing there. She was soaked. Hair hanging down in front of her shoulders. Just... standing there, like she belonged."

Andie felt the room sway around her.

"What did she do?"

Liz swallowed. "She turned. Just slightly. And then she was gone."

The silence that followed was heavier than the crash.

"You sure it wasn't—?"

"I know what I saw." Liz crouched to pick up the pieces of ceramic, but her knuckles were white. "Maybe I'm just tired."

Andie didn't believe that for a second.

Later, Liz found a single, smeared *handprint* on the inside of the bathroom mirror. She wiped it away without comment.

That night, she slept with the bedroom lamp on.

The mirrors were getting worse.

It wasn't just the lingering sense of wrongness anymore—it was movement. Timing. Mismatch.

Andie caught it first while brushing her teeth. Her reflection *lagged*, just by a second. She turned her head to spit, and saw her own image still staring forward, eyes locked on hers. The moment was gone in a blink, but the panic it caused clung to her like a fever.

At work, she checked every mirror she passed: the bathroom, the café's polished espresso machine, the wide glass panels behind the counter. Each one felt like a window into something that knew her name.

When Jacob reappeared, it was a relief. For a moment.

He stood behind the dumpster, jacket open to the wind, hands in his pockets. He looked different. Less composed.

"I didn't know Mark would act like that," he said, voice softer than usual.

"You didn't stop him."

"I should have. I told him not to come, but he's... difficult."

"You let him stay. You didn't say a word when he looked at me like that."

"I didn't want to make a scene."

Andie stepped closer, pulse hard in her throat. "You stood there like it didn't matter. That *matters*, Jacob."

His mouth twisted. "You're right." He hesitated. "You matter."

“To what?”

“To *me.*”

But his eyes never quite met hers when he said it.

Her world fractured again the next afternoon.

Andie had just finished stacking the sleeves of coffee cups when a wave of nausea hit her like a freight train. Her vision flickered—dim, then bright, then dim again. She dropped the cups. They rolled across the floor like scattered dice.

She gripped the counter, breath coming in shallow gasps. Her skin crawled, the sensation of being *watched* blooming behind her ears.

She blinked—and she wasn’t in the café anymore.

She was somewhere else. A corridor. Tight. Damp. The wallpaper was peeling, and the air smelled like mildew and copper. She recognized the hallway from a dream she hadn’t even remembered having.

A mirror stood at the end of the hall, tilted slightly.

It was cracked. Warped.

She stepped forward, her boots sticking to the floor. The mirror pulsed, a steady rhythm like a heartbeat.

Her reflection stood inside. But it wasn’t right.

Older. Paler. Mouth sewn shut. Fingers stained.

It tilted its head slowly—then raised one hand and *pressed* against the glass.

Andie screamed.

When she opened her eyes again, she was curled under the counter in the café. Her manager was standing above her, eyebrows raised in concern.

"You fainted," he said. "Jesus, Andie. You okay?"

She nodded.

She wasn't.

That night, she didn't speak to anyone.

She went straight to her room, locked the door, and took the old sheet from her closet. With careful precision, she draped it over her mirror, pinning it at the top and taping the corners down. She didn't want to *see* herself anymore. Not until she was sure it was still her.

Liz brought in a mug of tea without knocking. She set it down on the nightstand and hovered by the door.

"I found a new smudge," Liz said after a moment. "On the inside of my vanity mirror. I hadn't even opened it today."

Andie stared at her, eyes wide.

"You don't think maybe..."

"I don't know what to think anymore," Liz said.

They sat in silence for a long moment.

Then Liz spoke again, voice low and hoarse. "When I was seventeen, my mother told me something I never believed. She said our pain runs deeper than most. That women in our family... we carry something. It gets into the blood. Festers. And sometimes, it becomes *real.*"

Andie's skin prickled.

“She told me there was once a woman in our line who was *wronged*. So badly her sorrow grew teeth. Claws. And she passed it down.”

“Why didn’t you tell me?”

“Because I was scared of giving it power,” Liz whispered.

Andie stared at the covered mirror.

“It’s not waiting anymore,” she said. “It’s following me now.”

The front door opened with a groan that had started to feel like a warning bell.

Andie looked up from her homework, muscles tightening. Liz, across the room folding laundry, stopped mid-motion. Both of them listened as Patrick’s laugh burst in, thick with beer and breathlessness, followed by two other voices—louder, slurred, foreign in tone but familiar in weight.

Patrick’s friends.

“Girls!” Patrick shouted, as if it were a game. “We’ve got company tonight. Real gentlemen.”

Andie’s stomach turned. She rose quietly, gathering her notebooks as if armor could be made of paper. Liz, eyes narrowed, remained seated but straightened her spine.

The first to walk in was **Knotty Beard**, whose real name they’d never learned. His beard was gray in streaks, stained yellow near the mouth from years of cigarettes and chewing tobacco. His eyes were watery and glassy, never quite focused, as if always choosing between sleep or hunger. He wore a ragged camouflage jacket over a white undershirt stained brown under the arms, and he smelled like pickled onions soaked in gasoline.

“Evenin’, ladies,” he slurred. “Lookin’ real domestic tonight.”

The second, **Rabbit-Tooth Ricky**, followed—so nicknamed for his prominent front teeth and nervous, snorting laugh. He had thin hair that clung to his scalp like seaweed, and a leather vest over no shirt, showcasing sunburnt skin and a series of blurry prison tattoos. One of his eyes twitched constantly.

"Damn," Ricky said, leering directly at Andie. "She's grown into something fine, huh, Pat?"

Patrick didn't answer right away. He shut the door too hard and dropped his keys.

"Hey," Andie said sharply, stepping back. "Don't talk to me like that."

Knotty Beard gave a low whistle. "Mouth on that one. She always this spicy?"

Liz stood. "That's enough."

"Enough what, sweet Lizzy?" Ricky said. "Ain't nobody touchin'. We're just *talkin'*."

Andie could feel the rage rise behind her ribs, a cold pressure tightening her shoulders. She didn't want to breathe the same air as these men. She didn't want to live in a world where they had keys to the house.

Patrick lit a cigarette in the kitchen, the smell instantly clinging to everything—the walls, the worn-out curtains, even the pillows on the couch. Andie sat stiffly, arms crossed, watching from the far end of the room like she was trapped behind invisible bars.

"Hey," Patrick barked. "You girls don't gotta act so uptight. These guys helped me out when I needed it. Show some goddamn *gratitude*."

Liz's voice was quiet, tired. "You don't owe them this."

Patrick turned, eyes bloodshot. "I owe them everything. When I couldn't pay that ticket, Knotty lent me cash. When I needed a place to crash after the truck repo, Ricky gave me a couch. They've been there for me more than *you* ever were."

Ricky smirked. "We're real saints, huh?"

"Why are they here now?" Andie asked, not blinking.

Patrick exhaled smoke through his nose like a dragon. "They need a favor. I told 'em I'd talk to my family. It's temporary."

Liz took a step forward. "They're not family, Pat. And we're not your bargaining chips."

Knotty took a long swig from his flask and wiped his mouth on his sleeve. "You know, I don't think she appreciates what we've done for you, man. Maybe we should all sit down and talk it out. Family-style."

Andie could see it then—*this wasn't kindness*. This was a transaction. Patrick was *selling proximity*, testing boundaries, pretending these lecherous animals were just down-on-their-luck buddies.

And their eyes never stopped roaming.

Dinner was hell.

Not a real dinner—more like open beer cans, microwaved burritos, and old greasepaper spread across the coffee table. The TV blared a rerun of some game show, but no one watched it. All attention hovered around Liz and Andie.

"You girls always this quiet?" Ricky asked, peeling open another burrito with greasy fingers. "Feels like a funeral in here."

"We don't like sharing our table with strangers," Liz said, her tone measured.

Knotty laughed. “Strangers? C’mon. We’re *family* now, remember?”

Patrick didn’t laugh. He was too drunk. Eyes half-lidded, words slurring more by the minute, he flicked his ash onto the floor and leaned back in the recliner. “They’re not used to company. That’s the problem.”

Ricky nudged Patrick with a beer can. “You said Liz was a real firecracker when you met her. What happened?”

“Life happened,” Patrick muttered. “And bills. And kids.”

Andie clenched her jaw. She could *feel* the sweat gathering behind her knees, her throat tightening. The way they stared—like cats circling a cornered mouse.

Knotty leaned in toward Liz, his voice low and close. “Tell me, sweetheart... if you ever get tired of that hard bed and loud husband, maybe you want to spend a night with a man who knows how to listen.”

Liz stood abruptly. “Get out.”

Ricky’s smirk vanished. “The hell you say?”

“I said *get out.*”

Patrick stayed in his chair, arms slack. “They’re staying the night.”

The argument erupted after midnight.

Liz had tried to retreat into her room, but Ricky followed her down the hall under the pretense of asking for a towel. Andie had heard his laughter—mocking, sharp. Liz’s response was muffled, low and firm.

A door slammed.

Then came Patrick’s shout. “Don’t be rude, Liz! Jesus Christ!”

Andie rose from her bed, stepping into the hallway barefoot. The tension was so thick it buzzed in her ears.

Patrick and Liz were facing off at the edge of the kitchen. Ricky and Knotty were watching like vultures perched on barstools.

“You said they’d be gone,” Liz spat. “You said they were staying one night, not moving in!”

“Things changed,” Patrick barked. “I owe them, and they don’t have anywhere else to go!”

“This isn’t a shelter, Pat. It’s our *home.* My daughter sleeps here!”

Patrick’s face darkened. “She’s *my* daughter too.”

“Then act like it!”

Andie didn’t realize she was shaking until she noticed the tremor in her hands. Her back pressed against the wall. She wanted to scream. Throw something. Claw the walls. But she stayed still.

“They’re here until I figure it out,” Patrick growled. “If you don’t like it, leave.”

Andie locked eyes with Liz across the room.

They were both already planning it.

Andie didn’t sleep. Not even a little.

She lay in bed fully clothed, a metal flashlight clutched in one hand, her other arm draped protectively across her stomach. Every creak in the house made her flinch. Every muffled cough from the living room twisted her gut.

From the hall, she could hear one of them snoring—deep, phlegmy, like an animal hibernating inside the drywall. At one point she heard a floorboard groan just outside her room. She waited, holding her breath, not daring to move.

Nothing happened.

But that night was a *lesson*. The world didn't have to be supernatural to be terrifying. It could stink like beer breath, leer with bloodshot eyes, and linger too long in the doorway while laughing about things that weren't funny.

She stared at the ceiling and swore she would never forget how this felt. How powerless. How *trapped*.

But even in the silence, the fear twisted into something... focused.

In the morning, she would start moving money. She'd talk to Liz. She'd count bus routes, compare distances, look at bus stops with overhead cover. They couldn't afford a motel, not yet, but they could make *steps*.

They had to.

Because something worse than ghosts was in the house now.

And it wore flesh. Andie had always been a sharp observer. She noticed patterns, caught whispers of conversations not meant for her, saw bruises on arms that people tried to hide. She trusted her instincts.

But now, even she wasn't sure what was real.

It started with the **wisp**—a flicker of movement near the pantry door while she was pouring cereal for Billy. It passed fast, like smoke curling low to the ground. She turned, but nothing was there.

Maybe just a **floater**, she told herself. She blinked hard, stared at the floor. No smoke. No light tricks. Still, her skin crawled.

Later that same day, she reached across the counter for a spoon, only to find a **knife**—not in the drawer, but balanced near the edge of the cutting board.

She didn't remember pulling it out. But maybe she had. Maybe she had moved it while unloading dishes and forgotten.

Maybe.

She stared at the knife for a long time. The overhead light reflected dully off the blade, and something about the angle made her uneasy.

Liz walked in and immediately noticed the tension.

"You okay?"

"Just tired," Andie muttered.

She wasn't.

She was watching the world carefully now. Too carefully.

That night, the air in the house shifted.

It wasn't supernatural—just *off*. Like someone had rearranged all the furniture by an inch. It made walking through the living room feel wrong. The couch too close, the air too still.

Patrick had passed out drunk by eight. But Knotty and Ricky were still awake, parked in the living room with beers and dirty boots propped up on the table.

Andie entered only to grab her textbook from the side shelf, planning to disappear again without conversation. She kept her eyes forward. Focused.

Ricky whistled. "She even walks like her mom, huh?"

Knotty chuckled. "Told you, man. Sweet little thing."

Andie stopped walking. Her hands clenched at her sides.

“Don’t,” she said.

“Don’t what?” Knotty asked. “We’re *complimenting* you.”

“Yeah,” Ricky added, standing. “Just being friendly.”

He took a step toward her. Andie backed up, chest tight, legs stiff. Her heel caught the carpet.

Ricky raised his hands like he was calming a wild horse. “Relax. You’re safe. We’re just messin’ around.”

“Stay away from her.”

The voice came from behind them.

It was **Liz**.

She stood in the hallway, barefoot, her nightshirt rumpled. In her right hand, gripped white-knuckled, was a **paring knife**.

The silence that followed cracked like ice underfoot.

Liz didn’t move. The knife trembled slightly in her hand, but the look in her eyes was unshakable.

“I said stay away from her.”

Knotty and Ricky both turned, half-laughing, half-assessing the situation.

“C’mon, Liz,” Ricky said with a crooked grin. “We were just joking. Weren’t gonna touch her.”

“You moved toward her,” Liz said coldly. “You *cornered* her.”

Knotty scratched his beard. “It’s late. Emotions are high.”

"You think this is a joke?" Liz took a step forward. "Say another word. I dare you."

Andie hadn't seen her mother like this in years. Not since the early days—when Liz still had hope, still fought back.

Ricky put his hands up in mock surrender, backing away toward the kitchen. "Alright, alright. Shit. Don't get stabby on us, Mom."

Knotty chuckled, following. "Man, y'all are sensitive. We were just bein' neighborly."

Andie stepped beside her mother. Liz never dropped the knife.

The men moved into the hallway and disappeared into the backroom they'd been using. Doors shut. Laughter muffled.

The moment passed. But the *danger* didn't.

They had tested the line.

And Liz had drawn it in steel.

Patrick stumbled in twenty minutes later.

His shirt was unbuttoned halfway, revealing a dirty undershirt clinging to his chest with sweat. His breath reeked of whiskey and bitterness.

He saw the knife still in Liz's hand. He blinked slowly, as if assembling the story in pieces.

"What the *hell* is going on?"

Liz didn't answer.

Patrick looked at Andie, then the empty hallway, then back at Liz.

"Put the knife down," he said.

Liz's grip didn't loosen.

Patrick's voice rose. "I said put the goddamn *knife down!*"

"Your friends came after our daughter," Liz said. "I stopped them."

"Bullshit," he spat. "They were probably flirting. You just don't know how to take a joke."

"That's not a joke, Pat. That's *predatory.*"

Andie held her breath. She could feel the world tilting.

Patrick stepped forward. "You're trying to *embarrass* me? In my house? In front of my friends?"

"No," Liz said. "You did that yourself."

The slap came fast.

Not a wind-up. Not a warning.

A single, sharp crack across Liz's cheek that snapped her head sideways.

The knife fell to the floor.

The silence after the impact was unbearable.

Andie didn't scream.

She didn't run.

She moved.

Quickly. Efficiently. She stepped between her mother and Patrick, fists balled, tears welling—but her voice steady.

"Don't touch her again."

Patrick blinked, shocked not by what he'd done, but that someone **challenged** him afterward.

Liz held her face, eyes wide but dry. Her breath came in short gasps.

Patrick exhaled and took a step back, as if his anger had evaporated with the violence. He shook his head like he was clearing fog from his ears.

“Goddammit,” he muttered. “You always make everything worse.”

Andie stared at him. “You hit her.”

He looked away. “You think life’s easy? You think I wanted those guys here?”

“You *chose* them.”

“They bailed me out, Andie. You think money falls outta the sky? I told ’em I’d let ’em crash here while they figure out their shit. They’re all I got.”

“No. We were what you had,” Andie said. “You just gave us away.”

Patrick didn’t respond.

He stepped over the knife and disappeared into the bedroom.

The door slammed.

Liz dropped to the couch, clutching her face.

Andie sat beside her, wordless.

Both of them knew this wasn’t the bottom.

But they were getting close.

The café opened at 7 a.m., but Andie arrived at 6:15.

There was comfort in the silence before the day began—the soft hum of the espresso machine heating up, the filtered sunlight bleeding through the front windows, the smell of roasted beans and lemon cleaner. She liked the way it made her feel: invisible, capable, useful.

Home was unbearable. She avoided it now unless absolutely necessary. Liz tried to keep it stable, but with Patrick spiraling and his "house guests" always lurking, it had become a game of survival. One misstep, one eye contact too long, one joke mistaken for an invitation, and something could shatter.

At the café, she could breathe.

For a while.

Then Mark started showing up again.

Always with Jacob. Always uninvited.

Andie's stomach tightened the first time he walked in that week. He had that same smug expression, like the entire world owed him something and he was just here to collect. He wore expensive cologne that clashed with the coffee beans, and his clothes looked like they belonged to a catalog—not a teenager.

He slid into the booth across from Jacob with a dramatic sigh, glancing toward Andie with a smirk. "Still working the early shift, huh?" he said, loud enough for the room to hear. "You know, some girls do this to keep busy, others do it 'cause they *need* the money. Which are you?"

Andie didn't answer.

She just kept wiping the counter, but her hand trembled.

That afternoon, Mark brought someone else.

His name was **Billy**—though not the same Billy as her little brother. This Billy was tall, baby-faced, and *too clean*. The kind of rich-boy clean that looked scrubbed with bleach. His dark hair was slicked back, and he wore loafers with no socks, like some obnoxious prep school stereotype.

He didn't order anything. Just leaned over Mark's shoulder and whispered something that made both boys laugh before locking eyes with Andie.

"Jacob," Billy said, "you didn't tell us she was *cute.*"

Jacob looked mortified, opening his mouth to speak, but Mark interrupted him. "He tried. She doesn't like *talking.* Only glaring."

Billy tilted his head. "I like quiet girls. They're better at... listening."

Andie turned sharply and disappeared into the kitchen.

She didn't come out until she was sure they'd left.

Later that night, she found a sugar packet in her apron with the words "Sweet but silent ;)" scribbled on it in marker. Her hands shook as she threw it away.

The next day, she came in even earlier. She began double-checking the locks.

Her refuge was starting to rot.

Jacob tried to soften the discomfort the next time he came in—alone.

He sat at the bar instead of the booth, kept his hands folded, avoided looking at her too long.

"I didn't know they'd follow me," he said. "They were just supposed to grab lunch somewhere nearby. They saw me come in and... I don't know. Decided to tag along."

"You don't seem like them," Andie said, watching him pour sugar into his coffee.

"I'm not," Jacob replied. "I mean... I didn't grow up like that. I had to learn how to *talk* like them. My family's not poor, but we're not them. Not Mark. Not Billy. They're..."

"Entitled?"

He chuckled. "That's a polite word."

Andie gave a half-smile, but it didn't reach her eyes.

"You don't have to let them follow you," she said.

Jacob didn't respond right away. "Sometimes it's easier to let them think they lead."

"Until they step on someone else."

He looked up at her. "I'm sorry. For what they said. I didn't mean for you to feel... unsafe."

Andie nodded slowly. "But you didn't stop them."

The silence between them widened.

Friday afternoon brought **another** new addition: Sean.

He was quieter than the other two, but somehow worse. He didn't leer the way Mark did, or toss childish double entendres like Billy. Sean observed. Measured. His eyes lingered too long on Andie's wrists, her neck, her throat when she drank water. He never smiled.

The four of them took over the café corner booth like royalty slumming it in a dive bar. Mark cracked jokes at the staff's expense. Billy flicked sugar packets at the counter. Sean just watched. Jacob said very little.

Mark stretched his legs under the table and called out, "Hey, Andie. You ever think of modeling? I bet you could really sell a uniform if you tried harder."

Billy laughed.

Sean said nothing, just tilted his head, his eyes never leaving her.

Andie excused herself to the walk-in freezer, locked the door, and sat on a milk crate with her head between her knees.

She wasn't going to cry.

She was going to *remember* this. Every word. Every glance. Every time someone let it happen.

She had always been good at remembering.

After they left, Jacob lingered by the front door.

Andie wiped down the counter without acknowledging him.

He hesitated before speaking. "They're assholes," he said. "I know."

She didn't look at him.

"I don't even like them," he added. "I just… grew up near them. Got dragged into their circle. I'm not like them."

Andie stopped wiping. "But you let them sit here. You laughed at their jokes. You watched me disappear behind the kitchen door and you still came back the next day."

Jacob's face fell. "I was trying to keep the peace."

"Peace doesn't mean silence," she said. "Sometimes silence is just surrender."

He stepped back. "You're right. I—look, I'm sorry."

She nodded once.

But something in her had shifted.

Jacob had been the one bright spot, the one thread she held onto, but now even that was unraveling. He might not have *meant* harm, but meaning didn't erase consequence. She'd learned that too well at home.

As he left, she didn't watch him go.

And she didn't cry.

She just counted the napkins on the counter one by one, steadying her breath.

The coffee shop wasn't a sanctuary anymore, but it was still better than home.

Andie worked double shifts when she could, even took on some deliveries during the lunch rush for tips. Every single dollar mattered now. Her phone case had a slit in the back where she slipped bills—singles and fives, folded tight. It wasn't much, but she was building a way out, inch by inch.

She'd memorized the bus routes within a twenty-mile radius. Studied them like a final exam. She knew which ones ran past midnight, which ones had cameras, which ones stopped near shelters or clinics. She even started keeping a travel-sized deodorant and a granola bar in her backpack.

Liz was doing the same. They didn't talk about it in detail, but one look in the mirror—at the bruises, at the exhaustion—and they both knew time was running out.

Andie made a habit of walking part of the way home now. Not to waste time, but to *buy it*. She needed solitude to think. Needed space to map every detail in her mind.

And yet, the unease followed.

It started again with the notepad.

She always kept a green spiral-bound pad in her locker at work, left on the top shelf with her name scratched in Sharpie.

One morning, it was on the breakroom table. Open. Pages flipped. The pen cap was chewed.

She hadn't taken it out.

She told herself it was just a coworker. An accident. Someone grabbed the wrong pad. Still, her name was on it. Her handwriting.

She flipped through the pages and stopped.

There was a sentence she didn't write:
"He sees more than you think."

It wasn't her handwriting. But it looked like it could've been.

She tore the page out, crumpled it, and tossed it deep into the trash. But she couldn't stop thinking about it all shift.

Later that day, she stayed after closing to clean the espresso machine, alone. The others had gone. The front was locked.

Out of habit, she recorded a voice memo—something she did often when she was thinking through her plans.

"Bus 44 runs every twenty. Drops off past midnight near Crescent. No overhead lights at that stop. Bring flashlight."

When she played the recording back later that night in bed, it sounded normal—at first.

Then, just before the clip ended, something whispered:
"Don't run."

Andie sat straight up. Heart pounding.

She played it again. Again. But this time, it wasn't there.

Just silence.

She didn't sleep that night.

The house was worse than ever. Ricky and Knotty Beard had grown bold again—probably because Patrick had started drinking by noon and passing out by dinner. The men made themselves comfortable, wearing fewer clothes, taking over the TV, never knocking when doors were shut.

One morning, Andie came out of the shower wrapped in a towel to find Knotty standing in the hallway, pretending to look for a light switch.

"Oh," he said, eyes scanning her. "Didn't know you were in there. My bad."

He didn't move.

Andie stepped back inside and locked the door.

When she told Liz, her mother just nodded. "Two more days," she said. "That's all I need. Then we're gone."

Two more days.

They just had to make it.

That night, Andie noticed a glass had moved on the kitchen counter. Just an inch—maybe less. She'd put it on the far left edge, but now it was centered. She stared at it for five minutes, willing herself to remember moving it.

She couldn't.

But she also couldn't prove she didn't.

At this point, reality felt like wet paint—smudged, shifting, hard to trust.

At the café, she started watching the boys more closely.

Jacob still showed up, always quiet, always trying to offer small talk or apologies that rang hollow. Mark had grown more brazen, his jokes sharper, his smiles crueler. Billy was a ghost—there but empty. And Sean... Sean never looked at anyone but her.

It wasn't overt. Not anymore. They learned to behave when she was watching. But their presence filled the room like rot behind drywall.

One day, Jacob asked if she wanted to talk outside.

Andie nodded, curious but guarded.

They stood behind the café, near the dumpsters, out of view.

"I know they make you uncomfortable," Jacob said. "And I should've said something earlier."

"You said that already," she replied.

"I know. But this time I mean it."

Andie gave him a long look. "Then stop bringing them."

"I... I don't think I can."

That was all she needed to hear.

She stepped back. "Then stop coming too."

Jacob's mouth opened, but no words came.

Andie turned and walked inside.

She didn't look back.

After Jacob left, Andie sat in the breakroom and tried to breathe.

Her heart wasn't broken. Not really. Just sore. Bruised from hoping too much. Trust was like skin—it could only take so many scrapes before it hardened or tore.

She pulled out her journal and updated her plan. Bus routes. Departure windows. Which exits were closest to Liz's job. She even noted hiding spots—places to stall or disappear for a few minutes if someone followed them.

They would leave before the weekend. No more delays.

She tucked the journal back into her bag and stood, stretching her neck.

That's when she felt it—a pressure, subtle but present. Like eyes on the back of her neck.

She turned.

No one there.

But her apron had been moved from its hook. Folded. Placed neatly on the table.

Andie hadn't touched it.

She stood frozen, breathing shallow, heart knocking against her ribs.

She opened her locker. Everything else was untouched.

But inside, someone had left a *single sugar packet* with no writing—only a small dot of red ink in the corner.

Andie didn't scream.

She *memorized* it.

Because she was done forgetting. Andie walked for almost an hour before she realized where her feet were taking her. Past the church with the cracked bell tower, beyond the playground where the swings hung limp in the breeze, and finally to the worn stone steps of the town's old library. It stood at the edge of the block like a sleeping giant—quiet, forgotten, almost holy in its disuse. She hadn't been here in over a month.

Inside, it smelled the same. Dust. Aging glue. Dry wood. The ceilings were high, the windows tall, and the air was cool and undisturbed. She nodded politely to the older librarian at the desk, who smiled without speaking, then drifted toward the back where the shelves grew taller and the lights dimmer. Section 133.1—myth, mysticism, occult studies. She knew it by heart.

Her fingers slid across the spines until they stopped on a worn clothbound volume—no glossy cover, just faded gold letters pressed into navy: *Through the Veil: Supernatural Histories and Their Echoes*. It felt like it had been waiting for her.

Andie carried it to a tucked-away table beneath the largest window. Dust drifted through the fading afternoon light, catching in her eyelashes as she turned the pages. She found mentions of Celtic ghosts, South American shadow walkers, Scandinavian witches, women who wailed by rivers, cursed forests, burial mounds. It was academic, dry at times—but she was looking for patterns. Symbols. Any thread that matched what she'd been feeling.

Then she turned a page and froze. The heading read: *Charon: The Drowned Daughter*.

Her stomach clenched. The name felt... familiar. Not from school. Not from TV. From somewhere deeper.

Charon: The Drowned Daughter

Most commonly known in Greek myth as the underworld's ferryman, "Charon" has appeared in fragmented folklore as a feminine spirit in both Eastern European and Appalachian oral traditions. This female figure—often called *Shar-in* or *Carinne* in variations—was once believed to be a mortal woman betrayed, drowned, and bound to grief so strong it fractured her soul across generations.

In these stories, Charon is not a guide but a *witness*. She does not transport the dead—she waits for them. Her presence is marked by:
– **Dampness near mirrors**, especially when no source is visible
– **Emotional dissociation** or *memory blackouts*
– **Objects shifting location without explanation**
– **Dreams involving submerged corridors or unreachable exits**

Charon is drawn to those who are emotionally broken, especially **women in violent or repressive environments**. She is described not as a ghost, but as a living grief—moving through time via bloodlines and spiritual rupture.

In some traditions, she offers protection. In others, revenge. But always at a cost. Once awakened, she waits for the vessel to stop resisting.

"She does not whisper to the brave. Only to the hurt."

– *From "Women of Smoke and Salt: Forgotten Archetypes," pg. 211*

Andie stared at the page. She reread it twice. Her pulse thudded softly in her ears. She copied the entire passage into her notebook—every word. It wasn't about belief. Not yet. It was about recognition. She didn't know why the description affected her so deeply, but something beneath her skin stirred.

Maybe it was a metaphor.

Or maybe it was a warning.

Outside, the sky was the color of bruised lavender, clouds hanging low like they were too tired to climb any higher. Andie walked home slowly, her fingers curled tight around her notebook. Every few steps she glanced over her shoulder—not because she thought someone was following her, but because it *felt* like they could be. The kind of heavy quiet that made your bones hum.

She wasn't thinking about ghosts.

She was thinking about patterns. Mirrors. Moved objects. A shadow darting by. Maybe they weren't paranormal. Maybe it was stress. Sleep deprivation. Trauma making her mind stutter. That could explain everything. But even that thought didn't calm her. If it *was* trauma, it meant the world had warped in a different, cruel way—one that couldn't be exorcised.

She reached the front door and hesitated before turning the knob. She'd hoped Liz would be at work and Billy would be asleep. Maybe dinner would be started. Maybe she could pretend, just for one hour, that they lived in a house where nothing needed escaping.

Instead, she heard glass shatter somewhere in the back. A television buzzed from the living room—too loud, too bright, too normal. That's when she heard it—soft hiccuping cries. A child's.

"Billy?" she called, voice trembling.

No answer.

Her bag hit the floor. She moved quickly past the flickering TV screen, around the corner, into the hall. The door to the back bedroom was open. The light was off.

She stepped inside and froze.

Liz was on the floor, cradling Billy against her chest. Her face was blotched red and violet, the flesh above her cheekbone already swelling. Her lip had split open, dried blood crusting in the corner of her mouth. Her eyes were glassy but dry, refusing to cry in front of her daughter.

Billy's sobs came in shaky gasps. His little arms were wrapped around Liz's neck. His stuffed bear lay in the corner—eye missing, stuffing half-pulled from its side like a wound.

Andie dropped to her knees beside them.

"What happened?" she whispered.

Liz tried to shake her head, but Billy sobbed louder. Andie looked at her mother—really looked. Liz had bruises on her arms, like someone had grabbed her and not let go.

"Was it Patrick?"

Liz's eyes closed. She nodded.

"Was it—were they *all* here?"

"Knotty came by," Liz rasped. "I told him to wait outside. He wouldn't. Billy got scared. I told him to go to the room, and Patrick said I was 'making a scene.' I tried to get Billy away. I pushed the guy. And then..."

Her voice cracked.

Andie stared at the wall. The drywall near the closet had a fist-shaped dent in it. Just below that, a smear of blood—faint, as though someone had wiped it quickly and poorly.

"Did he hit Billy?"

"No," Liz said quickly. "Just me. Billy saw it. That's why he's—he's shaken."

Andie nodded, slowly.

She took the dish towel from the dresser and rose to her feet.

In the kitchen, Andie ran the towel under cold water and wrung it out carefully, as if trying not to tear the fabric. Her hands moved automatically, but her mind was burning—images she didn't want to hold on to, voices she couldn't unhear. She carried the damp towel back and pressed it gently to her mother's face. Liz flinched, but didn't protest.

Billy's cries had softened into whimpers, his head buried in his mother's collarbone.

"I'm okay," Liz whispered.

"No, you're not."

"I don't want you to worry."

Andie's voice didn't shake. "Too late."

They sat in silence for a moment, just the sound of the TV bleeding through the walls, some sitcom laugh track cackling like it didn't know what pain was. Billy clung tighter to Liz.

"We're leaving," Andie said, her voice like stone. "Tonight or tomorrow. No more waiting. I don't care if the money's not enough. We'll figure it out."

Liz didn't argue.

Andie rose again and stepped into the kitchen. She paused at the counter. Something was wrong.

The drinking glass—the one she'd left near the stove—was gone. She checked the sink. Empty. Checked the cabinet. There it was, top shelf, dry and spotless.

She hadn't put it there. She hadn't cleaned it. She stood still. Didn't move. Didn't breathe.

Then, calmly, she pulled the carrots from the fridge. And began to slice. The house was so quiet it felt staged, like someone had hit pause on a horror movie. Patrick was gone—he'd taken the car around noon, muttering about beer and lottery tickets—and the others hadn't returned. Liz stood at the foot of the bed with an open duffel bag, staring down at it like it might bite her.

Andie moved with precision. She didn't waste time. She folded what few clothes she needed, packed deodorant, socks, her work shoes. She put her notebook into a zipper pouch and tucked Billy's birth certificate beneath the liner of the backpack. The "escape bag" wasn't perfect, but it was real. It was happening.

"We can't bring too much," she said, kneeling to check the bottom drawer for clean jeans. "Just what we can carry. Nothing noisy. No shoes that squeak."

Liz nodded slowly. She hadn't packed much—some clothes for Billy, a change of underwear, an envelope of crumpled bills she'd been saving. But she kept glancing toward the door, like expecting Patrick to burst through it early and accuse them of betrayal.

Andie zipped her bag. "Tonight, after I close the café. We go. Whether he's here or not."

Liz's eyes filled, but she blinked it back. "Maybe... maybe we tell him. Let him know it's over. Maybe he'll accept it."

“Mom.”

“I just… I still want to believe he isn’t completely—”

“He is.”

That silence between them said everything.

Liz sat on the edge of the bed while Billy slept in the corner, curled in a ball with his tattered bear under one arm. His face was streaked with tears from earlier, but he slept hard now, like he’d finally collapsed under the weight of fear.

Andie stood by the doorway, arms crossed, watching her mother the way one might study a flickering flame—beautiful, dangerous, unpredictable.

“He’s going to feel like we tricked him,” Liz murmured. “He’ll say we stole something from him.”

Andie nodded. “He’ll say that no matter what we do. Whether we leave or stay, he’ll feel entitled to us.”

Liz looked up. “I should’ve left years ago.”

“You’re leaving now,” Andie said. “That’s all that matters.”

There was no rage in her voice. Just steel.

Liz rose slowly and hugged her daughter—something she rarely did. Andie stiffened at first, then let her arms fall around her mother’s waist. They stayed that way for a while. Not weeping. Not shaking. Just holding on.

At 4:15, Andie slung her backpack over one shoulder and grabbed her work apron.

"I'll be back by 10:30. Don't answer the door for anyone. And if he shows up early—go. Don't wait for me."

Liz hesitated. "And if he's here when you get back?"

Andie paused. "Then I walk through him."

The walk to the café was darker than usual. Clouds hung heavy over the streetlights, dimming everything in a pale orange blur. Andie kept her hood up, her steps brisk. She passed three men smoking near the corner bar—they didn't speak, but their eyes followed her. Always watching. Always calculating.

The café was mostly empty when she arrived. One couple sat by the window, eating in silence. A few high schoolers scrolled through their phones near the back. It was manageable. Calm.

She clocked in at 4:59 p.m., tying her apron with the muscle memory of routine. The act should've brought her comfort. It didn't. Not anymore. Nothing felt safe.

She tucked her hair behind her ears, adjusted her name tag, and moved toward the prep area. For two hours, she cleaned, prepped syrups, restocked cups. Everything mechanical. Everything still.

At 7:12, she refilled the sugar station and thought about the bus schedule. The last one that ran near the overpass left at 10:48. If she finished by 10:30, she could meet Liz and Billy and be gone before anyone noticed.

She exhaled slowly, watching the steam rise from a fresh brew.

That's when the bell above the door rang.

Four of them walked in.

Jacob entered first. His shoulders were hunched, his hoodie too large. He looked up and saw her immediately, then looked down again just as fast. No smile. No wave. No acknowledgment.

Mark followed, still wearing his signature smirk. He looked like he'd just walked off a yacht—white shoes, button-down shirt unbuttoned too low, sunglasses resting on his head like a crown.

Behind him came Billy—*their* Billy's name, but not *him*. This Billy had designer denim and an expensive watch, chewing gum like it was a weapon. He elbowed Mark and whispered something that made them both laugh.

Then came Sean.

Andie hated how silent he was. How his presence made her skin go cold. He didn't leer or speak. He just *watched*. Always. Like he was cataloguing her.

They picked a booth in the corner. Jacob sat apart from the other three, back to the wall, hands in his lap. Mark stretched out, tossing his keys on the table like he owned the place.

Billy tapped his spoon on the menu. "You think she's working tonight?"

"I saw her behind the counter, genius," Mark said, not whispering.

Sean just stared toward the register.

Andie hadn't moved.

She stood behind the espresso machine, breath caught somewhere between her ribs and her throat.

She hadn't expected this.

Not *tonight*.

She turned back to the grinder, pretending to adjust a setting. Her hands moved, but her fingers were numb. A deep chill settled between her shoulder blades. This was supposed to be her last shift. Her last *anything* here. And now the wolves had followed her into the den.

She reached for the coffee scoop and dropped it.

Metal clattered against tile.

The couple by the window looked up. She bent to retrieve it, her ears ringing.

They weren't doing anything wrong. Not yet. Just sitting. Ordering coffee like anyone else. But their laughter grated like nails on glass. Their presence *invaded* the space, shifting the atmosphere. Contaminating it.

Jacob hadn't looked up again. But she could feel the tension in him. She didn't know if it came from shame or something else. Something worse.

She stood, wiped her palms on her apron, and made her way toward their booth with slow, practiced calm.

Mark saw her coming and smiled. "Told you she couldn't stay away."

Andie didn't speak. Andie took half a step back. "If you're not ordering, I need to help other customers."

Mark whistled low. "Feisty." He reached out, as if to grab a napkin holder, but his hand veered just enough to brush hers. She jerked away.

The café owner, Donna, emerged from the back. Her steel-gray hair was pulled into its usual bun, and she was wiping her hands on a dish towel. She didn't need to ask. Her eyes caught the posture, the expressions, the temperature in the room.

"Gentlemen," she said, each syllable clipped. "This is a place of business. If you're not ordering, you need to leave."

Jacob didn't flinch, but the mask slipped for just a moment. His lips parted like he might challenge her—but then he shrugged. "Didn't mean to upset anyone."

"You did," Donna replied coldly. "Out. Now."

Mark's nostrils flared. "Seriously? For what? We didn't do anything."

"You were about to. Don't make me call the cops." Her voice had that finality adults used when they were done pretending to be nice.

Sean and Billy exchanged glances. Jacob gave Andie a last, unreadable look, then turned. "Come on, guys."

They left without another word, the bell above the door jangling with a different rhythm now. Donna waited until she saw them get into a car and pull away. Then she exhaled.

"You alright?" she asked gently.

Andie nodded, too quickly. "Yeah. I'm fine. They were just being... immature."

Donna didn't look convinced. "You know those boys?"

"Only one of them. He used to come in alone. He's changed."

Donna crossed her arms. "Listen. I can close tonight. You've already worked enough."

Andie shook her head. "No, really. I'm okay. I want to stay. I need the hours."

Donna softened. “Alright. But you call me the minute anything feels off. Understand?”

Andie offered a small, grateful smile. “I promise.”

The rest of the shift passed like molasses poured into a cold dish. Customers came and went, but the earlier tension hadn’t left. It clung to the air, hiding behind each chime of the door and hum of the refrigerator.

When Donna finally left for the evening, the quiet settled in. Andie washed dishes with shaky hands. She kept replaying Jacob’s voice, that hint of malice behind his smile. The boy who used to make her feel seen now made her skin crawl.

She closed the blinds, locked the front door, and reset the alarm panel just as Donna had shown her. The café felt like a tiny boat on a wide, dark ocean. Isolated.

Her thoughts drifted to the backpack in her closet, half-packed with the essentials—cash, some clothes, her mother’s birth certificate. Liz was waiting. She was sure of it. Just one more night. Just finish the shift.

She double-checked the back door, then returned to the counter. The air conditioner clicked on with a groan. A flicker of movement outside the front window made her heart skip, but it was just the reflection of passing headlights.

Andie made herself a small cup of chamomile tea, her hands still trembling. She leaned against the counter, letting the steam warm her face. The café’s dim evening lights threw soft halos on the clean tabletops.

She tried not to think about Jacob. Or what would've happened if Donna hadn't been there.

Andie reached beneath the counter and pulled out her well-worn notebook. She'd been trying to write again. Not poetry—nothing pretty. Just lines. Feelings. Like shedding old skin.

She flipped to the latest page and scrawled: *They don't look at me like I'm human. I'm a thing to poke, test, push. Like they want to see what I'll do.*

The pen scratched a little harder than intended.

A creak from the back hallway made her jump. Just the ice machine, she told herself. Still, she stood and walked over to check.

Nothing.

Returning to the counter, she caught sight of her reflection in the mirror behind the drink shelf. For a second, she didn't recognize herself. Pale. Tired. Older somehow.

Another flicker of motion. This time near the back alley window. She moved cautiously, peeking out. Again—just shadows. Nothing tangible.

Yet her gut told her something had changed. The line between watching and being watched was always thin. And now it was gone.

Andie put the tea down. Her hands were still shaking. She moved behind the counter and grabbed the emergency flashlight and small box cutter Donna kept tucked away near the register.

The weight of it in her palm felt both absurd and reassuring. She wasn't planning to fight anyone. But she didn't plan on being helpless either.

Outside, the wind picked up. A newspaper skidded across the pavement. A nearby trash can clanged, and she flinched, adrenaline spiking.

Her phone buzzed. A message from Liz. *We're good here. Be safe. Call me if anything changes.*

Andie smiled faintly. Then jumped again when the café's front door rattled. Not opened. Just... tested.

She moved quickly to the front, staying behind the counter. Nothing visible through the glass. She flicked the outside light on.

Empty sidewalk.

Still, the buzzing in her ears didn't stop.

She gripped the box cutter tighter. Not tonight. She wouldn't let them take tonight.

And then—three loud knocks on the front door.

Andie's breath caught in her throat. She leaned to look—

Jacob stood there. Alone. Hands in his pockets. Staring straight at her. Expression blank.

She didn't move.

He didn't either.

Then he smiled, slow and deliberate.

Andie backed away from the door, turned off the front light, and disappeared into the kitchen, the box cutter gripped like a talisman.

Chapter 3

The rest of her shift passed in a dull, static hush. No more knocks. No more figures at the window. Just the sounds of the café: the hum of the fridge, the buzz of the light overhead, the clink of dishes being stacked. But the silence didn't soothe—it only gave the earlier tension more room to breathe.

Andie wiped down the tables for the third time. She scrubbed at invisible crumbs, rinsed the sink twice, even re-organized the napkin dispensers. Anything to keep her hands busy.

At 11:58 PM, she clicked off the open sign. By 12:10, the place was locked, alarm armed, and keys pocketed. She stood in front of the glass door for a moment, pressing her forehead to the cool surface.

The street outside was empty. No music from the nearby bar, no couples laughing, no late-night cyclists. Just wind whispering across the asphalt.

She took a breath and stepped out into the night.

The walk from the café to her house wasn't long—just two blocks across the parking lot, past the closed pharmacy, and around the back of the auto shop. But tonight, each step felt amplified. Shoes scuffing the sidewalk. Distant barking. Her own breath, too loud in her ears.

She kept her hoodie up and hands in her coat pocket, clutching the little box cutter like a sacred object.

Andie had just reached the halfway mark—where the streetlamps thinned and the shadows thickened—when she heard it.

Tires on pavement. Slow. Deliberate.

Headlights washed across her back like a floodlight.

She didn't turn around at first. Maybe it was just a night driver. Maybe someone making a late grocery run.

Then the engine revved. Once. Twice.

She turned. Jacob's car.

The windows were down. Mark leaned out the passenger side, his mouth already twisted into something gleeful and cruel. "Hey! You need a ride home, sweetheart?"

Jacob sat behind the wheel, one arm resting casually out the window. Billy and Sean were in the backseat, both grinning like jackals.

Andie didn't respond. She just kept walking.

The car crept beside her, matching her pace.

Jacob's voice slithered out. "Come on, Andie. We were just talking earlier. Thought we had a connection."

Sean chimed in, laughing, "Yeah, you looked *real* happy to see us."

Mark pretended to pout. "Don't ignore us, Andie. That's rude."

She picked up her pace. Her heart pounded against her ribs, adrenaline souring her tongue.

The car swerved slightly ahead, cutting her path. Jacob leaned forward and opened the passenger door.

"Get in," he said, too quietly.

Andie froze.

Her hand tightened around the box cutter in her coat. Her breath came shallow and fast.

Jacob smiled, but it didn't reach his eyes. "Seriously. Get in. You're out here alone. It's not safe."

Mark mimicked her voice in a high-pitched falsetto. "What if something happened?" Then he and Billy erupted into laughter.

Sean said nothing, just watched her with that glassy-eyed stare.

Andie stepped back. "Move the car."

Jacob's foot tapped the gas just enough to lurch the vehicle forward. He didn't close the door.

"What's your problem?" he asked. "We're just trying to be friendly. Like old times."

"There were no old times," Andie snapped. Her voice sounded smaller than she wanted. "You need to leave me alone."

Jacob's expression turned. Not anger—worse. Disappointment. As if she'd broken some unwritten rule of theirs.

He nodded once to Mark.

Mark slid out of the car.

Andie's instincts screamed. She turned on her heel and ran.

She didn't scream. Not yet. Screaming made it real. Screaming made it *worse*.

She ran toward the alley between the pharmacy and the warehouse next door—narrow, dark, her feet barely touching the ground.

Behind her, she heard Jacob curse and the car door slam shut.

"Mark! Just grab her!"

Footsteps pounded after her.

The alley was cramped—trash bins, broken crates, cracked pavement. She hurdled a tipped-over shopping cart, ducked beneath a drooping power cable, and tore around the corner—

Only to skid to a halt.

A chain-link fence. Locked.

She turned—

Mark rounded the corner, panting, smiling. "Almost had you."

She pulled the box cutter from her coat.

He saw it.

His smile widened. "What are you gonna do, huh? Gut me?"

Andie's grip didn't waver.

"Don't," she said.

Mark took a step closer. "You think I'm scared of a little girl with a toy knife?"

And then she moved. Fast.

She slashed forward—not deep, just enough to graze his forearm.

He yelped and stumbled back.

Andie ran again, slipping past him while he clutched his arm and cursed.

The parking lot behind the warehouse was empty. Just cracked asphalt and an old rusted bike rack. Andie sprinted across it, lungs burning, shoes slipping on broken glass.

Behind her, Mark was still shouting. "You crazy bitch! You cut me!"

She didn't look back.

Jacob's car peeled around the far end of the alley, its tires squealing. The headlights found her again—white, blinding.

Andie darted into the next alley, weaving between dumpsters, not even sure if she was going toward home anymore. She just had to get *away*.

A cat hissed and bolted from under a trash bin.

She tripped but caught herself.

Then—another corner. A loading dock. She ducked beneath it, crawling into the gap between its foundation and a stack of crates.

Dark. Tight. Safe.

The car rolled by. Slower this time.

Jacob's voice floated out: "You think you can run forever, Andie? This is just the beginning."

She didn't move. Didn't breathe.

They didn't find her.

Eventually, the car faded into the distance.

Andie stayed there until her legs cramped and the night felt still again.

When she finally emerged, the moon had shifted. She walked the rest of the way home in silence.

Her box cutter stained with blood.

Her heart no longer racing. Just *cold*.

She hadn't even reached the corner before she heard the tires. The crunch of rubber over gravel. Headlights painted her shadow across the wall of the mini-mart, tall and monstrous. She turned too late. Jacob's car came to a stop with an angry hiss of brakes, cutting her path off at an angle.

Doors opened. Not slammed—opened slowly.

Jacob stepped out of the driver's side, his silhouette fluid in the night, like the shadows welcomed him. Mark, Billy, and Sean followed, each boy moving with a loose, dangerous confidence.

Andie's chest locked up. She backed away, but the sidewalk narrowed behind her, blocked by dumpsters.

"You run good," Jacob said. His voice wasn't mocking this time. It was quiet. Even. Controlled. "But I told you... this doesn't end until I say so."

Mark cracked his knuckles. "We're just here to talk, right?"

Andie reached into her coat, her fingers finding the box cutter again. She pulled it slowly, eyes darting between them. Her hand shook, but she held it out in front of her. "Don't."

Billy let out a high, nervous laugh. "She's serious, dude."

But Jacob didn't laugh. He stepped closer. "You know this won't work. Not with me."

When she slashed the air between them, it was desperate, wild. Mark caught her wrist. Twisted it hard.

She cried out as the box cutter hit the pavement.

They swarmed her.

Andie's screams were muffled by a hand. Her body buckled against the pavement, knees scraping concrete.

Her mind began to fold inward. Her legs kicked outward.

The world turned into fragments—familiar voices, terrifying and far away. The smell of sweat and asphalt. The pressure of weight. The cold burn of humiliation.

She didn't black out entirely. That would've been mercy. Instead, she drifted. She floated above herself. She became two people: one watching, one enduring.

Their laughter felt unreal, warped by their grunting only added to the panic and tears. Someone whispered something in her ear, but her ears had started ringing. Her body didn't respond anymore, even as it fought internally to survive.

When it was over, she wasn't sure how long she lay there. Minutes? Hours?

She couldn't cry. She couldn't move. Just lay curled in on herself, shaking, her face against the pavement.

A car door slammed again in the distance. Then the sound of a vehicle speeding away.

Silence crept back in.

Somewhere far off, a car slowed down.

Then stopped.

A door opened. Footsteps. A woman's voice, trembling but firm. "Oh my God—miss? Are you okay? Can you hear me?"

A warm hand touched Andie's shoulder. She flinched. The woman gasped. "I'm not going to hurt you. Help's coming. Stay with me."

More lights arrived. Red. Blue. White.

Radios crackled.

Then gloved hands, gentle but practiced.

An EMT leaned over her, his voice steady but his face tight with emotion. “Andrea? You’re safe now. We’re going to help you. I promise.”

She didn’t speak. She didn’t nod. But a tear slipped from her left eye.

Inside the ambulance, everything was blinding and sterile. The lights buzzed softly overhead. A white sheet had been draped over her like a fragile shroud, but it didn’t stop the shaking.

The paramedic closest to her—mid-30s, dark eyes—kept talking to her. Not questions, just soft affirmations. “You’re okay now. You’re not alone. We’ve got you.”

She clutched the sheet tightly to her chest.

Another paramedic made notes. “Female, seventeen. Lacerations on knees and hands. Possible signs of sexual trauma. Responsive but nonverbal. Call ahead—Mercy General.”

The female EMT, kneeling at her side, squeezed her hand. “Andrea, you don’t have to say anything. Just hold on.”

She did.

The ambulance wail rose again, screaming for her. She stared at the ceiling the whole way. Every bump in the road made her flinch.

At the hospital, they were met by two officers and a trauma nurse. Questions flew back and forth over her as they moved her inside.

“She was found behind Wexler’s Mini-Mart.”
“No ID on her. Only her name tag.”

"She's seventeen. The woman who found her recognized her from the café. Andrea Montgomery."
"Get the SART nurse. We need the kit ready. Call in crisis response."

They rolled her down a corridor. The ceiling tiles blurred together like falling snow.

A nurse held her face between gentle palms. "Can you look at me, sweetie?"

Andie blinked. Her lips trembled.

The nurse nodded. "We're going to take care of you. All of us."

They wheeled her into a quiet exam room and began the process. Slowly. Carefully. With gloves. With cameras. With dignity.

Outside the exam room, Officer Haley began filling out her report. She was new to the precinct, maybe mid-twenties, but her face bore the wear of what she'd already seen tonight.

She asked the EMTs for their logs. Recorded the names of witnesses. Interviewed the woman who'd found Andie—a local music teacher who'd been on her way home after a rehearsal.

"She looked like a broken doll," the woman said, voice trembling. "She was just... left there. What kind of animals would do that?"

Meanwhile, a nurse searched Andie's clothes for identification and found her café badge.

The name was clear: *Andie Montgomery.*

They found the emergency contact number she'd written on her employment file.

A nurse, her voice shaking but composed, made the call.

It rang four times.

"Yeah?" Patrick's voice answered, thick with alcohol and irritation.

"Mr. Montgomery, this is Mercy General. Your daughter—"

"What's she done now?"

"Sir, she's been sexually assaulted. She's in the hospital. We need you—"

"You sure she didn't start it?"

Silence.

The nurse cleared her throat. "She's traumatized. Physically injured. She needs family—now."

Patrick grunted. "Figures. That girl's always looking for attention."

Then he hung up.

The nurse stared at the phone for a long moment, her hand tightening around the receiver before she slowly placed it back in the cradle.

Back at the Montgomery home, Liz had been half-awake when the phone rang. She didn't hear the full conversation, but Patrick's tone told her enough. She emerged from the bedroom as he tossed his phone onto the couch with a grunt.

"What was that?" she asked.

"Your daughter's in the hospital," he slurred. "Says she got jumped or something. Probably lying."

Liz froze. "What happened?"

Patrick waved it off. "Said she got herself into something. Probably led 'em on. You know how she is."

Liz stared at him in horror. "You're blaming her?"

"She's been running her mouth for months. Hanging around with boys. What'd you think was gonna happen?"

Liz turned, grabbed her coat and purse. "I'm going."

Patrick moved to block her. "Where do you think you're going?"

She didn't speak. She stepped sideways, toward the kitchen.

He followed. "Don't be dramatic."

She opened the drawer and pulled out the butcher knife.

Patrick froze.

Liz's voice was cold and sharp. "Get. Out. Of. My. Way."

Patrick stepped closer. "Put it down."

She didn't.

He lunged.

The slap came fast, explosive. Her cheek flared, her vision blurred.

But she didn't let go of the knife.

She slashed him—clean, diagonal, across the chest.

Patrick howled.

Liz grabbed Billy from his bed. Carried him to the car in her arms.

Patrick stumbled into the front yard, shirt darkening. "You'll pay for this!" he screamed.

Liz didn't answer. She was already driving away. With her hands shaking and the baby crying loudly, Liz could not concentrate on the drive to the hospital. Her eyes were swollen from the punches by Patrick, and they filled with tears as she struggled to keep the car in the proper lane. A glare of high beams from oncoming traffic temporarily blinded her, causing her to miss a swerve in the road, sending her vehicle into oncoming traffic. Both mother and child died at the scene of the accident.

The hospital hallway was quiet that morning, muted by the insulation in the walls and the heavy hush of grief that seemed to follow Andie everywhere she went. She sat upright in bed, knees tented beneath the thin cotton sheet, arms folded over her stomach. Her hair hung limp over her face, unbrushed, unwashed, clinging to the dried sweat at her temples. She didn't care.

Sunlight seeped in through the blinds, dust swirling in the golden beams. It was after ten. Visiting hours had started.

Any minute now, Mama would walk through the door.

Andie told herself that over and over. Mama was probably filling out forms. Maybe they stopped for gas. Maybe Billy had one of his little tantrums about the car seat—he hated the way the buckle rubbed his shirt. Andie smiled at that thought, just for a second. She could hear his tiny voice fussing, and Mama trying to calm him. That's all it was. A delay.

But deep down, in the quiet space between her ribs and her breath, something darker whispered.

She pressed her palm against her chest and tried to smother the fear. The hospital room smelled like antiseptic and plastic. Her legs were still sore. Bruised. But the nurses said her body was healing. They didn't ask if her mind was.

The clock on the wall ticked so loudly she thought it might crack.

Time passed like syrup. Nurses came and went, checking her vitals, offering her pills, smiling with their lips but not with their eyes. She watched the door every time it opened.

No Mama.

She didn't say anything. She just waited. Curled into the bed like a child trying not to exist. When a young aide brought in a tray of scrambled eggs and a bruised banana, Andie stared at it, then turned to face the wall. Her stomach clenched at the smell of food.

Where was Mama?

The silence around her began to feel like pressure. Her thoughts turned inward. Maybe Patrick wouldn't let her come. Maybe he hit her again. Maybe...

No. She would've come anyway.

Andie imagined Mama at home, pacing, dialing the hospital, being told she couldn't visit. Or maybe she was on her way. Stuck in traffic. Crying, just like Andie was. That had to be it.

Outside the room, a voice on the intercom mumbled something indecipherable. Then silence again. Just the dull hum of fluorescent lights. Her fingers clenched around the blanket edge, twisting the fabric tight.

She started counting. Her heartbeats. The seconds between blinking. The tiles in the ceiling.

She made it to 114 before the phone rang in the hallway.

She strained to hear. The phone was picked up, then muffled voices exchanged a few quiet sentences.

Her door opened. A nurse stepped in—older, kind face, tired eyes. The same one who'd sat with her after the forensic kit was completed.

Andie sat up straighter. "Is that my mom? Did she call?"

The nurse paused. Not long. Just enough. She shook her head gently. "No, honey. That was just housekeeping. I'll let you know as soon as someone arrives."

The way she said it—soft and practiced—made Andie's stomach churn.

"I think... she's on her way," Andie said, needing to hear the words out loud. "She wouldn't just not come. Maybe something came up."

The nurse hesitated. "Of course. I'm sure she's doing everything she can to get to you."

But it was a lie. Not a cruel one, just the kind adults tell when they don't know what else to say.

The nurse fluffed Andie's pillows and gently smoothed the blanket across her legs. "Try to rest, alright? I'll be back to check on you soon."

The door clicked shut behind her.

Andie's hands trembled. She pressed her forehead to her knees. Her body felt heavy again.

Mama should've been here by now.

At that exact moment, not far from the hospital, the sky flashed with high beams reflected off wet asphalt. Tires screeched.

A silver sedan swerved across the dividing line. It clipped the shoulder, overcorrected, then spiraled—full speed—into oncoming traffic.

There was no warning. No horn. No time. Just impact. Metal screamed against metal. Glass exploded outward like ice shattered from a rooftop. A truck swerved, trying to avoid the collision. It couldn't. The driver had no chance.

Back in the hospital, Andie stared at the wall.

A warmth spread down her cheeks again—tears she didn't remember starting.

"I'm sorry," she whispered into the pillow. She didn't know what for. Just that something inside her had broken again.

She pressed her hands over her ears to shut out the ticking clock, the drip of the IV, the world.

Outside, people pulled to the side of the road. Emergency services were dispatched. Two bodies were pulled from the wreckage, one adult and one small child. Neither showed signs of life. The paramedics worked anyway. It's what they always did.

Andie felt a sharp pain in her chest.

It wasn't physical. It was deeper. An ache that made no sense—like part of her had just vanished.

She curled tighter into the bed and prayed a wounded person's prayer.

The next morning, no one told her anything. The silence that greeted her was more deafening than any siren. No new visitors. No phone calls. No messages.

She sat beside the window, tracing the cracks in the sill with her fingernail.

When the nurse returned, Andie asked again. “Did my mom call?”

Another gentle smile. “Not yet, sweetheart.”

Her heart caved in a little more.

By early afternoon, a social worker entered the room with a clipboard and a sad voice. Her name was Ms. Alvarez. She wore soft colors and smelled like hand sanitizer and lavender.

She introduced herself, explained the protocol. “Since you’re still a minor, we need to confirm a guardian can pick you up when the doctor discharges you. Has your father made contact?”

Andie didn’t answer.

Ms. Alvarez waited. “If no one comes, we’ll coordinate a temporary placement. I’ll stay with you while we sort it out.”

Andie stared past her, out the window, at the motionless trees.

It was her silence that said everything.

Ms. Alvarez got the paperwork moving. By late afternoon, they had a temporary release. A voucher for a taxi. A small bag of donated clothes.

When she left the hospital, the world was too bright. Her body ached from the weight of absence.

Andie didn’t know yet that her mother would never walk through any door again.

Chapter 4

The taxi ride from the hospital felt longer than it should have. Andie sat in the backseat with her hands balled into her lap, fingers white from clenching. The driver didn't speak to her, which she appreciated. He had looked at her once through the rearview mirror, registering the bruises on her face, the faded hospital ID band still around her wrist—but said nothing. No music played on the radio. Just the soft hum of tires on pavement and the distant sound of wind brushing against the windows.

The city rolled by outside, but she didn't look at it. She stared at her knees, tracing the seams of the cheap jeans the hospital gave her. They were too long and cinched awkwardly with a knotted string. Her hoodie was old, donated from a charity bin, faded pink with a school mascot she didn't recognize.

When they reached her street, the driver cleared his throat. "This it?"

Andie nodded, but her voice didn't come out. She opened the door with one hand and clutched the voucher in the other. He waited as she stepped out onto the curb, then pulled away before she'd even made it to the porch.

The house looked unchanged. Still weather-worn. The yard, still unkept. The sagging front door, still bearing the dent Patrick had left during one of his rages years ago.

Andie swallowed the lump in her throat. Her legs felt heavy. Her body was tired. But somewhere deep in her gut, she had hope. Maybe Mama was inside. Maybe all of it was a mistake. Maybe—

She opened the door and stepped inside.

The smell hit her first—alcohol, stale food, sweat, and something metallic she couldn't place. The living room was dim. The blinds were drawn tight, letting in only slits of gray daylight. On the couch, sprawled in his usual stained t-shirt and jeans, was Patrick. Passed out, mouth hanging open, one arm dangling over the side of the couch. His chest rose and fell in deep, snoring breaths.

Andie stood in the entryway, frozen. Her feet didn't want to move forward. She wanted to call out for Mama—but the word caught in her throat. She couldn't say it. Not yet. Not until she was sure.

She crept down the hall, quietly checking each room. The kitchen was empty. The bathroom door hung open. The bedroom—her mother's bed was made, too neatly. No sign of her things. No purse, no keys, no signs of life.

The panic started slowly, like rising water. Andie backed out of the bedroom, turned, and walked with purpose toward the couch.

Patrick's body groaned as she shook his shoulders. "Daddy?" she said softly. No response. "Daddy, where's Mama?"

His eyes fluttered, bloodshot and unfocused. His breath reeked of cheap whiskey.

She shook him again. "Daddy, where's Mama? Where's Billy?"

He blinked and looked around like a man trying to remember what year it was.

Then he sat up suddenly and grabbed her in a hug.

His arms wrapped around her like iron bars, holding too tight. Andie didn't hug him back. She stiffened under his grip, shocked at the sudden contact. It had been years since Patrick had hugged her—if ever. She wasn't even sure he knew how.

He held her like he was desperate. When he pulled back, there were tears in his eyes.

“Your mama...” he began, his voice cracking. “She and Billy... they were killed in a car accident on the highway.”

Andie blinked at him. Her lips parted, but no words came out.

“When?” she finally whispered.

“A few days ago,” he muttered, already glancing around for a bottle. “She was on her way to see you at the hospital. Car got struck. Spun out. Hit a truck. Died right there.”

Her mind couldn’t hold the information. It crashed against the walls of her brain, trying to make sense of it. It didn’t feel real.

She staggered back and sat on the arm of the recliner, her knees giving out.

“She—Mama—was coming to see me?”

“Yeah,” Patrick said. “Because of you.”

He took a swig from a bottle he found on the floor, then fixed his glassy eyes on her. “They’re dead. Because of you.”

Andie couldn’t breathe. The room closed in. The walls pressed closer. Her chest shrank to nothing. Her hands trembled.

“I didn’t—I didn’t ask her—” she tried to say.

Patrick stood and took another step toward her.

“You think you didn’t have a hand in this?” he said, voice rising. “You think she would’ve gone anywhere that night if you hadn’t gotten yourself raped?”

Andie recoiled like he’d hit her.

Patrick tossed the empty bottle aside. It rolled across the floor and struck the baseboard with a hollow thunk.

"I gotta deal with the morgue now. The funeral home. The feds asking questions. I gotta bury my wife and my boy, all because you don't know how to dress decent or keep your legs closed."

The words cut deeper than any slap.

Andie didn't respond. She couldn't.

The lump in her throat had turned to stone.

Patrick's face twisted into something cruel. "Now I gotta pay all this money to get them out of cold storage and into the ground. And people are looking at me like I did something wrong."

His voice cracked into a laugh—bitter, hollow, hateful.

She stood up slowly, trying to make it to her room. But Patrick wasn't finished.

He stepped forward, grabbed her by the arm, and spun her back to face him.

"Look at me when I talk to you!"

Andie turned her face up just in time to feel the slap.

Her head snapped sideways, and she stumbled back, her ear ringing.

"Did you hear me, girl?" he bellowed. "You're the reason my wife is dead!"

Her cheek throbbed. A red-hot sting radiated down her jaw. Andie clutched her face, staggering backward toward the hallway. Patrick followed.

"You dress like a slut. You act like a whore. You brought shame into this house." His words tumbled over each other, faster and louder, like an avalanche that wouldn't stop. "You ruined this family, and now I gotta pick up the pieces!"

Andie turned and ran.

Her bare feet pounded against the hardwood as she rushed down the hall, rounded the corner, and slammed her bedroom door shut. Her hands fumbled with the lock, heart pounding, eyes stinging.

He banged on the door once—twice—then cursed and stomped away.

She slid down the door until she hit the floor, curled her legs to her chest, and let the tears come.

This wasn't grief. It was something worse—being punished for grieving. For surviving.

She sobbed into her knees, small and alone in the darkness.

For the first time, she stopped praying for it to end.

She prayed for something else entirely.

The rage, buried deep, began to stir.

The day of the funeral came cloaked in overcast gray, as if even the sky refused to show emotion. Andie sat in the back seat of a borrowed sedan, the only car in the driveway that still ran. She wasn't sure who had arranged the transport—one of the hospital social workers maybe—but the keys had been left in a manila envelope taped to the front door. Patrick hadn't spoken a word to her that morning. He just grunted when he emerged from the bedroom already dressed in his old black suit.

It was the same suit he wore to job interviews long ago, back when there were still jobs to apply for. Now, it hung from him like a borrowed skin. The jacket's shoulder seams drooped. The sleeves extended past his wrists. His tie was tied wrong, too short and cockeyed. He didn't fix it. He didn't look at her either.

Andie stared out the window as the town rolled by. Storefronts with CLOSED signs. A few people walking dogs. Potholes in the streets she used to ride her bike down. They passed the elementary school—Billy's would-be kindergarten next year—and her stomach clenched. She rubbed her palms together, trying to forget the sound of his voice, high and eager, whenever he said her name. *"An-dieee!"* She bit her bottom lip hard until the sting chased the memory back.

When they arrived, the small church lot was already half full. Patrick parked at an angle, too far from the curb, but didn't fix it. He stepped out and lit a cigarette, ignoring the No Smoking sign beside the door.

Andie followed behind, each step a mile.

The church smelled like cedar polish and artificial lilies. Rows of wooden pews lined the sanctuary, and at the front, under the dull glow of chandelier light, stood the caskets: one full-sized for her mother, and one heartbreakingly small for Billy. They were surrounded by towering bouquets—red roses, white lilies, forget-me-nots—each arrangement bearing ribbons of condolences from people who didn't really know them.

Andie stood frozen at the back of the room. Her feet wouldn't move. The sight of the caskets stole her breath. The small one in particular made her knees weak. She gripped the edge of a pew to steady herself. Her eyes locked on the soft blue of Billy's casket trim. She hated it. It was too cheerful. Too bright. It felt like mockery.

Patrick moved ahead of her, nodding vaguely at people he didn't seem to recognize. His handshake was slow, automatic. There were tears in his eyes, but they didn't look real. Not to Andie. It felt like a show. A mask.

A man in a dark blazer motioned for Andie to come forward. She shook her head once. He frowned, then gently approached her.

"You're family, aren't you? You should be near the front."

"I'll stay back here," she whispered.

The man hesitated. "Your brother and sister are expected. They'll be sitting up front too."

She turned her face away. "I'll move when they get here."

The man didn't press. He simply nodded and left her alone again.

She stood still, watching the empty space beside the caskets, waiting for her family to fill it.

Jarrod arrived first. His tall frame entered the sanctuary like a gust of cold air. He wore his Army service uniform, everything sharp and formal—polished shoes, pressed slacks, brass gleaming on his chest. His face was expressionless, but his eyes searched the room the moment he stepped inside.

When he spotted Andie near the back, he didn't hesitate. He made his way to her, boots echoing on the hardwood. He stopped in front of her, standing awkwardly. Neither moved for several seconds. Then he leaned forward and hugged her.

It was brief. Just enough to count.

"You okay?" he murmured.

Andie shrugged, which was the only answer she could muster.

He didn't press. "They want us up front."

Together, they walked toward the caskets, taking their place in the second row—immediate family. Andie flinched when she had to sit beside Patrick, but Jarrod's presence beside her dulled the edge.

Moments later, Kayan appeared at the entrance. Her belly had grown round and prominent beneath a flowing navy dress. Her face was drawn, her eyes ringed with exhaustion. She moved slowly, one hand resting protectively on her stomach. She sat beside Andie, squeezing her hand briefly. No words. Just the gesture.

Gerard wasn't with her. Andie wasn't surprised.

The service began. The pastor, a gray-haired man with a Bible thick enough to crush bone, welcomed the congregation and asked them to rise. Andie stood when they did, mouthing the hymns but not really singing. The notes caught in her throat like thorns.

And all the while, her eyes returned to the smaller casket.

The eulogies started with her mother. The pastor spoke first, recalling Liz's soft nature and her years at the pharmacy, how she knew every customer's birthday and handed out candy to children during flu shots. A woman from the church read a poem. A neighbor spoke about Liz's "quiet dignity" and "God-fearing spirit." All of it felt wrong.

No one talked about the bruises. The nights she cried behind locked doors. The moments Andie watched her cover up another black eye or flinch when someone raised their voice. They turned Liz into a saint in that room, but not the kind Andie knew. Not the tired woman who once whispered, *"I'll get you out one day, baby. Just hold on."*

No one remembered *her* Liz.

When the focus shifted to Billy, the tone cracked. Even the pastor's voice faltered. "He was so young. A bright light. Just five years old, and already charming the world around him."

Andie stared at the polished wood of his casket and imagined his little feet curled up beneath the blanket. She couldn't picture his face anymore without remembering what she never got to say.

I'm sorry.

I love you.

Please don't go.

When the service ended, the crowd formed a slow-moving line to the front. People placed flowers on the caskets. Some knelt in prayer. Some just touched the wood and walked away.

Patrick stood there, accepting hugs and condolences. Andie sat still, invisible in her own skin, every touch around her feeling miles away.

The worst part wasn't the loss.

It was that no one saw her in it.

After the final hymn, people began to trickle outside. The air was cool, and the sky finally gave way to a drizzle—light enough not to cancel the graveside gathering, but heavy enough to feel symbolic. Umbrellas bloomed in the parking lot like somber flowers.

Andie stood beside Jarrod and Kayan under the portico. They waited for the pallbearers to prepare the caskets for transport. Patrick was nowhere to be seen.

"I don't know where he went," Jarrod muttered, glancing around. "Checked the lot. Restrooms. Nothing."

Kayan snorted. "Probably found a bar or a bottle somewhere."

Jarrod's jaw tightened. "I'd teach that bastard something if I had the time."

He looked at Andie. "How are you holding up?"

Andie didn't respond. Her arms were wrapped tightly around herself.

Kayan stepped closer. "You see how she is. I bet he's been wailing on her every chance he gets."

Jarrod turned fully toward Andie. "Is he still hitting you?"

Her gaze dropped to the concrete beneath her shoes. Her silence said everything.

Jarrod's fists clenched, but he let out a shaky breath instead of exploding. "I wish I could take you with me, but I live in a damn barracks. It's not a place for you."

Andie turned to Kayan, her voice thin. "Then can I come with you?"

Kayan hesitated. "I would... but the baby's almost due, and Gerard—he wouldn't be okay with it. The house is a wreck."

Andie nodded slowly. Each refusal was a brick. By the end of the conversation, she was already buried beneath them.

The road home felt longer than it ever had before. After the final condolences were whispered and her siblings vanished in different directions—Jarrod to a waiting bus back to base, Kayan to a taxi bound for the airport—Andie found herself alone at the church gate. No ride. No farewell. Just her, the wet gravel underfoot, and the silence of a world too busy grieving itself to care what happened next.

She walked.

The funeral shoes someone had loaned her were a half-size too small. Blisters had already formed by the third block, but she didn't stop. Her hoodie, borrowed from a box of clothes left by a kind nurse at the hospital, soaked through slowly as the drizzle picked up. Her hair clung to her cheeks. Her breath fogged in the cool air. With each step, the houses became more familiar—until the dread started to bloom.

She passed Mrs. Hayward's rusting wind chimes. The mailbox shaped like a dog with one ear missing. The old oak tree she used to hide behind during hide-and-seek with Billy. Every memory bit at her heels like cold wind.

As she turned the corner onto her street, she froze.

A sheriff's car was parked at the curb in front of her house. The blue stripe along the side was faded, but the light bar on top reflected the overcast sky like polished bone.

She slowed her pace but didn't stop. Her stomach twisted with panic. Her mind filled with all the wrong possibilities.

The door creaked open just as she stepped onto the porch.

The sheriff stepped out.

He was a broad-shouldered man with a square jaw and a permanent scowl etched into his brow. His name tag read ***Miller***, and Andie remembered him only vaguely—from school assemblies and town parades. But up close, he radiated something colder than authority. Something *watchful*.

He glanced at her as she approached, his eyes sweeping over her soaked hoodie and funeral dress with quiet judgment.

"You're Andie, right?" he asked, voice flat.

She nodded.

"I was just talking to your daddy. Store manager down at Grover's said he caught him knocking beer bottles off the shelf, stumbling around.

Didn't have a penny on him." He frowned. "Guess he tried to walk out with a few."

Andie swallowed hard, her hands clenching into fists inside her sleeves.

"I figured, considering everything y'all been through," he continued, "I'd bring him home instead of booking him. Sympathy, you know?" His tone suggested he didn't offer that very often.

She said nothing.

"Manager's got a receipt. He wants the damages covered. Said if he don't get the money, next time he'll press charges."

He pulled a folded receipt from his chest pocket and held it out. She took it silently.

The number scrawled in pen made her stomach tighten.

"You got that?" Sheriff Miller asked.

She nodded faintly and dug into her pocket. Hospital discharge voucher money, ten crumpled singles, and a wrinkled five. She handed it over.

Miller took it without thanks. "He's passed out now. Might give you some peace for the evening." He paused. "Best have something for him to eat when he wakes up."

He stared at her for too long. Then left.

The sheriff's cruiser pulled away, its headlights washing over her like a cold x-ray. Andie stood on the porch, motionless, her hand still clutching the doorknob. The damp funeral dress clung to her like skin. She listened until the cruiser turned the corner, the hum of the engine swallowed by the wind.

Inside, the house was dim. The smell hit her immediately: sweat, beer, and old laundry. Her fingers brushed the light switch, but she didn't flip it. Darkness felt safer now.

Patrick's snoring echoed through the house like a warning siren muffled by drywall. She moved through the narrow hallway as quietly as possible, her shoes squeaking faintly against the floor. She tiptoed past the living room, where his body sprawled across the couch in a heap. A half-empty bottle of rum rested on his chest, one arm draped over the side.

She reached her room, closed the door gently, and leaned against it. Her chest ached. Her hands trembled. She stepped out of the wet clothes, peeled them off layer by layer, and dropped them into a growing pile in the corner.

She looked up at the mirror above her dresser—and froze.

Outside the window, something shifted.

She moved to the curtain and peered out.

Nothing but darkness.

Still, the sensation lingered—eyes watching, breath fogging the glass.

She yanked the curtain shut and stepped back. Her heart thudded so hard she thought it might bruise her ribs. The room smelled like mildew and damp wood. But underneath it all... was that smoke?

No. Just nerves. Just her imagination.

She turned toward the bed.

The door burst open.

Patrick stumbled into the room, wild-eyed and weaving, the bottle still in his grip but nearly empty now. His shirt was untucked, half unbuttoned, stained with something that could've been ketchup or dried blood. He reeked—of sweat, whiskey, and something older, something rotting in the corners of his soul.

Andie backed up, arms crossed tightly over her chest. "Daddy... please don't."

His voice cracked through the air, guttural and drunk. "You damned witch. You cursed this house. You cursed *me*. My wife's dead. My boy's gone. And it's *your* fault."

"No," she whispered. "I didn't do anything. I miss Mama too."

"Don't lie to me, girl!" he roared, flinging the bottle toward the wall. It shattered, glass and liquor exploding against the drywall like a gunshot. Andie flinched but didn't run. There was nowhere to run.

Patrick stormed forward. "I'm your father! You will *respect* me!"

Andie stepped back, bumping into the dresser. "Then EARN IT!"

The words came out louder than she expected—clear, sharp, defiant.

He lunged.

The slap hit her across the face with a sickening crack, knocking her into the dresser. She slid to the floor, her head spinning. Then came the first kick.

She curled into a ball.

Another.

Then another.

She tasted blood.

She felt herself slipping out of the moment, out of the pain, out of her body.

No longer a girl praying to be spared.

Now—just something full of rage, rising.

The beating blurred together, a rhythm of impact and silence, bones meeting wood, breath stolen with every blow. Andie lost track of how many times he kicked her. Three? Five? Ten? Time bent around her pain. Her ribs ached, her back burned, her face throbbed with every thudding heartbeat.

Then—quiet.

When she opened her eyes, he was gone.

Just like that. The room echoed with the aftermath, like a concert hall left hollow after the musicians left. Her ears rang. Her muscles spasmed. Her nightstand had tipped over in the fight, and the drawer had spilled open—its contents scattered like bones across the floor.

She stayed on her side, barely able to breathe.

Her right eye began to swell shut. Blood crusted her lips. Her hands twitched but wouldn't obey.

She didn't know how long she stayed like that.

An hour? A lifetime?

Then she noticed something.

A smell.

Smoke.

But not the sharp burn of something on fire—no. This smelled... old. Ancient. Like the sulfur pits Mama used to tell her about in Bible stories. Like what you'd expect Hell to reek of.

She blinked through the haze, slowly turning her head toward the mirror.

And froze.

The mirror reflected her broken room—but in the center of it, swirling behind her, was smoke that didn't exist in the real world.

Within it—eyes.

Not human. Not possible.

Bright yellow. Flickering like candles. Watching.

She didn't scream. She just stared.

A voice filled her mind.

"Andrea Montgomery... you have been forsaken. Embrace what comes."

Andie didn't rise so much as unfold.

Her limbs moved like they were waking up from something deeper than sleep—muscles crackling with stiffness, but under them, a new awareness hummed. She exhaled slowly, feeling her ribs protest the motion, but she didn't wince. Pain was still present, but it was dull now, distant—as if it had slid beneath her skin to make room for something else.

She sat upright, placing one hand flat on the wooden floor to steady herself. The floorboards felt cooler than they should have. The air smelled faintly of ozone and smoke, like a lightning strike had just missed her.

The mirror across the room still reflected her shape, but the mist within it had thinned, like fog peeling back from glass. She saw herself clearly now: bloodied lip, bruised eye, dried trails of tears on her cheeks. But she wasn't afraid of that image anymore. She was studying it. Understanding it. Owning it.

She thought about the book she'd found—*Supernatural Histories of the Ancient Dead*. It had mentioned Charon in the margins of a chapter about judgment, not death. Not the ferry across the Styx, but the collector of pain unaccounted for. She'd dismissed it at the time as myth.

Now, she wasn't sure anything had ever been more real.

Andie stood, joints clicking like rusted hinges. She moved toward her bedroom door, each step measured, purposeful. Her bare feet glided over the uneven floorboards, the calluses on her heels catching splinters but not reacting.

The hallway awaited—dark, narrow, crooked in the corners like it had shifted during the night. She paused at its threshold.

Somewhere in the house, something had changed.

The hallway stretched forward like a tunnel. Shadows pooled at the baseboards, stretching upward like fingers. Andie didn't rush. She stepped slowly, deliberately, her hands grazing the wall for balance—not because she was weak, but because she was *feeling* it. The wallpaper beneath her fingertips was slightly textured, bubbled from water damage, and faintly warm.

The air was thick. Heavier than it had been earlier. The silence wasn't absence; it was *pressure*. Like something was waiting.

She turned right at the junction where the hall split into the kitchen and utility room. A narrow archway framed the laundry area, and beyond that, the old boiler room—where the wall curved unevenly to accommodate the foundation.

That's where the air was pulling her. Not by wind or sound—but by instinct.

She passed the coat closet. Her shoulder brushed the crooked door. It opened a sliver on its own, but she ignored it. She passed the kitchen without looking in. She didn't need to. Her destination was set.

The door to the utility room creaked when she nudged it open. Inside, the space was cold. A cracked tile floor. A leaning shelf of expired detergents. A busted mop handle propped like a cane against the wall.

But it was the back wall that drew her gaze.

She didn't register what she was seeing at first. It didn't compute. Her mind tried to shape it into something familiar—plumbing maybe, or insulation torn loose.

But no.

As she stepped closer, the truth became clear.

Her father was in the wall.

At first glance, it looked sculptural—like something chiseled into the brick, deliberate and grotesque. But the longer she stared, the more she saw the human in it. Patrick's body wasn't slumped or collapsed. It was *fused*.

His back protruded from the wall in twisted relief, muscles warped, vertebrae unnaturally arched, arms spread wide like a grotesque crucifixion. One shoulder jutted higher than the other, and the fingers on his left hand clawed upward in a final, impossible grasp. His knees were bent beneath him, fused into the brick like kneeling stone.

The skin was darkened, shiny with some resinous texture—part flesh, part masonry. His head tilted forward, pressed into the wall itself, leaving only the suggestion of his jawline and a single wide eye. It stared into the wall. Or through it. Mouth open. Mid-scream.

Andie's breath caught in her throat—not from horror, but from something else. *Relief.*

The tension in her spine slackened. A long, quiet exhale escaped her lips.

Then—against all reason—she smiled. It was small. Not joyous. But real.

She took another step forward, observing the way the brick pulsed faintly around his ribs. As if the wall had *breathed* him in and hadn't yet exhaled.

She whispered, "Guess the house finally had enough of you too."

Her mind scrambled for logic. Maybe he'd tried to crawl into a crawlspace. Maybe the heat warped his body. Maybe—

But the thoughts died.

There was no logic.

Only completion.

She stood silently, acknowledging what was done. Not grateful. Not mournful.

Just... balanced.

The room settled into stillness around her. Andie remained planted, arms crossed loosely across her stomach, watching the unmoving body of her father disappear inch by inch into the wall's dull, dark face. The sigh she'd released just moments earlier hadn't left her entirely—it lingered, like the end of a hymn, slowly trailing off.

Part of her mind still sought explanation. Perhaps he had overdosed, fallen backward and cracked through the wall somehow. Maybe the damp rot in the foundation had swallowed him up. Maybe he'd hallucinated and done this to himself. Maybe...

But the way the bricks curved around his shape... it wasn't collapse. It was consumption.

Something had taken him. Intentionally.

She tilted her head and narrowed her eyes. In the reflection of the broken dryer door, she caught her own shape standing near the wall, posture strangely calm, like a statue in thought. She looked older in the reflection. Taller. More... solid.

That amused her too.

This was his grave. Unmarked. Ungrieved. Unmissed.

Andie moved closer. She extended a hand—not out of reverence, but out of instinct. Her fingers brushed the brick where his ribs once were. The surface was warm, almost pulsing. She pressed harder.

The wall hummed beneath her skin.

Not with sound. But with rightness.

And something in her responded.

A quiet voice inside her—a voice that sounded like hers, but deeper, ancient—whispered, *"This is balance. You are its vessel now."*

She pulled her hand away. The warmth lingered on her fingertips.

No fear. No sadness.

Only direction.

Andie turned and walked toward the hallway again.

Each step back down the hall carried new weight—not like burden, but like presence. The house felt smaller now. Not because it had changed, but because Andie had grown—internally, invisibly. The crown of her awareness stretched higher. Her breath sat deeper in her lungs.

She passed the cracked coat closet again. It didn't open this time. It respected her now.

The living room lay in half-shadow. Bottles on the floor, a torn cushion on the couch, and the indelible stink of Patrick still hung in the air. But the weight of him was gone.

Andie paused in the doorway of her bedroom. She touched the frame with two fingers. The wood had splintered when he'd kicked it open. Now it was a mark. A scar. A boundary she'd never need again.

Inside, her room was untouched. The mirror still leaned against the wall above the dresser, but something shimmered in it now. A thread of mist clung to the edges, coiling lazily.

Andie moved to it, slowly. Her reflection met her gaze without blinking. Same bruises. Same swollen lip.

But her eyes—they burned faint gold.

She looked down. Her hands were steady. Her heart didn't pound.

She was ready.

She turned away from the mirror and sat on the bed. Her fingers folded gently in her lap, her shoulders square, her posture regal without realizing.

Charon had not spoken. Had not overtaken her.

He had *merged with her.*

And Andie—what remained of the girl she once was—would never beg again.

Andie didn't blink. The mirror no longer showed just her reflection—it shimmered faintly around the edges, rippling like water disturbed by breath. Her muscles were tight, her fingers curled over her knees. She stared, waiting for the yellow light to return to her eyes.

And then came the voice.

It didn't come from the mirror. It didn't come from the walls. It came from *inside her head.*

Soft, intimate. Too close.

"Andrea Montgomery..."

She flinched. The words slid along her spine like wet silk.

"You have been forsaken by your faith..."

Her body went still.

"Your family has abandoned you... Your loved ones taken. Your virtue stolen."

Andie's breath caught. Her chest locked. Her jaw trembled, but she didn't speak.

"You know no justice for that which has befallen you... and your suffering knows no comfort."

She clenched her teeth. Her fingernails dug into her jeans. Her vision blurred as the air around her grew heavy, like the very room was leaning closer to listen.

The voice was smooth—soothing—but coiled around each syllable was something sinister. Something *reptilian*.

"Andrea Montgomery, you can finally find the retribution you deserve..."

Her pulse thundered in her ears.

"Embrace it."

The plea was gentle. Enticing. Almost *tender*.

"Receive the power offered... and you will be a victim no longer."

Andie's shoulders began to tremble. Her throat clenched tight. Tears slid down her cheeks without sound.

She shook her head, as if the motion alone could cast out the voice.

But the words echoed on.

And they would not leave her.

Images exploded behind her eyes—memories she hadn't summoned, hadn't wanted. Each one slammed into her consciousness like waves crashing against rock.

She saw the alley.

Jacob's hand at her throat.

Mark's laughter echoing in the dark.

Billy's little sneakers in the back seat.

Her mother's hand going limp as the car spun into the path of another.

The cracked, empty hospital room.

The caskets. The smell of roses masking rot.

Patrick's hand. His boot. His belt.

Her siblings' backs turning, each with their own excuse. Each walking away while she drowned.

Andie squeezed her eyes tighter. She rocked forward on her bed, trying to make it stop. But the voice returned—softer, more persistent now.

"Let go."

"Let me help."

"Let them pay."

Andie gasped—short, ragged. Her body convulsed once, arching sharply. Her fingernails raked across the blanket beneath her. The mist in the room thickened, rising around the bedposts, curling into her nose and mouth like breath that didn't belong to her.

Her knees buckled beneath her. She fell forward, arms stretched out like wings, shaking violently.

A scream built in her throat but never escaped.

And then—she collapsed fully.

Her body convulsed again, limbs flailing once, twice, before going still. Her fingers twitched. Her head lolled to the side.

The mist wrapped around her now like a second skin.

Andie lay on the bed, unmoving. A still figure at the eye of a storm.

She didn't hear the voice anymore.

But she *felt* it.

Waiting.

Darkness folded around her like a velvet curtain, warm and endless. It wasn't death. It wasn't sleep. It was between—a space untouched by time or breath. Andie's thoughts floated inside it, fragmenting like leaves caught in swirling water.

Then, from the thick void, he came.

She didn't see him arrive. He was simply *there*, occupying space that hadn't existed a moment before. A tall figure—smooth, lean, entirely black—like obsidian carved into the shape of a man. Yet he wasn't a man. His face bore no defined features. His eyes burned with a dim yellow glow, their depths unreadable. His presence wasn't loud. It was absolute.

Charon.

She knew the name. Not from introduction. From recognition.

He stood beside the bed. The mist in the room bowed toward him, as if aware of its master.

Andie's body remained still. But her spirit rose, hovering within the space where dreams live and gods linger.

Charon did not speak with a mouth. He spoke directly into her essence.

"I am Charon."

"And I have the power to give you the justice you desire."

She didn't answer.

She didn't need to.

He extended a hand—long-fingered, elegant, glowing faintly with ancient light.

"Merely promise me the spoils of your vengeance..."

"And my power will be yours."

Andie stared at the hand, suspended in her dream-state, trembling within herself.

So many things she could have said.

But all she did... was reach.

Her fingers closed around his.

And the pact was made.

The rush that followed wasn't a jolt—it was a *flood*. A surge of energy that filled every inch of her soul. Andie felt herself expand, pulled upward and inward at once, stretched between her past and something eternal.

Pain unraveled inside her—layer by layer—memories transforming from wounds into tools. Grief became weightless. Rage became warmth.

Every heartbeat pulsed with purpose.

Charon's face drew closer, though he had no face to speak of. He was darkness wrapped in reason. Power without fury. Authority without forgiveness.

"You are mine now," he said—not as a command, but as a truth spoken aloud.

Andie nodded within the silence.

The pact did not bind her. It freed her.

Charon released her hand and stepped back. With each step, his form dissolved into strands of mist and gold, disintegrating into the room, into *her*. He wasn't leaving.

He was becoming part of her.

When she awoke, it was with a sudden inhale. Her chest rose sharply. Her back arched. Then she dropped against the mattress with a whisper.

Eyes open.

Awake.

Andie blinked once.

The ceiling stared back.

No smoke. No figure. No voice.

But the echo remained.

She sat up. Her breathing was even. Her muscles no longer trembled. Her ribs ached faintly, but the pain no longer owned her.

Charon was silent now.

Because she understood.

Andie stood slowly. Her body obeyed with ease.

She walked to the closet and began to pack.

No tears.

No hesitation.

Just intention.

The old backpack from ninth grade still hung on the closet hook, half-forgotten, coated in dust. Andie pulled it down, wiped it off with her sleeve, and unzipped it. The sound of the zipper tearing open felt louder than it should. Sharp. Final.

She filled it with what she needed. A change of clothes. Two granola bars. A water bottle. A flashlight. Socks. A utility knife she'd hidden years ago beneath her dresser drawer for "emergencies." This counted.

She moved with care, but not panic.

No more looking over her shoulder.

No more flinching at footsteps.

She didn't check the wall to see if Patrick was still there.

She knew.

He was part of this house now—fused into its bones like a fossil. The echo of his cruelty silenced by consequence.

She walked to the window, pushed it open with a slow, steady breath. The cool night air swept in, brushing across her cheeks. It smelled like damp leaves and pine and something deeper—metallic, like the moment before a storm.

One leg over the sill. Then the other.

She dropped into the yard below, landing in a crouch.

Andie didn't look back at the house.

There was nothing left for her inside it.

She walked toward the tree line that framed the edge of the neighborhood. Her shoes crunched over gravel.

The wind stirred her hair.

Above her, the sky was black and wide.

As she stepped into the woods, she whispered four names:

"Jacob... Mark... William...Sean."

She vanished beneath the branches.

The reckoning had begun.

Chapter 4

The house on Sycamore Lane stood still, its windows dark and empty. The neighbors hadn't seen any activity in days. Mail collected in the rusting box out front. Trash bins hadn't been rolled to the curb. A dog barked intermittently from two yards down, but otherwise, the neighborhood had gone quiet.

Sheriff Douglas Miller pulled his cruiser onto the patchy grass out front, tires crackling over gravel. He stepped out slowly, adjusting the strap of his service belt. The chill in the late October air nipped at his neck. He wasn't dressed for a cold snap—just his brown uniform shirt and a thermal undershirt. No jacket.

He stood at the foot of the porch and sighed. "Damn it, Patrick," he muttered.

Two weeks had passed. People in town hadn't seen Patrick for a while and wondered where he might have run off to. The deputy wanted to ask Andie if she knew anything about her father's absence from the community. The town was used to Patrick Montgomery disappearing for benders, but something about this one felt off. The school had called—Billy was absent, not that he'd ever enrolled properly. Andie hadn't been seen since the funeral. And when a neighbor swore they saw "smoke or fog" pouring from the upstairs window at 2:00 a.m. two nights ago, Miller figured it was time to check in.

He knocked.

No answer.

"Sheriff's Department!" he called. "Patrick? You in there?"

Still nothing.

He tried the knob. Unlocked.

The door creaked open.

The smell hit him like a wall.

Rot. Decay. And something worse—something chemical and burned.

Miller pulled his radio from his shoulder holster. “Dispatch, this is Sheriff Miller. I’m at the Montgomery residence. I’m going inside.”

The interior was dim, the curtains all drawn. Dust hung in the air, stirred by his entrance. The living room was strewn with empty bottles, a coffee table covered in cigarette burns and mildew stains. A couch cushion had been flipped over—its underside damp and torn.

Miller stepped in cautiously, one hand near his holster. The smell intensified the farther he walked.

“Patrick?” he called again, slower this time.

No reply.

He moved past the living room, stepping over a crushed beer can, and rounded the corner into the hallway. His boots creaked on the warped floorboards. The air here was thicker—humid, almost oily. He followed the source of the smell toward the back of the house.

The utility room door was cracked open. He nudged it wider with his boot.

Then he froze.

At first, he didn’t register what he was seeing. His brain rejected the image.

A human body—muscled, male—was fused into the far wall covered with flies and maggots.

The torso protruded out of the bricks, arms spread wide as if caught mid-struggle. Knees embedded. Spine contorted. The back of the head was pressed so hard into the wall it looked like the skull had been swallowed by concrete.

Miller gagged. His hand flew to his mouth.

The body was blackened—not charred, but unnatural. Hardened. Like tar had poured through the mortar and replaced the skin.

He stumbled backward, hit the doorframe, and nearly dropped his radio.

He keyed the mic. "Dispatch—this is Sheriff Miller. I've got... I need backup. Possible homicide. And you better call the Feds."

By the time the local crime scene unit arrived, the property had been taped off. The yard filled with flashing lights and hushed voices. Officers milled about the driveway, trying to make sense of the scene without stepping too far inside. Some leaned close to the front door, eyes wide. Others stood back, arms crossed tightly, unsure whether to believe the sheriff or call it in as a prank.

A forensic photographer emerged pale-faced from the utility room, refusing to speak until he'd finished two full cigarettes.

Miller leaned against his cruiser, sipping burnt coffee from a styrofoam cup, the sour taste forgotten beneath the weight of what he'd seen.

He barely noticed the black SUV pull up until it idled to a stop behind the coroner's van.

A man stepped out—tall, clean-cut, wearing a long dark coat over a pressed suit. No sunglasses. No smirk. Just cool, focused eyes and a straight back.

He moved through the chaos without hesitation, flashing a federal badge with one smooth gesture.

"Special Agent Damian Nash, FBI," he announced.

Miller straightened. "You're the one they sent?"

"Yes, sir," Nash replied. "Got the alert from the Bureau's Anomalous Crime Division. My cell lit up like a Christmas tree."

Miller narrowed his eyes. "You saying this is federal?"

Nash offered the faintest smile. "No, Sheriff. I'm saying it's *not local*."

He turned to the house. "I'd like to see the body."

Miller hesitated. "You're not gonna believe it."

"I hope I don't," Nash said, already walking.

Inside the house, Nash moved like a man accustomed to walking among trauma. He stepped over the same beer can Miller had, his sharp shoes silent on the creaking boards. His eyes scanned everything—framed photos on the wall, peeling wallpaper, the scattering of cheap cigarettes in an ashtray. He wasn't looking for signs of a struggle. He was reading the **person** who had lived here.

The utility room door was still open. The smell had worsened since Miller first entered.

Nash paused at the threshold.

His face remained unreadable.

Then he stepped inside.

He stood still for a full minute. His eyes swept the walls, the floor, the embedded body. His breath fogged faintly in the room—though the house wasn't cold.

He moved closer. The body was perfectly still. Patrick's arms outstretched. Fingers half-clenched. A faint black sheen coated his shoulders and spine. Nash noted the bruises on the wrists, the warping of brick around the knees.

He crouched.

"Sheriff," he called back.

Miller entered reluctantly, already rubbing his temple.

"Tell me no fire damage was reported."

"None."

"No accelerants?"

"Nothing we could detect."

Nash stood, slowly.

"Then this man didn't just die."

Miller frowned. "What does that mean?"

Nash stared at the corpse, then turned toward the hallway.

"It means something **put** him here."

The next two hours blurred together—crime scene specialists took more photos, local deputies kept the crowd at bay, and the coroner's crew stood scratching their heads. No one could figure out how to remove the body from the wall. Every time someone got close with a chisel or hammer, their tools cracked—or worse, the wall *repaired* itself.

Nash had seen a lot in his years with the Bureau, most of it classified. But this...

This was new.

He stood just outside the house now, writing in a notebook. He kept it analog—no digital trail. The sketch he'd drawn of Patrick's position was eerily accurate.

He flipped the page and wrote a single line:

"Subject appears to have been fused at a molecular level with foundation materials. Possible non-human interaction. No trace of Andrea Montgomery."

He looked up as Miller approached again, his face pale.

"The neighbors say the girl's been missing since the funeral," Miller reported. "Nobody's seen her leave. But the back window was open."

Nash nodded once. "No blood trail?"

"None."

"She didn't run," Nash said. "She **moved on**."

Miller rubbed his neck. "You think she did this?"

Nash tucked the notebook away. He shrugged his shoulders.

"I think something happened to her," he said. "Something that didn't *just* break her."

He looked back at the house.

"I think it *changed* her."

Nash returned to the Montgomery house the following morning. This time, alone. He preferred it that way. He moved through the rooms methodically, scanning the environment not for immediate clues but for *behavioral evidence*. Every stain, torn paper, and displaced object told a story. He had a knack for spotting patterns where others saw chaos.

The hallway bore smudged fingerprints—some too small for Patrick's calloused hands. Nash knelt beside a scuff mark against the baseboard just past the bathroom door. A footprint, faint but fresh. Size 7 or 8. Women's. Trailing toward the back window.

He followed it to the small bedroom. Andie's.

The air here felt different—tense, heavy. Not like trauma. Not like grief.

It felt... **charged**.

The bed was stripped, the sheets gone. Nash scanned the bookshelf and nightstand. A half-filled journal sat crooked beneath the bed, mostly blank but for a handful of scribbled entries. Her handwriting was small, neat, but slanted sharply, almost aggressively. One phrase repeated in the margins:

"No one will come for me."

He turned it over and spotted a tear in the bottom lining of the mattress. He reached inside and pulled free a folded piece of paper—worn with age. A photocopy of a book page. Greek myth. The name "Charon" underlined in ballpoint pen.

He studied the passage: *Ferryman of the dead. Collector of souls. Giver of retribution.*

Nash stared at it for a long moment.

Then he whispered aloud: "What did you read, Andie?"

He took the copied page and the journal, careful not to disturb the room further. Back in the hallway, he paused. His eyes lingered on the trail of darkened smudges on the floor—like someone dragging something heavy from the kitchen to the back window.

But there was no body. No sign of a struggle.

Only Patrick's impossible death fused into the wall, and now this sense of deliberate absence.

She hadn't run.

She'd **planned**.

Nash stepped outside and pulled his coat tighter around him. The late morning sun had little warmth. He climbed into the black SUV and started the engine, his mind already retracing her path. If she fled on foot, she would've needed shelter. Food. A place to recover.

But more than that—she would need *purpose*. People like Andie didn't just run.

They moved with intent.

He tapped a few commands into the dashboard tablet and pulled up Patrick Montgomery's background. A small network of bar buddies, former coworkers, and occasional drinking partners popped up. Most of them lived within twenty miles.

Nash zoomed in on the three closest: Rick Danner, Bud Leary, and a man named Carl Simmons—each with priors for minor assault, DUIs, and disturbing the peace.

His jaw tightened.

"If she's not hiding," he murmured, "she's hunting."

Rick Danner was found two days later, hanging by his ankles from a rusted pipe in the back of an abandoned warehouse outside town. The scene baffled local law enforcement. There was no sign of forced entry. No witnesses. But the body showed signs of psychological torture—deep scratches across the chest, the word "ENABLER" etched into the skin.

Nash stood under the flickering ceiling light as forensics worked around him. The odor of urine and rust mingled with the industrial scent of old motor oil. He glanced around the room, noting how clean it was otherwise—no blood spatter, no broken glass, no chaos. Just... intent.

He took a photo of the body on his private phone. He wasn't supposed to, but this wasn't a normal case.

Outside, he dictated a quick memo into his secure recorder:

"Subject Danner appears to have been subdued without resistance. Restraints were improvised, body hung with calculated balance. No rage, no panic—just execution. Killer likely has emotional control. Objective not revenge alone, but *message delivery*."

He stopped the recorder and checked the time.

Then he checked a second name: Bud Leary. Last known address: mobile home park near the river. No utilities paid in three months.

Still, Nash decided to visit.

Andie was moving fast. But he was gaining ground.

The mobile home sat tilted slightly to one side, as if drunk or defeated. Paint peeled from the aluminum siding. The porch sagged at the corners. Nash stepped carefully onto the loose wood and knocked once on the thin metal door.

No response.

He knocked again, louder. "FBI. I need to ask you a few questions."

Still nothing.

He twisted the knob. It was locked.

Nash walked the perimeter, noting the curtains had been drawn closed with duct tape in some places. The rear door was unlatched. He slipped a glove on and eased it open.

The smell hit him immediately—foul, but not the sweet rot of death. This was something different. Oily. Chemical.

Inside, the walls were covered in crude drawings—symbols scratched into every available surface, carved with keys or knives or nails. A smear of what looked like tar dripped down the length of the hallway wall.

Nash advanced slowly.

He found Bud Leary in the bathtub.

Fully clothed. Eyes wide open.

Not dead.

Just... broken.

Rocking slowly, muttering a word over and over.

Nash crouched beside the tub.

"Bud? Do you know who I am?"

Leary didn't respond. He just kept whispering: "She glowed... she *glowed*... like her eyes were fire."

Nash leaned in, not disturbed—just intrigued.

He whispered, “Andie?”

Leary began screaming.

Bud was taken into custody under psychiatric hold, rambling incoherently the entire time. Nash followed the ambulance to the hospital but didn’t accompany the orderlies inside. Instead, he waited in the parking lot, replaying the man’s words again and again.

She glowed. Her eyes were fire.

He’d heard similar delusions before—victims of trauma inventing supernatural explanations. But Leary wasn’t just describing a vision. He was describing **fear**. A fear so complete it rendered him catatonic.

Back at his SUV, Nash began to trace timelines. Rick Danner’s death. Bud Leary’s breakdown. The spacing wasn’t random. They weren’t hiding places. They were *stops* on a planned journey.

Each man linked by one thing: Patrick Montgomery.

The question wasn’t who was next?

Where was it Andie had learned to do this? Based on town people description, someone as petit as Andie couldn’t have hoisted a grown man upside down. Let alone encrust one in a wall.

He tapped again into the FBI’s restricted database and pulled up a flagged name: *Charon*.

He cross-referenced it with occult cases, missing person reports, and psychological profiles. At least twelve similar murders across the country over the last decade. Every time: isolated victim, symbolic execution, supernatural suggestion.

But Andie was different. Younger. Still learning. Still unraveling.

He looked up from his screen and spoke quietly into the silence of the car.

“Where are you, Andie?”

The boy’s name was William Sutter.

Two years ago, he was just another smirking face in a crowd of boys who didn’t think of girls as people. Now, he was a young man with polished sneakers, a student ID, and a carefully curated social media presence. His life had been reset. Fresh start. College out of state. Clean slate. New friends. New dreams. His sins buried beneath transcripts and tuition payments.

But Andie remembered. Not just the act, not just the pain, but the small cruelties. The mocking glances. The laughter. The dismissiveness afterward—as if what they did to her had been inconsequential, an inconvenience at most. That particular memory stayed sharp. Not the screams or the hospital lights, but the silence that followed. The deafening void where justice should have lived.

She tracked William like a predator, but not through magic. Not entirely.

The supernatural was in her now—yes—but it was not always what guided her hands. Practicality did. She started by hacking into school district records, a skill she picked up during long nights of stolen Wi-Fi and cracked screens. She found his full name in the case transcripts buried in her old high school’s administrative files. The school had tried to erase the incident, fearing scandal. But paper trails have long shadows.

She combed alumni networks. Fake scholarship boards. Digital yearbooks. Bits and fragments of data tied together like blood vessels on a forensic map. A cousin's wedding post tagged him at a specific university. A friend's graduation story mentioned the name of a dorm. A fraternity's public Instagram showed his arm slung casually over a keg at an initiation party, his name tagged without thought. People were careless online. William especially. He was the kind of man who believed bad things happened only to other people.

From there, she narrowed the search.

College schedules were mostly open-source if you knew where to look. Dorm layouts. Campus security blind spots. And once she was in town, it took her only a few days to memorize his schedule—not just where he walked, but how. His gait. His rituals. The nervous check of his phone. The way he double-knotted his laces before heading into the gym.

Money came in odd ways.

She took what she needed. Sometimes she worked—temporary gigs under stolen names, delivery jobs, bar-back shifts where no one asked questions if you kept your mouth shut and your head down. Other times, she skimmed—abandoned wallets, careless phones, half-watched tip jars. She didn't call it stealing. She called it survival. The world owed her far more than what she took.

She'd learned to move through society like a glitch in the system—present but unreadable. She avoided places with cameras unless she was the one watching. She layered herself in anonymity. Wigs when needed. Glasses. Hoodies. She had dozens of IDs, forged or found, and she knew how to speak in dialects that lowered suspicion. She understood how to blend—not as a ghost, but as noise. Nothing memorable. Nothing distinct.

She didn't look for kindness anymore. She didn't even look for fairness. Those were myths—fairy tales adults told children to keep them soft. What she sought now was *equilibrium.* Not justice. Not revenge.

The word vengeance resonated more truthfully with her.

Justice was performative. It played out in courtrooms with lawyers and rules, in systems built to serve those already protected. Justice was the illusion that if you followed the process, someone would answer for what was done to you. Andie had seen where that led. Hospitals, interviews, shrugs. Her rapists had walked free. Justice had watched it happen and said nothing.

Revenge, on the other hand, was personal. Messy. Emotional. It felt good—but it wasn't sustainable. It burned out too fast. It relied on satisfaction.

Vengeance was different. Colder. More sacred.

Vengeance had rules.

It demanded precision. It didn't scream or cry or self-destruct. Vengeance *waited.* It observed. It planned. It made sure the pain echoed—not just once, but again and again until the soul broke apart like old stone. She wasn't here to satisfy her anger. She was here to erase rot. To punish in proportion not to her wounds—but to their *arrogance.*

And William?

He had no idea.

She watched him now from across the campus green. Hidden beneath the awning of a quiet bookstore café, a copy of *Dante's Inferno* open in her lap like a silent joke. She sipped her tea slowly, her fingers tracing the rim of the cup. Across the lawn, William laughed with a group of boys, pushing one playfully in that hyper-masculine way they mistook for friendship. They were dressed for a mixer. Hair gelled. Collars crisp. Every one of them a variation of the same lie.

William didn't know he was already marked.

She had no plan to confront him yet. That wasn't how this worked. Not anymore. She would observe. She would chip away at the illusion he had built around himself—that he was safe, untouchable, absolved.

First, she would learn his fears.

Then she would introduce them to him again, one by one.

Until he begged to remember who she was.

Until he remembered everything.

The motel sat on the fringe of town like a half-forgotten memory, weather-beaten and sagging, the sign missing three letters and flickering when the wind pushed against the wires. Andie didn't pick it for comfort. She picked it for what it lacked—attention, surveillance, accountability. No cameras. No night clerk that asked questions. No other guests that made eye contact. Room 6 was hers for as long as she paid in cash. She kept her presence as thin as the mattress she slept on.

The carpet smelled of mildew. The bathroom faucet never stopped leaking. The window's lock was broken, so she wedged a screwdriver beneath the sill. The closet door didn't close. The paint peeled like molting skin. None of it bothered her. It felt like the outer world had been tailored to match the inside of her mind—disordered, silent, barely held together. She took comfort in the decay.

Every night, she returned to the room with stiff limbs and quiet breath. She never took the same path twice. One night she walked in from the train depot. The next, she looped behind gas stations and alleyways.

She was methodical. Untraceable. Her boots had learned to move without making sound. Her coat never came off, even indoors.

The first thing she always did was cover the mirror. A hand towel, taped at the corners, blotting out her reflection. It wasn't that she feared what she'd see. It was that she feared she wouldn't see anything at all. The girl she used to be had bled out slowly, over months, and now all that remained was this unfamiliar shadow that carried her shape.

Andie no longer cried. It wasn't defiance—it was impossibility. Her body simply didn't respond that way anymore. The tears used to rise in waves, hot and sudden. Now? Nothing. Just pressure behind her eyes, like a thunderstorm that refused to break. She'd tried once, lying curled on the mattress, to summon it—to force tears. But her chest remained still. Her jaw clenched. Her fingers twitched against her thigh, waiting for release that never came.

She told herself it was because of the pain. The trauma. The loss.

But late at night, when the motel was silent and she could hear every creak of the warped walls, she wondered if it was something else.

If the thing inside her—the force that had whispered to her beneath the earth, that had twisted her father's body into a warning—had slowly replaced her capacity for grief. Like sapwood hollowed by beetles, she feared she had been devoured from the inside. Not all at once. A little more every time she acted. Every time she made someone pay.

She sharpened a blade by hand, working slowly, deliberately, breathing in time with the scrape. She didn't need it, not really. But the ritual gave her purpose. Sound. Focus.

In this room, in this life, there were no tears.

Only preparation.

And the waiting.

The bed was too soft, so she slept on the floor. A sheet folded into a narrow rectangle beneath her spine, a hoodie rolled beneath her head. The floor was cold, but honest. It didn't shift beneath her like a mattress. It didn't pretend to be gentle. Her knife was always beside her right thigh, handle facing the door. Her boots stayed on. One eye half-open. She slept as a sentry would—ready to rise, to react, to kill if needed.

The walls weren't thick, but they muffled most sounds. Occasionally she'd hear a car pull in, an argument flare and fade, a door slam and remain closed. It didn't matter. She'd stopped responding to noise long ago. What kept her awake wasn't outside. It was inside—images that floated behind her eyes when she tried to rest. Not memories. Not exactly. More like echoes.

Some nights, she saw their faces—William, Sean, Mark, Jacob. Their expressions blurred, as if caught between recognition and oblivion. Their mouths moved without sound, their eyes glowing faintly in shades of copper and ash. Other nights, she saw herself—not the girl she had been, but the thing she had become—standing barefoot in a shallow pool of dark water, staring up at a black sky pulsing with veins of fire.

And always, the voice.

It didn't speak in sentences anymore. It murmured in impressions. It pressed against the edges of her skull like steam, curling into her blood, making her fingers twitch when her thoughts turned toward those who had hurt her. The voice had no gender, no tone. It was simply there—patient, powerful, ever-watching.

She no longer asked if it was real.

What mattered was that it had become part of her.

By day, she moved among people like a shadow. She used different names depending on the register. Sometimes she stole coffee. Sometimes she left cash where no one saw. She bought burner phones, discarded them after three days. She memorized passwords, patterns, and plates. She understood how to disappear into the fabric of society by becoming unmemorable. Smiling just enough. Speaking just little enough. Clothes slightly worn but never suspicious.

People didn't see her unless she wanted them to.

They saw a girl with dyed hair and earbuds. Another student. Another waitress. Another nobody.

She saw them.

Their lies. Their glances. Their potential for cruelty.

At night, she returned to this room, her sanctuary of dust and silence. She sat cross-legged, scribbling patterns into her journal. Not words. Just lines. Circles. Shapes she didn't remember learning. Symbols that came to her in dreams.

She didn't pray anymore.

But sometimes, before she laid down, she whispered: "I remember."

And the walls whispered back.

Some mornings, she didn't move for hours. She'd lie there staring at the ceiling, counting the stains, memorizing the spiderweb of cracks that bloomed out from the single flickering lightbulb. Her body would feel like stone—too heavy to lift, too inert to stretch. Not from exhaustion. Not from fear. From *absence.*

It wasn't depression. She knew what that was. She remembered what it used to feel like. The heavy fog. The numb grayness. The clawing desire for anything that resembled meaning. This wasn't that.

This was precision.

A cold, internal switch that knew when to shut down her system. Conserve energy. Recalibrate. She didn't waste movement anymore. She didn't fidget. Her body only acted when the moment required it. Everything else was stillness.

She once tried to meditate, sitting on the floor in perfect silence, her spine straight, eyes closed, hands resting palm-up on her knees. She thought she could control the noise inside her. Thought she could master it, perhaps find peace. Instead, her mind descended into something she hadn't prepared for.

She saw herself—blood dripping from her fingers, standing in a field of mirrors. Every reflection showed a different version of her. Younger. Older. More monstrous. More empty. In one of them, her eyes weren't hers. They were fire, molten and flickering, and in her mouth was a voice that wasn't hers, laughing without sound.

She opened her eyes and vomited into the corner trash can. Her nose bled for an hour.

That was the last time she tried.

Now she stuck to repetition. Fold the hoodie. Unlace the boots. Sharpen the blade. Check the journal. Clean the sink. Wash the knife. Sit. Breathe. Write. Wait.

Sometimes she wrote letters. Not to mail—just to exhale. One was addressed to Liz. Another to Billy. Dozens sat in her backpack, folded and unfinished, written in messy script that grew darker with every page.

She never signed her name.

Not "Andie."

Not "Andrea."

She didn't know if she deserved a name anymore.

Names were for people. She was... other now.

Her thoughts had stopped orbiting what had happened to her. They had begun to orbit what she would *do.* The space between cause and response had narrowed. It used to be that she had to remind herself why she was hunting. Now, it was her natural rhythm.

She watched the world like a hunter watches its prey. Eyes behind glass. Quiet. Focused.

She didn't hate the world.

She just didn't trust it to do the right thing.

That had been proven.

The justice system was a machine with clogged gears and broken levers. Its levers were men like her father. Its gears were boys like William. Its oil was the blood of girls like her.

So no, she didn't seek justice.

She sought *rebalancing.*

One victim at a time.

One reckoning at a time.

Sometimes, in the quietest hours, she asked herself the question she feared the most: *Was this vengeance, or was this something else entirely?*

The word vengeance still sounded human to her—rooted in emotion, forged in the crucible of grief and rage. Vengeance was a daughter standing over her abuser's grave, spitting out the words no courtroom would let her say. It was a girl walking away from the ashes of her own innocence and choosing not to die with it.

But this?

This thing inside her—this presence, this *companion*—it didn't feel like vengeance.

It felt older.

It felt like ritual.

Like a force too vast to belong to any one person. Too ancient to be born out of her suffering alone. She hadn't just become something new—she had become *part* of something older. Something whose patience made her seem impulsive by comparison. Something that had waited for centuries to find her.

She didn't know if she had invited it in... or if it had always been waiting.

Her reflection—when she allowed herself to see it—showed her skin grown paler, lips redder, the faintest shadow beneath her eyes that never left. Her body hadn't aged, but it had altered. Refined. Her features had become sharper. Beautiful, in a way that unnerved her. Ethereal, in a way that scared others.

She looked like someone you didn't want to follow into the dark.

And that suited her just fine.

People left her alone now. They didn't know why—they just did. Clerks looked past her. Men avoided her eyes. Other women looked confused when they crossed her path, sensing something that didn't fit, didn't *belong*. She'd become a walking dissonance. A frequency no longer on the human dial.

She sometimes tested it.

Once, she stood on a sidewalk in a busy square, completely still, and watched as people subtly parted around her without noticing. Like water around stone. No one bumped her. No one made contact. She was invisible—but not in the way of shadows.

She was untouchable.

And she was beginning to believe that this was the point.

That maybe she was meant to be *dislodged* from society. Pulled from it like a thorn from skin. That her pain had created space for something unnatural to take root—and now it lived alongside her, breathing through her lungs, watching through her eyes, feeding on the moral weight she carried.

And it had no interest in mercy.

Mercy was a human thing.

This wasn't.

Whatever had joined her, it didn't want her to feel peace.

It wanted her to deliver *balance*.

And balance required fear.

It required permanence.

It required her.

By the time dawn colored the sky in soft bruises, Andie was already awake, seated on the motel's roof with her back against the rotting A/C unit. Her breath fogged faintly in the air, but she didn't shiver. Cold had become a concept to her—not an experience. She wore the same black coat, same jeans, same scuffed boots. She looked like a statue sculpted from asphalt and shadow.

She watched the street for patterns. Always patterns.

The jogger who passed at 6:14 a.m. sharp. The coffee truck that arrived ten minutes later. The woman in the green scarf who walked her dachshund like clockwork. These people moved through their lives unaware that the monster they feared might not crawl out of the woods or hide in alleys. It might live above them. Behind them. Within the ones they wronged.

She could still fake a smile, if she needed to.

She had done it twice last week. Once when she paid for toothpaste. Once when she asked for a lighter at the gas station. The smiles felt brittle. Thin. Like masks made of glass.

But no one questioned her.

They never did.

The fire inside her was slow now. Not an inferno—but a kiln. It shaped her day by day, hollowing out what she didn't need, hardening what she did. The softer parts—empathy, forgiveness, hope—they were evaporating.

She felt it. Not with regret.

With *clarity.*

Sometimes she sat with her journal open, and nothing came out. No words. No drawings. Just the faint thrum of her pulse syncing to something older, more mechanical. The silence between entries spoke louder than ink ever could.

She didn't fear losing herself anymore.

She feared she'd already lost the wrong parts.

Still, sometimes—just sometimes—her hands trembled when she thought of Billy's voice. Or Liz's perfume. Or the way sunlight used to feel on her face before the night took her. When that happened, she clenched her fists, forced herself to stand, and turned her eyes to the sky.

She would not cry.

Not because she was strong.

Because she no longer could.

And maybe that was what terrified her most.

That she wasn't healing.

She was *changing*.

Not into a survivor.

Into something *else*.

It happened on a Thursday, late afternoon. The air was dry, crisp with the approaching cold snap, and the college quad was dotted with students shuffling between classes and coffee. Andie hadn't intended to be there. She wasn't following William that day—at least, not actively. Her loop had ended. She had already logged his schedule, confirmed his routines, and drawn up his three-mile radius in the notebook she never let leave her side.

She was supposed to return to the motel. Rest. Repeat.

But something—maybe the wind, maybe the whispering presence inside her—pulled her toward the east walkway, a shortcut between the science buildings and the student union. She kept her head low, the brim of her hood casting a shadow across her face. She didn't think. She moved like fog, silently, effortlessly, feet barely touching the brick path.

That was when she saw him.

William Sutter, walking with his friend—Eli, if she remembered correctly—laughing, mouth full of smugness and charm, wearing a puffer vest over a plaid shirt like some catalog cutout of collegiate masculinity. His backpack hung off one shoulder, earbuds looped around his neck, and his eyes scanned the scene around him like he owned it.

And then they landed on her.

The moment froze.

He didn't recognize her. Not really. Not consciously. But something in his body reacted before his brain caught up. His laughter slowed. His pace hitched. His mouth stayed half-open, but no words came out. He looked straight at her, caught in that exact second of strange, magnetic attention.

She stopped walking.

Their eyes locked across the narrow walkway. The crowd moved around them—students passing, bicycles weaving through—but for a moment, it was only them. His brow furrowed slightly, like he was searching his mind for context, for memory. He didn't find any. Of course he wouldn't. The girl standing in front of him wasn't the one he and his friends had left sobbing on the edge of a nightmare two years ago.

This one was taller in posture, colder in presence, draped in dark fabric and lined with invisible armor. Her skin was paler now, her cheekbones sharpened, her hair longer and dyed into shades of ember and rust. But it was her eyes that made him pause—eyes that didn't move when he did, didn't blink, didn't flinch. They just stared. Unwavering.

"Uh... hey," William said, his voice dropping into that performative charm he used when he spotted someone attractive. "You new around here?"

Andie didn't answer. She didn't even tilt her head. She just stared at him with that hollow, unreadable calm. Behind her silence, a storm churned. Her fingers twitched faintly at her sides—not in nervousness, but in restraint. The presence inside her hummed with expectation, but she kept it still. Not yet.

William gave an awkward chuckle, rubbing the back of his neck. "Sorry. Thought I... I don't know. You just looked familiar."

Andie smiled.

Just barely.

A crack in marble.

It was enough.

He blinked, suddenly uncertain.

Then his friend called him from the other end of the quad.

William hesitated. His body angled toward his friend, but his eyes stayed on Andie. She saw the confusion settling in behind his gaze, the slow tick of instinct crawling along his spine. He wasn't remembering—not yet—but he was *feeling*. Something ancient and buried was stirring in him, something tied to fear. Or perhaps shame. Maybe the line was thinner than most people wanted to admit.

"I'll see you around?" he asked, voice lighter now, trying to cover the unease.

Andie didn't respond. Didn't move.

William offered a final, hesitant smile and turned to leave.

She watched him go.

She didn't turn away, didn't even exhale until he disappeared behind the line of concrete pillars by the business building. Then, and only then, did she reach into the inside pocket of her coat and pull out her black journal. She flipped to the page already marked with his name. Her pen hovered over the margin for a moment before she added a single detail: *Saw me. Did not know me. Felt something.*

Then she closed the book and tucked it away.

She resumed walking in the opposite direction of William, allowing herself to blend once more into the nameless noise of the campus. The encounter had not been part of her strategy. But it hadn't harmed it either.

In fact, it had proven something she'd hoped.

She wasn't invisible.

She was *unrecognizable.*

And yet somehow... unforgettable.

She felt it in the way he looked at her.

She had entered his mind.

Now she would *haunt* it.

Back at the motel, Andie's hands trembled for the first time in weeks.

Not from fear. Not from weakness.

From control.

From the sheer effort it had taken not to lunge at him when he smiled. To not whisper his name into his ear, or drag him into the dark between breath and memory. Her body ached not with need—but with the suppression of power. The presence inside her had grown hungry with proximity.

"You waited," it seemed to whisper.

Andie ignored it, stripping off her coat, letting it slump to the stained carpet. She sat down cross-legged on the floor, opened the journal, and stared at William's name. Her pen hovered again. She didn't want to write. She wanted to remember the silence. The look on his face. That brief, unspoken pull between them—like he could feel the debt he owed, but hadn't remembered the loan.

She hadn't spoken a word to him.

And yet he had heard her.

Felt her.

She replayed the encounter again and again, dissecting it with surgical calm. His body language. His breathing. The drop in his tone when she didn't respond. The nervous smile. The retreat. All of it meant something. Andie didn't just watch people anymore—she *read* them.

And he had read her, too.

Not for who she was.

But for what she had become.

He felt the shadow.

She would now begin the slow descent of his sanity.

The first crack had been made.

Now she would pry it open.

That night, she didn't dream.

Not in the way humans do.

She lay awake long past midnight, eyes fixed on the ceiling, her body perfectly still except for the slow, rhythmic rise and fall of her chest. The motel buzzed with its usual broken hums and metallic hisses, but she didn't hear them. Her mind was somewhere else. Far beyond the sagging ceiling tiles and mold-choked walls.

She thought of William.

Not in a sentimental way.

Not even in hatred.

But as a puzzle.

A living riddle of arrogance and denial, now fractured by a single glance from a woman he didn't remember breaking.

She wondered what his dreams would be like tonight.

If they would be tinged with her silence.

If he would wake up sweaty, unsure why the shadow in the corner had eyes.

If her face—unfamiliar yet impossible to shake—would haunt the edges of his day.

She hoped so.

This was only the beginning.

She would not rush. Vengeance was a tide, not a bullet.

And like all tides, it would rise.

She rolled over, pulled the blanket halfway across her hips, and closed her eyes. No fear. No doubt. Just the cold stillness of someone who no longer believed in justice—but had learned to *become* consequence.

Tomorrow would be the next step.

But tonight?

She would let the silence wrap her like armor.

She smiled into the darkness.

And the thing inside her smiled back.

Chapter 6

It started at the bookstore.

Andie didn't wander in by accident. She had studied his habits for weeks—watched him move through town, the places he visited, the times he lingered. He came here every other Thursday around four. Always alone. Usually after class. He'd skim the new releases or leaf through battered paperbacks in the philosophy aisle, half-reading, half-waiting for someone to notice how thoughtful he looked.

This time, someone did.

She positioned herself near the front, pretending to be absorbed in a coffee table book of surrealist art. She let her presence be quiet, but not invisible. Her hair was different now, thick and dark, with sharp bangs that shadowed her face just enough to keep it suggestive, not familiar. Her clothing was tasteful but form-fitting. Nothing obvious. No red flags. Just enough to catch a glance.

It took twelve minutes. He noticed her as he headed toward the register, catching only her profile. He slowed his steps—not stopping, just enough hesitation to say he was curious.

She gave him nothing.

The second time was two days later. The weather had shifted—damp, humid, the sky like wet ash. She timed it so they crossed paths outside the coffee shop across from campus. She was already seated on the stone bench, a paper cup in hand, legs crossed, pretending to read a folded page of something handwritten. A list of books, or maybe a poem.

He stepped out, blinked at the dull light, and saw her. Again.

This time, she looked up.

The glance she gave was brief, warm, and dismissive in a way that made him want more. He hesitated again. His lips parted—maybe to say something, maybe just to draw breath—but she returned her gaze to the paper in her lap before he could speak.

He left without saying a word.

But he looked back.

That night, in her temporary room above the antique shop—one she rented under a false name with cash earned from "returned favors"—Andie stared into the cracked mirror above the sink. The face looking back at her was familiar, but not hers. The same eyes. But older. Sharper. A face carved by intent. She touched her cheek, pressing down until it hurt, until a flash of heat pulsed at her fingertips. A dead fly buzzed once, then fell from the windowsill.

She didn't sleep.

Not because of nightmares—but because she no longer dreamed.

The third encounter felt like chance. To him.

Andie made sure of that.

It was midday. The campus lawn buzzed with early spring noise—students playing frisbee, someone strumming a guitar near the steps, laughter carried by warm gusts of wind. William emerged from the Humanities building with two classmates, talking about something banal—film scores or podcast ideas. She was already there, seated under the shade of an old oak, sketchbook open on her lap, though she hadn't drawn a single thing.

He spotted her instantly.

A flicker crossed his face. Recognition mixed with delight, tempered by confusion. Like seeing a dream step into daylight. He slowed, let his friends move ahead without him. He hesitated near the tree as if pulled by some invisible thread.

"You're here a lot," he said finally.

She turned her gaze upward, slowly, with the hint of a smile tugging at one corner of her mouth. Not warm. Not cold. Just enough.

"Am I?" she replied, voice low and musical. "Maybe I like the quiet."

He laughed, awkward. "That's ironic. This place is never quiet."

She closed her sketchbook deliberately, letting her fingers linger on the cover. "Then maybe I just like the illusion."

That threw him. His head tilted, intrigued. He was clearly trying to place her, maybe from a dream, a blurred memory, or a past life his mind couldn't fully catch.

"I'm William," he offered, extending a hand.

She didn't take it.

Instead, she glanced at his outstretched palm, then looked back into his eyes and said, "I know."

A flush touched his cheeks, not embarrassment, but heat—stimulated, curious. He let the hand drop with a sheepish grin. "Do I know you?"

"No," she said. "But maybe you will."

With that, she stood. Her fingers trailed the edge of her skirt, her posture loose, comfortable, every movement controlled. She didn't look back as she walked past him, only letting her perfume—rose and sandalwood, faint and haunting—catch in the breeze behind her.

William stood alone under the tree, still watching long after she vanished from view. His hand lingered near his chest where hers hadn't touched. The sound around him—laughter, guitar strings, even the buzz of traffic—faded into a hum, like background noise on a broken cassette.

From a window above, hidden behind a thin curtain, Andie watched. Her heart didn't race. Her skin didn't flush. There was no thrill in the contact—only the knowledge that it had worked. He was hooked.

And still, deep in her chest, something fluttered. A shadow of something old. Maybe it was guilt. Maybe it was pity.

Or maybe it was just the lie beginning to settle. He came looking for her the next day.

Andie made sure she was easy to find, seated alone at the edge of the botanical garden on campus, a place few students bothered to visit this early in the semester. The benches were damp from the morning dew, but she didn't mind the cold. She sat perfectly still, a small paperback resting open on her knee. She didn't read it. She simply let it be seen.

William approached cautiously, his hands in his jacket pockets, his hair slightly tousled by the breeze. He smiled as though greeting someone he already knew, not asking permission—just assuming presence meant invitation.

"You always sit alone," he said, trying to sound casual.

"I like being left alone," she replied, turning a page.

He faltered for a beat, then took a chance. "Yet you keep turning up where I am."

She raised her eyes at that, the flicker of amusement so brief it might've been imagined. "Maybe it's the other way around."

He laughed, the sound softer this time, more sincere. He sat down beside her—not close, but not far either. The bench creaked slightly under his weight. He leaned forward, elbows on knees, glancing at her book.

“What are you reading?”

“Camus,” she said. “But I already know how it ends.”

“Let me guess,” he said. “Someone dies, and it doesn’t matter.”

“Not quite.” She shut the book slowly and looked at him. “Someone dies... and it matters too late.”

That silenced him. The words lingered in the space between them. He nodded slowly, as though trying to catch up to what had just passed between them. Something about the way she spoke made him feel like she saw straight through his armor—into the small, ashamed places most people kept buried.

“You always talk like that?” he asked.

“Only when someone’s worth the words,” she said, standing before he could ask more.

He stood with her, instinctively. “Hey, I’m glad I ran into you.”

“You didn’t.” She tilted her head, her gaze unwavering. “You came looking.”

He didn’t deny it. He smiled like it was a compliment. “I still don’t know your name.”

Andie stepped closer, just enough that he’d have to notice the heat of her presence, the faint smell of something floral and old. She looked into his eyes and said, “Maybe I’ll tell you... when you’re ready to hear it.”

Then she walked away again, slow and deliberate.

Behind her, William stood rooted, eyes fixed on the curve of her retreating form, a slight grin pulling at his lips. He hadn't noticed the dead sparrow on the path behind the bench, its neck twisted, eyes wide open. Nor had he noticed that the garden clock above the entrance had stopped ticking three minutes ago.

Only she had.

That weekend, rain fell in a steady curtain over the college town—thin, cold sheets that blurred the windows and kept most indoors. Andie waited near the library entrance, sheltered beneath the arched overhang, her arms crossed, a thin sweater clinging to her frame. She looked like someone who hadn't checked the weather. Vulnerable. Exposed.

She saw him before he saw her.

William jogged across the quad beneath a too-small umbrella, soaked halfway through, backpack bouncing against his spine. As he neared the steps, he paused and blinked the rain from his lashes.

Their eyes met.

"You again," he said, out of breath, smiling with what he probably thought was charm.

"Me again," she said softly.

He climbed the steps, shaking water from his sleeves. "You waiting on someone?"

She looked out into the rain. "Not anymore."

It hung in the air for a moment—an invitation dressed as resignation. He picked up on it. She could see the way his posture changed, the angle of his shoulders, the ease that slipped into his stance.

"I've got an umbrella," he said, holding it out toward her. "If you need to be somewhere."

She hesitated, then stepped under it without a word.

They walked together across the quad, closer now. Rain tapped rhythmically above their heads. She let her shoulder brush against his, her breath quiet and deliberate. William said something about the rain reminding him of childhood, about backyard puddles and muddy jeans. She smiled—an empty smile, polished but hollow. She knew how to make it look real.

He didn't stop talking.

He didn't realize she hadn't said a word in over two minutes.

When they reached the far side of the lawn, she slipped slightly—just enough for her ankle to wobble. William caught her by the elbow without hesitation.

"You okay?"

She nodded, favoring her foot. "I guess I wasn't paying attention."

He looked concerned. It was automatic, unfiltered. "You want to sit?"

They stepped under another overhang, this one near the science hall. She leaned against the stone wall, lifting her foot as if testing it. William crouched beside her.

"Let me see," he said. "I used to do first aid for track in high school."

She let him. Let him touch her ankle lightly, gently. Just fingertips, no pressure. He examined it like it mattered. She watched him with an expression she had practiced for weeks—soft, open, tinged with silent gratitude.

"You're really sweet," she said quietly.

He met her eyes again, visibly taken aback by the compliment.

"You think?" he asked.

She nodded. "I think people don't say that enough. Especially to someone who just wants to help."

He beamed. Actually beamed.

The rain hadn't let up. In fact, it had grown heavier—but neither of them noticed the air had turned strangely cold, unnaturally so. The lamplight above them flickered once, then steadied.

And in the puddle at William's feet, their reflections shimmered—but only hers blinked. Later that night, she stood in front of the mirror in her borrowed room, brushing her hair slowly, each stroke even and deliberate. The rain still whispered against the glass, but inside, everything was silent. The kind of silence that pressed on your ribs.

The girl staring back at her looked whole. Composed. Pretty, even. Her eyes carried no weight. Her lips formed the faintest curve, a lingering ghost of the smile she'd worn all afternoon.

It scared her.

Not because she was pretending.

But because it no longer felt like pretending.

The ease with which she'd let William catch her fall. The way she'd let him touch her skin—just enough to make him feel like the protector, the gentleman. The words she'd chosen. The silence she had shaped. All of it flowed too naturally.

Andie set the brush down.

She studied her own face the way someone might examine a painting they hadn't seen in years—recognizing the shape, the color, but not the soul behind it. Her lips parted, as if she meant to say something to the girl in the mirror. But nothing came.

A tremor ran up her spine. The light above the mirror flickered.

She didn't flinch.

She leaned forward, watching closely. Her pupils dilated. Her breath fogged the glass for a moment. She drew a finger through the condensation, trailing a slow, curved line across the surface.

"I could've been this girl," she whispered. "Before."

Before Patrick. Before the fire in her chest. Before the night they took everything.

The room grew colder.

She turned, slowly, and saw nothing. Just the same walls, the same dull furniture, the same closed window.

But she felt it.

Something ancient, breathing just beneath the skin. Watching. Waiting.

She sat on the edge of the bed, resting her hands in her lap. Her fingers flexed slowly, the skin pale and cool. She thought about William—how he'd looked at her, like she was something rare, maybe even sacred. He didn't see her. Not really.

And maybe that was the point.

She hadn't lied. Not outright. She hadn't promised anything. But the way she'd moved, the way she'd played her role—it had drawn him in. And now he was circling, helpless to understand why.

Andie closed her eyes.

Chapter 5

The mask no longer pressed against her face. It didn't suffocate. It didn't sting.

It fit.

She didn't know if that made her strong.

Or if it made her something else entirely.

They met for coffee on a Tuesday.

He texted her now—innocent, polite messages, punctuated with emojis and small talk. She responded just enough to keep the thread alive. Never too eager. Never too cold. She let him feel like he was steering. In truth, he was drifting exactly where she wanted him.

They sat across from each other near the front window of a small café just off campus. The rain had stopped, but the air still hung heavy, the sky tinted in shades of pale slate. She cupped her drink with both hands, her nails pale and perfect. He sipped his black coffee like it mattered.

"I still don't know your name," William said with a grin, half-flirting, half-frustrated.

She smirked softly, shaking her head. "Not yet."

"Come on, mystery girl. You know everything about me."

"I know just enough," she said. "The rest... I can read."

He tilted his head. "Oh? What do you read?"

She set down her drink and leaned in ever so slightly. "You're overconfident. But not arrogant. You want to be seen as good. Not just liked—respected. You second-guess your instincts when it comes to people like me. You tell yourself you're above it, but here you are."

He blinked.

She leaned back again, letting the pause speak.

"You're... good at that," he said. "Observing."

"I've had time to watch."

Their eyes locked. For a moment, he seemed to search hers for something—recognition, perhaps. A flicker of doubt crossed his expression, but it vanished just as quickly as it had come.

Then came the environmental shift.

The lights above them dimmed briefly—not enough to draw attention, but enough to make William glance up. The clock on the wall behind her had stopped ticking, stuck at 2:16. She didn't look. She didn't have to.

Outside, a small bird flew directly into the windowpane near their table. A sharp *thump*, a smear of feathers and motion. William startled and turned.

Andie didn't move.

"Jesus," he muttered, leaning to look. "Did you see that?"

"I heard it," she said quietly. "Some things don't notice glass until it's too late."

The metaphor hung in the air.

He turned back toward her, unsettled but trying not to show it. "You always talk like that?"

She smiled, gentle and smooth. "Only when I mean it."

He laughed nervously. "You're intense."

"I'm honest."

Their drinks sat forgotten for a moment. His knee bounced under the table. She stilled his movement with the lightest touch of her hand against his leg.

"I like talking to you," he said. "I feel like... I don't know. Like we have this weird connection."

She tilted her head. "Maybe we do."

He smiled again, warmed by the idea.

She looked past him, through the window, at the rain-darkened world beyond.

And quietly, the shadows beneath her eyes deepened—just for a second.

They met again the next evening. Not planned—at least, not from his perspective.

Andie sat on a bench near the reflecting pool, the campus fountains gone still for seasonal maintenance. Lights from the nearby admin building shimmered across the water's glassy surface. She wore a soft gray sweater, her hair loose this time, shoulders tucked slightly forward as if she were smaller than she was. She looked like someone thinking about something heavy. Someone worth approaching.

William spotted her from the walkway. His smile was immediate, unguarded.

"You again," he said, like it was a gift.

She gave him a half-turn, a subdued smile. "Looks like fate wants us to keep running into each other."

He sat beside her without asking. "I'm starting to think you're right."

She glanced at him, then back at the water. "Do you believe in fate?"

He hesitated, as if weighing the cost of sincerity. "I don't know. Maybe. I believe in... moments. Connections. Like when you meet someone and it just... clicks."

Andie looked down at her hands. "That doesn't happen often."

He nodded. "Exactly. But when it does, it feels like a sign."

"You like signs," she murmured.

"I like clarity."

"Clarity is dangerous," she said. "It makes people stop asking questions."

He chuckled. "And what's so bad about that?"

"It makes them easy to lie to."

She didn't smile when she said it. He blinked, unsure whether to laugh. Then she softened, leaned just slightly closer, as if letting him glimpse a truth beneath her armor.

"But you're right," she said. "There is... something. Between us."

The words hit their mark. His shoulders loosened. His grin returned, tentative but pleased. He didn't realize she hadn't said *what* that something was.

"Do you feel it too?" he asked.

She turned to him fully now, eyes catching the reflection of streetlights. "Don't you?"

He flushed slightly, nodding. “I feel like I’ve known you longer than I have. Like we’re on the same page without having read the same book.”

“That’s a nice line,” she said softly. “Did you come up with that just now?”

He laughed. “Yeah, I guess I did.”

She reached out and gently brushed a speck of lint from his jacket shoulder. Her hand lingered a heartbeat too long. His breath caught.

“I don’t usually do this,” he said.

“I know,” she said.

He leaned back, looking out over the water again. “It’s weird. Being this into someone when you don’t even know their name.”

“Names are just labels,” she whispered. “They’re the first thing people learn to lie with.”

He looked at her, lips parted slightly. But he didn’t argue.

In the stillness that followed, a streetlamp across the path buzzed, then flickered out. The breeze chilled. Neither of them moved.

Andie smiled faintly, a perfect mimicry of romantic promise.

But inside, she felt nothing.

Only the quiet tremor of power humming beneath her skin—and the ticking of a clock that wasn’t there. “I don’t tell people this,” William said, voice lower now, eyes on the darkened surface of the pool. “Not even my friends.”

Andie watched him carefully, her posture relaxed, her breathing measured. Every line in her body projected openness, safety. She had spent days weaving the illusion—and now he leaned toward her like a moth drawn into soft firelight.

"My dad died when I was fourteen," he continued. "Heart attack. It was sudden. My mom—she didn't handle it well. We had to move a lot after that. Different schools, different cities. I got good at starting over. At pretending things didn't bother me."

His hands rested between his knees, fingers twitching slightly with memory. She didn't interrupt. That silence was part of the seduction—letting him fill the gaps with truth while she remained a canvas for his confession.

"It messed me up," he admitted. "I acted like I was okay, but I kept everything inside. Still do, I guess."

She nodded slowly, her voice a whisper. "You carry it well. But I can tell."

His head tilted slightly. "Tell what?"

"That there's a sadness in you," she said. "Not the kind that makes people weak. The kind that makes them feel too much."

He swallowed. His eyes shimmered—no tears, but a distant ache. It was almost endearing. Almost.

Andie leaned closer, letting her hair fall to one side, the scent of her skin drifting into his space. "You want to be seen. You want someone to really *see* you. Don't you?"

He nodded, breath shallow.

"I see you," she said.

The words landed like a soft punch to the chest. His eyes fluttered shut for a moment, then opened again—wide, clear, vulnerable. She could feel the shift happen, like the final clicks of a padlock.

He was hers now.

"Thank you," he murmured. "You don't know what that means."

She tilted her head. "Maybe I do."

She let her fingers graze his hand—just enough to feel the heat of his pulse, just enough to make his skin react. His hand didn't grab hers. He let it rest there, trembling slightly.

Inside her, the hollowness deepened.

This was easier than it should've been.

She had imagined this part would bring her pain, dredge up pieces of the girl who once longed to be held, seen, protected. But that girl was gone. What sat in her place was something else entirely—an observer, an actor, a shadow with her voice.

Andie looked down at their hands. His fingers moved slightly, as if asking permission.

She pulled away.

"Not yet," she said, smiling gently. "We're still writing the first chapter."

He smiled through the disappointment, masking it with hope.

She looked back at the pool.

In the water's reflection, his face glowed faintly.

But hers... didn't appear at all.

By Thursday, he was messaging her constantly.

Short, eager texts in the morning: *"Hope I see you today."*
Jokes and observations during class: *"Some guy just asked if Aristotle invented democracy."*

Late-night admissions, half-flirt, half-confession: *"I think I sleep better after talking to you."*

She replied with brevity. A single word here, a thoughtful sentence there. Just enough to stir him. Her restraint was a drug—every response from her fed the illusion of pursuit rewarded, desire reciprocated.

William didn't realize he was playing a part in something already written.

They met again that evening under the bridge near the music building, where the brick wall bore old murals no one had touched in years. She leaned against the worn stone, shadows stretching behind her like smoke, the buzz of a nearby security lamp low and pulsing.

He arrived breathless. Smiling.

"You always look like you're waiting for me," he said.

"Maybe I am," she replied, voice velveted.

They stood close. He said something about wanting to show her a song he'd written. Something soft and melancholy. He pulled out his phone, fumbled through his voice memos. His hands shook slightly. He wanted her to see him—his art, his effort, his soul.

Andie didn't listen to the melody.

She watched his face.

There was a light in his expression—a warmth she could've once craved. He looked at her the way boys used to look at girls in movies. Not like prey, not like property. Like a person worth unfolding.

It should've mattered.

But it didn't.

All she could think about was how easy it was. How easily the mask stayed in place. How easily she had become the kind of girl people trusted, even adored.

And how much of it wasn't her anymore.

He finished the song, sheepish. "It's not much. Just something I've been working on."

"It's beautiful," she said. "You are... very good at showing people who you are."

"Only to you."

She turned away slightly, letting the words sit in silence. A gust of wind swept through the underpass. Leaves skittered across the walkway like tiny bones.

"Can I ask you something?" he said, gently.

She nodded without facing him.

"Why me?"

The question stung more than she expected.

Not because she had an answer.

But because, for a moment, she didn't.

She had picked him because of what he was—one of them. Because of his smile, because of what he hadn't done, because of the life he got to keep. Because his name tasted bitter in her mouth. Because he had been nearby and free and untouched.

But now, now that she saw him this close—now that he looked at her like this—she wasn't sure if it was revenge she wanted.

Or exposure.

Or maybe just to see if he would break too. William invited her over the next night.

He tried to sound casual about it, but Andie could see the anticipation in every word he typed, the subtext hidden behind his offer: *"Movie night? Just us. No pressure."*

She said yes.

His apartment was small, clean, and carefully arranged—half-masculine, half-childish, as if still afraid of looking too grown. The walls held band posters and framed prints of films she never cared to watch. A guitar leaned against the bookshelf. His bed wasn't made, but the sheets were fresh.

He lit candles.

She didn't comment.

He offered her tea.

She accepted.

They sat on the couch, a narrow two-seater that forced closeness without contact. The movie played, something slow and forgettable. He pretended to be watching. She pretended to be interested.

But all her focus stayed on *him*.

The way he shifted slightly toward her, like gravity had begun to bend. The way his knee bumped hers and lingered. The way he glanced over, not at her eyes, but her lips. Like a question he hadn't earned the answer to.

Andie leaned her head lightly on his shoulder. Not for comfort. For calibration.

He exhaled softly, relaxing under the weight.

"You're warm," he whispered.

"So are you," she replied.

Outside the windows, the wind had stilled. Inside, the apartment felt oddly hushed—like it had exhaled and hadn't taken a breath since. The flickering candlelight stretched their shadows long across the wall.

"You ever feel like you were meant to meet someone?" he asked.

She didn't answer.

He turned his head slightly, trying to meet her gaze. She kept hers on the screen, unreadable.

"I feel like I've known you longer than I actually have," he said. "It's strange."

"It's not strange," she murmured.

"No?"

"It's just what happens when someone gives you exactly what you need."

He was silent. The movie crackled on, forgotten.

Then he turned, slowly—face hovering close. His breath brushed her cheek. His hand touched her knee.

She didn't recoil.

But she didn't lean in either.

Instead, she placed her fingers gently on his chest, firm and still. A barrier.

"Not yet," she whispered, the words soft but final.

He nodded, immediately pulling back, ashamed of the impulse. "Sorry. I didn't mean to—"

She touched his cheek, silencing him. "It's okay. I just... want to make sure it's real."

He smiled, awkward and sweet. "It feels real."

She nodded, but said nothing.

Later, after he fell asleep with a blanket over his chest and the empty mug still on the coffee table, Andie stood in the dark hallway, watching him.

The candle had gone out.

The room was shadowed, still, quiet.

She didn't blink.

She didn't move.

She only stared.

And somewhere, inside the silence, a picture frame cracked without being touched.

She stayed there for nearly an hour.

In the shadowed hallway, arms crossed over her chest, bare feet silent on the hardwood floor. William's breathing came slow and steady from the couch—deep, trusting, utterly unaware. The faint ticking of the kitchen clock was the only rhythm in the apartment, yet even that began to slow.

Andie tilted her head.

She had the power now. All of it. He was open to her. Receptive. Malleable. Every barrier he'd built over years of grief, loss, and adolescent survival—she had slipped past them without force. Just grace, suggestion, and timing.

She hadn't threatened.

Hadn't needed to.

And yet she wondered—*is this worse?*

She stepped closer, one silent pace at a time, until she stood directly behind the couch, looking down at him. His eyelashes flickered in dream. His lips parted slightly, murmuring some half-formed word. The blanket had slipped off one shoulder, revealing the soft hollow where neck met collarbone.

She could reach out now.

Touch him.

End him.

And it would be *so easy.*

But that wasn't the plan. Not yet.

She turned away and walked to the window. The glass reflected her shape, though the light was too faint to capture her face. Just a dark outline in motion. Behind her, William stirred but didn't wake.

Andie stared out into the street below.

A stray cat slinked through the alley. A flickering streetlight danced overhead. The night felt stretched—too long, too quiet. It had the weight of something *waiting*.

She felt it building inside her again—the slow, coiling energy. A pulse beneath her ribs, not quite hers. Something old. Watching. Wanting.

But not yet.

She closed her eyes and whispered to herself, "Not yet."

A low groan echoed from somewhere in the walls—pipes maybe, or something else. Andie didn't turn.

Instead, she opened her eyes again and looked at her reflection in the window. The figure staring back was not the girl she used to be. That girl would've cried tonight. That girl would've collapsed onto the floor in confusion, shame, or rage.

This version of her didn't cry.

She studied the image carefully, tracing the sharp edges of her new face, the stillness in her eyes. She was becoming something else entirely. Not hollow. Not broken.

Sharper. Colder. More precise.

She could smile when needed. Laugh when expected. She could offer warmth and tenderness like a script she had memorized. But none of it rooted. None of it grew.

The mask had fused. She no longer wore it.

She *was* it.

Behind her, William shifted again and sighed her name in his sleep—though he didn't know it.

She turned away from the glass.

Walked quietly to the chair across the room.

And sat.

Watching.

Waiting.

Morning brought a pale gray light that filtered through the blinds, striping the apartment in uneven lines. The candles had long since burned out. The television screen glowed faintly with the blue "Are you still watching?" prompt. William blinked awake with a small stretch, arms above his head, hair wild from sleep.

Andie was already awake. Still. Seated across from him in the old armchair, legs crossed, her chin resting lightly on one hand.

"You stayed?" he asked, rubbing his eyes.

"I did."

He sat up quickly, searching her face. "Did we... I mean, did anything—?"

She smiled.

Not a laugh. Not mockery.

Something between promise and restraint.

"No," she said. "You were a perfect gentleman."

He flushed, nodding. "I just... I wasn't sure. It felt..."

"Like something could've happened?" she finished for him, tilting her head.

"Yeah."

"It could have."

The air between them changed—just enough to make him sit straighter. His heart rate quickened; she could see it in the pulse just below his neck.

He licked his lips. "But it didn't."

"Not yet," she said, with a soft smile that carried heat behind it. "Some things are better when they're earned."

He exhaled a shaky breath, both relieved and hooked deeper. He moved closer along the couch cushion, hand instinctively brushing the edge of the blanket between them.

"I want to see you again," he said.

"You will."

"I mean soon."

"You're already seeing me," she whispered.

She reached for the coffee mug on the table—the one he'd left half-full the night before—and lifted it to her lips as if it belonged to her. A subtle claim. A small intimacy. The kind that made someone believe they were falling into something mutual.

William watched her every movement now, eyes following her like he couldn't help it.

"You're dangerous," he said with a grin.

"I am," she replied, not grinning back.

The silence after the words was thick, deliberate.

Then she shifted in her seat, letting her sweater fall slightly off one shoulder. She made no move to fix it. Let the illusion deepen.

"You ever feel like something's inevitable?" she asked.

"I do now," he said.

She set the mug down. "Good."

A flicker passed through the room—something beyond candlelight, beyond morning shadows. The overhead bulb gave a small *pop,* not enough to darken the room, but enough to be noticed.

William blinked. "Did you see that?"

"Must be the fuse," she said, already standing.

She didn't give him time to speak again. Instead, she leaned in, kissed him on the cheek—just the cheek—and let her hand rest briefly on his chest.

His hand reached for her waist, hopeful.

She stepped away, not rejecting—just retreating.

"Next time," she said.

Then she was gone.

William sat back, dazed, smiling to himself.

Behind him, the clock on the microwave had reset to 00:00.

William couldn't keep it to himself.

By the following afternoon, he was already telling someone—his roommate, a quiet pre-law major named Josh who barely left his room unless it was to refill his coffee or complain about the Wi-Fi. They sat in the common area, a pair of reheated burritos on paper plates between them, ESPN murmuring low on the TV.

"She's... different," William said, smiling down at his plate, poking at it with a fork. "In a good way. It's like... being around her makes everything else feel fake."

Josh raised a brow. "You met her last week."

"I know, man. But it's not like that. I don't feel like I'm chasing something temporary."

"You know her name yet?"

William chuckled. "Not exactly."

Josh gave him a long, flat stare. "You're serious?"

"I'm telling you—it's not weird. It's kind of her thing. Mysterious. But not in a fake way. It's more like she's... above the games."

Josh grunted. "Or she's playing a really good one."

William shrugged off the comment but didn't respond right away. He was still glowing with the warmth of last night. Her touch. Her closeness. That kiss on the cheek. And the way she'd left—like she'd decided it, not him. That somehow made it feel more real.

"She's not like other girls I've dated," William said, mostly to himself.

From outside, across the street, Andie stood under the eave of the laundromat, a hood pulled lightly over her head. The glass pane of the apartment window distorted the figures inside slightly, but she could see enough—his posture, his grin, his animation. She knew that look. It was what came after affection and before vulnerability.

It meant the hook had set.

She didn't smile.

Instead, she watched in silence as William stood, probably headed to class, still talking as he walked. She slipped around the corner before his eyes could drift toward the window. Not that he ever looked out.

People rarely looked out when they were warm inside.

She walked the sidewalk slowly, fingers trailing along the brick wall beside her, as if listening for something buried in the stone. She could hear her thoughts clearer when she moved—especially thoughts she didn't want to speak aloud.

What am I doing?

The question came with no answer. It wasn't guilt. Not remorse. Just distance—like the question belonged to another person asking from inside a well.

A low hum followed her, just under the sound of traffic and wind. Not real noise. Vibrations. Like something alive in the concrete beneath her feet.

A dog barked once from an alley behind her.

Then whimpered.

And went silent.

She kept walking.

That night, Andie didn't go back to her rented room above the antique shop.

Instead, she walked for hours, drifting through the city's edges—beneath freeway overpasses, along the border of the old train yard, past the shuttered gas stations that always seemed trapped in some forgotten decade. The streets were nearly empty, the kind of quiet that settled too easily, as if something had frightened the noise away.

She liked it here.

There were no mirrors. No windows to catch her reflection. Just cracked pavement and windblown trash. The real world peeled thin around the edges in places like this. And that was where she felt most like herself.

Or whatever *self* was now.

She stopped beside a graffiti-covered loading dock and sat, the concrete cool beneath her. A half-moon hung above the skyline, jaundiced and cracked by distant clouds. Her fingers toyed absently with the hem of her sweater, her eyes fixed on nothing.

What am I becoming?

Not the victim anymore. Not the girl cowering in corners or apologizing for her own breath. That version of Andie was gone, atomized by flame and screams and silence. But what had replaced her wasn't easy to name.

Predator?

Possessor?

Protector?

Each mask she wore now—whether coy or warm or broken—fit too well. She had learned the pitch of her own false laughter, the weight of suggestive silence. Learned how to say just enough. Offer just enough. Keep them always leaning forward.

Was it acting?

Or was the role always hidden inside her?

Her breath fogged briefly in the air, despite the mild night.

Across the street, a lamppost flickered once, then dimmed completely. A second later, the one next to it buzzed and joined it in darkness. Only hers remained lit, humming faintly. A perfect spotlight.

She looked up at it and whispered, "Stop."

The light went out instantly.

She didn't flinch.

Instead, she closed her eyes and felt the quiet rush into the space left behind. It wasn't power that coursed through her veins—it was control. And control felt cleaner than rage. More permanent than fear.

But it was lonely.

She'd spent her whole life wanting someone to understand her. To love her without condition, without demand. And now... someone almost did. William. With his soft hands and sad eyes. With his open heart and fumbling honesty.

He didn't deserve what was coming.

And yet, he'd be the first to see it.

Not because he had harmed her.

But because someone had to.

Andie stood, slowly, brushing the dust from her jeans. The streetlight above her flicked back on, casting a harsh white glow over her figure.

She didn't look back as she walked away, disappearing into the dark with silence as her cloak.

The message came just after midnight.

She saw the screen light up from across the room, a soft rectangle of blue in the dark. She didn't move to grab it. Instead, she waited—watched the light fade, then return as the next line appeared.

William: "I hope I didn't say anything weird today. You looked kind of distant. If something's wrong, you can tell me. I won't judge."

And then, a minute later:

William: "I know you're not mine. I'm not trying to push anything. I just feel like I care about you, and maybe that matters."

Andie sat on the floor, legs folded, spine straight. She stared at the screen from where she was, watching the glow pulse once more before settling into silence.

He meant it.

Every word.

She could feel the weight behind them—not rehearsed or performative, but real. An offering. A small, fragile truth being held out in trembling hands.

Her thumb hovered over the phone for a moment. Then she picked it up, opened the message thread, and read the words again.

Care.

She tried to remember what it felt like to believe in that word. To want it. To accept it as something without danger tied to its tail. But the only memory that surfaced was the sound of her mother's scream the night the car flipped. The blur of flames. The way her body had refused to move, to cry, to *feel.*

You're not mine.

The line stuck with her. It wasn't possessive. It was vulnerable. *He wanted her,* but he didn't expect her. Didn't demand.

She hated that it almost moved her.

The part of her that had been remade in blood and silence stirred. *Feel nothing. Give nothing. Take what you need, then leave the pieces behind.* That was the rule now. The new code. She had survived by burying the girl who wanted to be held. Who whispered *maybe he's different* when the lights went out.

Still, she typed.

Andie: *"You didn't say anything wrong. I'm not used to this. It's hard for me to believe when someone's being real."*

A moment passed.

Then he replied:

William: "I get that. And I'll prove it, if you let me."

She stared at those words for a long time. Not because they confused her, but because they didn't. He would try. He would try with all his heart. And he would fail. Because it wasn't about what he gave—it was about what had already been taken from her. What could never be returned.

But let him try, she thought. *Let him get close.*

She typed again.

Andie: *"Maybe I'll let you in. A little."*

Then she turned off the phone.

And sat alone in the dark.

No smile.

No tears.

Just the hum of something old and final rising in her bones.

It was raining again.

Not a downpour, just the soft hiss of water brushing against the windows, steady and rhythmic. The kind of sound that made people believe the world was gentler than it was. William's apartment was dimly lit, a single floor lamp casting a golden cone across the couch where they sat, close—closer than ever before.

Andie let herself lean into him. Not out of affection. Not out of strategy.

But out of curiosity.

Can I still feel anything?

William was warm beneath her hands, his body responsive, cautious but hungry. When he kissed her, it wasn't greedy—it was reverent. Slow at first, then deepening, like he thought she might shatter if held too tight. She didn't shatter. She didn't tremble. She didn't melt.

She simply allowed it.

His hand slipped beneath her shirt, fingertips ghosting along her ribs. His breath quickened, lips trailing across her neck. Her body responded—mechanically. Muscles tensed, eyes closed, heart steady. She kissed him back. Let her hands drift up his back, then under his shirt.

It was heat.

It was movement.

But it wasn't *real.*

Not for her.

He pulled back just slightly, his voice thick with breath. "You sure?"

Her answer was a kiss. Deeper. Harder. She let her legs wrap around his waist as he leaned into her, as their bodies tangled and the world shrank to skin and breath and pressure.

But then something happened.

Nothing.

She felt nothing.

Not discomfort. Not disgust. Just… emptiness.

No fear. No longing. No electricity beneath the skin. His hands were there. His mouth. His weight. But none of it touched her where it used to count. Where it would've once made her ache or gasp or laugh.

Andie opened her eyes.

She saw his face, eyes shut, lost in the moment. Trusting. Wanting. Human.

And she felt like a shadow in the shape of a girl.

Her hands slid from his back. Her legs unwrapped.

He noticed the change instantly, blinking at her, confused. "Did I—?"

"No," she whispered, gently pressing her palm to his chest. "You didn't do anything wrong."

He sat up slowly, watching her. Concerned.

She sat too, legs drawn close, eyes fixed on the floor. "I thought maybe I could feel it again. That maybe there was something left to reach."

William didn't know what to say.

She looked at him—not with anger, not with regret, but with the kind of sadness reserved for strangers in passing trains.

"I'm not who you think I am," she said. "And this… this isn't what you think it is."

He opened his mouth, but no words came.

She stood, calmly adjusting her shirt, her movements quiet and clinical.

"I'm sorry," she said. "For pretending I was still whole."

Then she walked toward the window and stared out at the night.

Behind her, William sat frozen, the warmth between them dying into silence. The silence between them stretched, thick and fragile. William sat motionless, his expression caught between confusion and wounded pride. Andie remained at the window, watching the rain blur the world into streaks of gray.

She knew what came next. The doubt. The withdrawal. The emotional unraveling of a man unsure if he had pushed too hard or simply wasn't enough. The shift in power—once handed to her—might begin to slip away. She couldn't allow that.

Not now.

Not yet.

She turned back toward him slowly, softening her face with practiced care. Her voice dropped to a whisper as she walked back across the room, each step unhurried, deliberate.

"I didn't pull away because I didn't want you," she said, crouching beside him. "I pulled away because I don't know how to *deserve* you."

His eyes flicked to hers—hope fighting its way through the fog.

She touched his hand gently, letting her thumb run over his knuckles. "You make me feel like I'm still real. Like I'm not just... broken pieces trying to look like a girl."

He swallowed hard. "You're not broken."

She tilted her head, eyes glinting in the low light. "Then promise me something."

"Anything."

"Don't give up on me."

He nodded quickly, leaning toward her, desperate to be useful, to be the anchor she appeared to need.

“I mean it,” she said, laying a hand flat on his chest again, pressing lightly against his heartbeat. “This scares me. But you make me want to try.”

William’s hand covered hers, fingers closing around her wrist with a tenderness that nearly made her flinch—not from pain, but from its sincerity.

“I’m here,” he said.

She leaned in slowly, brushing her lips against his—just once. Not lingering. Just enough to reignite the illusion of intimacy. When she pulled away, she rested her forehead against his.

“Goodnight, William.”

“Stay,” he whispered.

“I can’t tonight.”

He nodded, but she could feel the disappointment coiling inside him, along with the desperate hope that she’d return. That there was still something to win. Something to fix.

She had re-established the balance.

As she stood and moved toward the door, she paused, glancing back over her shoulder.

“When I come back,” she said, voice velveted, “you’ll really know who I am.”

He smiled, dazed by her promise.

She left quietly, letting the door close with a soft click behind her. Once outside, the cold air hit her lungs like ice water. The sky overhead churned with thick clouds. Wind tugged at her hair, but she didn't feel it.

She walked.

No destination. No pause.

Just the night swallowing her step by step.

Not with shame.

Not with guilt.

But with the certainty that whatever *love* had once meant... it was no longer a language her heart could speak. The streets were nearly empty at that hour, save for the distant hiss of wet tires and the faint hum of neon signs still clinging to life. Andie walked with no umbrella, no destination. The rain clung to her hair, soaked into the shoulders of her sweater, and still she kept moving, her pace even, her steps silent.

She didn't feel the cold anymore.

Didn't notice the wet.

Only the *absence.*

There had been a time—*before*—when moments like the one in William's apartment would have cracked her open. Her body would've flushed with anticipation, her chest would've fluttered with nervous possibility. She might have trembled under someone's touch. Might have felt *alive.*

But now?

Now his fingers on her skin had felt like cloth through water. Dim. Distant. Echoes passing through a house no longer inhabited. No fear. No thrill. Just weight and breath and heat—*tolerated,* but never *felt.*

That terrified her more than anything.

Not the power. Not the entity that whispered in her blood. Not even the promise of vengeance.

But this hollowness.

The soft, sterile vacuum where her soul used to be.

She stepped off the curb and crossed an intersection lit only by a flickering streetlamp. Her shadow danced around her ankles like something trying to keep up. A cracked neon sign above a pawn shop buzzed and spit sparks. The rain intensified for a moment, coming down in needles.

Still, she didn't flinch.

She remembered William's eyes as she'd left. So full of promise. Still believing. Still *hoping*.

She hadn't wanted to hurt him.

But she also hadn't cared if she did.

That was the fracture she couldn't ignore. The clearest sign of what she was becoming. She could *mimic* love now, as well as she once mimicked silence. Could wear empathy like a veil, just thick enough to convince anyone who dared look closer.

But the emotion itself—the *feeling*—was gone.

Somewhere between the flame and the scream and the night she was *remade*, something had burned clean through her center. What filled it now was something else entirely. Not demonic. Not holy. Just... void.

She reached a church at the edge of town, dark and locked, its wooden doors towering above her like a challenge. She stepped onto the stone steps and stared at the stained-glass window over the entryway. A faded image of St. Michael. Sword raised. Face serene.

She hated it.

Hated the lie of peace in its eyes.

Thunder rolled once behind the clouds. The light overhead blinked and went out.

Andie turned from the doors.

And kept walking.

The echo of her steps was the only sound left. The alley behind the old convenience store hadn't changed.

She remembered it too well. The tilt of the dumpster. The sagging fence. The streetlamp that buzzed but never lit right. It was the first place she saw him again. Not a stranger. Not a coincidence.

Billy.

No one called him that anymore. Now he was William. College boy. Clean-cut. Aspiring something or other. He wore guilt like a distant dream, if he wore it at all.

She watched him that day from the shadows—saw the way he smiled at a girl, charming and unbothered. It made her stomach twist. Not with fear. Not even with rage. With purpose.

Because he'd forgotten her.

But she had *never* forgotten him.

She could still hear the laughter echoing in that room. Feel the weight of him pressing her down. The hot breath, the slurred names, the careless way he passed her back like a used thing. And when he left her there—broken, bleeding, still and shaking—it hadn't been with remorse.

It had been with pride.

She had seen it in his eyes.

And now, years later, he looked at her again—different hair, different name, different voice—and didn't see the girl he'd destroyed.

He saw a mystery.

He saw *opportunity*.

That's what turned her stomach now. That he could look into her eyes, so close to the same ones he forced shut that night, and still see someone to *charm*. Still think he could win her. That he *deserved* her.

Her fingers curled into fists.

She hadn't sought love in William.

She'd sought confirmation.

To see if the fire inside her could be extinguished. To see if the monster he helped create could still be reached. Could feel something besides this cold, calculating hunger. Could fall into the lie of romance just long enough to pretend it hadn't all happened.

But the moment his lips had touched hers, the truth ignited behind her ribs.

There was no love left in her.

Not for him.

Not for *anyone*.

She hadn't found Billy by accident. She had *tracked* him. Hunted him. The night she saw him again, the plan was born before the breath left her lungs. Get close. Make him want her. Make him *need* her. Then show him what it felt like to be stripped bare and helpless.

And now?

Now the mask was secure. He trusted her. He felt *safe.*

He had no idea.

She leaned her head back against the brick wall, rain trickling through her hair, eyes open to the black sky.

Her heart didn't race.

It hadn't in years. Three nights passed before she returned.

William didn't expect her—he hadn't heard from her in over forty-eight hours, and he'd sent three messages that went unanswered. But when she knocked softly on his door just after nine, hoodie pulled up, hair damp from the light drizzle, he opened it like a man forgiven.

"Hey," he breathed, unsure whether to smile or apologize.

She stepped in without a word, brushing past him. The scent of her—faintly sweet, oddly earthy—lingered as she moved into the center of the apartment. She didn't look at him immediately, just stood there for a moment, as if listening to something only she could hear.

He shut the door behind her, heartbeat rising. "I wasn't sure if I'd see you again."

"I wasn't sure either," she said.

Her voice was quiet but not uncertain. She turned to him then, eyes softer than he remembered—less guarded, but unreadable. Like she'd reached some internal conclusion and wasn't sure how much to share.

"I've been thinking," she continued, pulling down the hood and letting her hair fall loose, strands clinging wet to her cheeks. "About us. About whether I'm capable of doing this."

William stepped closer. “You don’t have to explain anything. I get it—whatever it is, I’m just glad you’re here.”

She tilted her head, studying him. “Are you?”

“Of course,” he said, smiling now. “I care about you, Andie. I’ve never connected with someone like this. Not so fast. Not so—deep.”

She didn’t respond immediately. Her gaze moved past him to the couch, the blanket half-folded from their last night together. She walked over and sat down, pulling her knees up slightly, as if shrinking into herself.

He followed, sitting beside her but giving her space.

“I’m not used to people staying,” she said.

“Well,” he said gently, “I’m not going anywhere.”

She looked at him with a faint smile, the kind that might’ve once meant something. “That’s what they always say.”

He didn’t ask who “they” were.

“I wanted to see you,” she said after a moment. “To try. To see if... something inside me could feel again.”

William reached for her hand. She let him take it.

“I want that too,” he said. “For you. For us.”

“I brought something,” she said, reaching into her bag and pulling out a small glass jar filled with folded slips of paper.

He raised an eyebrow. “What’s that?”

“Thoughts I was too afraid to say out loud. I write them down, fold them up, and seal them away.”

He took the jar, turning it in his hands.

"You want me to read one?"

"No," she said, voice cool. "Not yet."

She reached over, gently took the jar back, and set it on the coffee table in front of them.

"I just wanted you to see it. Know that there are parts of me even I'm afraid of."

He nodded slowly, mesmerized.

Her fingers laced with his again.

And this time, she didn't pull away. They sat in silence for a while, the jar between them like a forgotten offering. William's thumb traced the ridge of her knuckles, slow and deliberate, as if touching something rare. Andie let it happen. She didn't flinch. She didn't recoil.

But inside, she measured every breath he took.

"I missed you," he said quietly. "More than I thought I would."

She gave a small nod, but her gaze remained fixed on the glass jar. She wasn't thinking about the words trapped inside it—she was thinking about the way his voice softened when he spoke to her. How it trembled ever so slightly. The same voice that had once laughed in a basement room while she bled silently into the floorboards.

He didn't remember.

But she did.

"You ever wonder," she said slowly, "what parts of yourself you'd bury if you had to start over?"

He blinked. "I mean, yeah. Everyone has regrets."

"No," she said, turning to face him. "I don't mean mistakes. I mean the parts of you that can't exist anymore. The parts you have to kill to survive."

His lips parted as if to speak, but he hesitated.

She smiled gently, falsely. "Never mind. I'm being dramatic."

"No," he said quickly. "You're not. I just don't know how to answer that."

She leaned her head on his shoulder then, letting her weight rest there. It wasn't comfort she sought—it was closeness. To feel him breathe. To listen to the beat of the thing she would soon still.

"You always talk like you've been through hell," he said.

"I have."

He chuckled nervously. "Well, I'm here now. And I'm not afraid of whatever came before me."

She tilted her head slightly to look at him. "You should be."

The words were soft. Almost playful. But his smile faltered.

A draft passed through the room. Not from the window. Not from the door. The kind of cold that slithered up through the floorboards, quiet and unearned. William shifted in his seat.

"Did you feel that?"

She nodded, eyes unreadable. "Sometimes things just... pass through."

The overhead light dimmed for a moment, then returned. A low hum from the fridge cut out mid-cycle.

William stood up, brushing his hands on his jeans. “I’ll grab a blanket. You cold?”

“I’m fine,” she said.

As he stepped into the hallway closet, she turned toward the coffee table, lifted the glass jar again, and removed one folded slip of paper. She unfolded it slowly, her eyes scanning the words she had written months ago:

“He smiled after. That was the worst part.”

She folded it again and slid it into her back pocket.

William returned with the blanket and sat beside her once more. He draped it over them both, instinctively pulling her close.

Andie leaned in, resting her head against his chest, listening.

Still beating. Not for long.

His heartbeat thumped steadily beneath her ear, calm and rhythmic. To him, it probably felt like safety. Like something unfolding naturally. But to Andie, it was a metronome counting down. A soft, biological drumbeat marking the last stretch of a life he’d already forfeited.

She wondered what it would sound like when it stopped.

William’s fingers traced small circles across her back. His breath had slowed, deepened—not with sleep, but with comfort. Desire lingered in the air between them, warm and stupid. He didn’t know he was on the edge of a grave he helped dig.

“I don’t deserve this,” he said suddenly, voice low.

She lifted her head slightly. “What do you mean?”

“You. This. I don’t know what I did to be lucky enough to have you here.”

She blinked slowly. "You were in the right place. That's all."

He chuckled. "Then thank God for bad coffee and bookstores."

She smiled, but it didn't reach her eyes. She ran her fingers along his collarbone, slow and idle. Her touch was featherlight. Controlled. She could feel his skin warm under her hand, his body responding to her as if he were choosing the moment.

But he wasn't.

This moment didn't belong to him.

William leaned in, brushing his lips along the side of her neck. She let him. Not because she wanted to be touched, but because she wanted to know what it felt like to *tolerate* it. To see if she could become ice in motion. She closed her eyes and allowed the illusion.

His hand moved under her shirt again. She let him.

She even kissed him back.

For a few breaths, the world compressed—just heat, skin, breath, friction.

Then she opened her eyes and felt the weight of what was missing.

There was no spark. No flutter. No warmth. His mouth could've been air. His hands might as well have belonged to a mannequin. His body pressed against hers, trembling with hope and desire, and all she could feel was *nothing*.

A dull static buzzed in her ears.

His lips reached hers again. She did not respond.

When she pulled away, it was slow. Controlled. Surgical.

He paused, blinking at her. "What's wrong?"

Andie sat up, rearranged her shirt. "Nothing."

"Did I—?"

"You didn't do anything," she said, standing.

He looked small now, still half-covered by the blanket, hair tousled, lips slightly parted like a question left unanswered. "I thought..."

"You thought wrong," she said gently.

She stepped into the kitchen without explanation and opened the fridge—not because she was hungry, but to fill the space with something other than him.

Inside, the light flickered.

The milk had curdled. The eggs had cracked in their carton.

He followed her, hesitating at the threshold. "I don't understand."

She closed the fridge and turned to him. "I know."

And that was the cruelty in it—he never would. Andie stood still in the kitchen, the stale fridge air wafting around her. William lingered by the doorway, shifting from one foot to the other like a boy afraid of being sent away. His eyes searched hers for explanation, for mercy, for the softness she'd shown just minutes ago.

She gave him neither.

Instead, she stepped toward him slowly and placed a hand on his chest. His breath caught. The tension in his shoulders eased, just a bit.

"I told you I'm complicated," she said softly. "But you keep looking at me like I'm something you can fix."

"I don't want to fix you," he whispered. "I just want you to let me in."

She tilted her head. “You think you’re already in.”

“I know you’re holding something back.”

“I’m holding *everything* back, William.”

He flinched a little at that—at the honesty of it. Still, he didn’t retreat. His hand reached up and gently touched hers where it rested against his chest. She let him hold it.

“I don’t care what happened to you,” he said. “Not in the way that makes me pity you. I just… I just want to know you now. The you that’s here.”

Her eyes narrowed slightly.

“And what if the me that’s here isn’t real?”

His mouth opened. No answer came.

She leaned forward, pressing her lips gently to his forehead. Not affectionate. Not even tender. Just precise.

“You don’t know me,” she whispered. “You know what you want me to be.”

“I’m trying,” he said.

“I know,” she said. “That’s the worst part.”

She pulled away and walked past him into the living room. The room felt heavier now. The lights dimmer. Even the walls seemed to lean inward, as if listening.

William followed slowly, uncertain.

Andie sat down on the couch and patted the cushion beside her. “Come here.”

He did. Eager. Hopeful. Desperate to understand the rules again.

She leaned into him, resting her head against his shoulder. Her fingers moved over the inside of his wrist, feeling the pulse.

"So steady," she murmured.

"What is?"

"Your heartbeat."

He laughed awkwardly. "Is that a good thing?"

"For now," she said.

He didn't notice the flicker in her tone.

"Can we just sit like this?" he asked. "No pressure. No expectations."

She nodded against him, closing her eyes. "Of course."

He relaxed fully, finally. His head rested lightly against hers. He didn't speak again, as if worried anything he said would unravel it all.

Andie's breathing slowed. Her body softened against his.

But inside, the numbness only deepened.

This was how it would begin—the death not in the scream or the struggle, but in the stillness. The comfort. The illusion of closeness. She wouldn't strike like a flame. She would extinguish him like a lullaby. And he would never see it coming.

She waited until his breathing matched hers—calm, slow, syncing into something intimate. The kind of rhythm that made men believe they were understood. Accepted. Loved.

Only then did she begin.

Chapter 6

"Do you ever think about the people you've hurt?" she asked quietly.

William shifted beside her. "What do you mean?"

She kept her voice even. "I mean... really think about them. Not just in passing, not just in apology, but in *detail*. Their names. Their faces. What they looked like after you were done."

He blinked. "That's a heavy question."

"You don't have to answer."

"No, it's okay." He hesitated. "I mean, yeah—there are things I regret. Stupid things. Hookups that went too far. Times I acted like an asshole. But I never wanted to hurt anyone."

"You think intention matters more than impact?"

"I think it matters," he said. "Don't you?"

She turned to him. Her eyes were too calm.

"No," she said.

He studied her for a beat. "Is this about something I did?"

She smiled faintly. "Everything is about something you did, Billy."

His brow furrowed. "Billy?"

"Yeah," she said. "That's what your friends called you in high school, right?"

He stiffened slightly. "Yeah, I haven't heard that in years."

"I remember it," she said. "I remember a lot of things people think are long gone."

William sat up a little straighter. "Did we... know each other then?"

Her head tilted slightly. "Does it feel like we did?"

He nodded slowly. "A little. I thought that the first day I saw you."

She leaned in, her face close to his, whispering so softly it barely moved the air between them. "Memory's funny. It hides what hurts until it's safe to remember."

He pulled back just slightly, confusion rising behind his eyes. "What are we talking about, Andie?"

She didn't answer right away. Instead, she reached into her pocket and retrieved the same slip of paper she'd folded earlier. She handed it to him.

He opened it, reading the line written in neat, deliberate ink.

"He smiled after. That was the worst part."

He stared at it, eyes scanning it once, then twice more.

"What... is this?"

"Do you recognize it?"

He shook his head, but not confidently. "No... no, I don't. What is this?"

"It's a memory," she said. "Not yours. *Mine.*"

His face paled. "I—I don't understand."

"I know," she said softly.

She stood up and walked to the window, arms crossed. Rain had started again, tapping the glass like impatient fingernails.

Behind her, William read the slip again.

And began to feel something like dread crawling up from his stomach.

She turned back, her eyes fixed on him. Not angry. Not triumphant.

Just awake.

“You don’t get to forget,” she said. “Not anymore.”

The paper trembled in William’s hands. His fingers tightened around it, creasing the edges. He read the sentence again, his eyes slower this time, as if afraid the words might change.

He smiled after. That was the worst part.

He looked up at her, and for the first time since they met, he didn’t know what to say.

Andie stood by the window, unmoving, watching the streetlights bleed down the wet pavement outside. The air between them stretched thin, charged with something deeper than discomfort. It wasn’t anger. It was revelation.

“Is this some kind of... story?” he asked, voice hoarse.

“It’s a memory,” she replied. “Mine.”

William blinked rapidly. “And you’re saying... I—”

She turned, slowly.

“I don’t need you to say anything. I just need you to *remember*.”

His eyes darted around the room, as if some object might save him from what was coming. “I... I don’t know what you think I did—”

“I *know* what you did,” she said, cutting him off. Her voice wasn’t loud, but it sliced through the space with precision. “And I think—no—I *know* you’ve spent years convincing yourself it didn’t mean anything.”

He opened his mouth again. Closed it.

"There were four of you," she said, stepping toward him. "You smelled like bourbon and Axe. There was music in the background, something with too much bass. I remember the ceiling tiles. I remember the taste of blood. I remember you."

"No," he whispered.

"Do you remember laughing?"

"I didn't—"

"You did," she said. "And when it was over, you smiled. Not out of cruelty. Out of pride."

"Stop," he whispered. "Please. I don't remember that."

"You *chose* not to," she said.

He stood, knocking over the jar on the table. It shattered, shards skittering across the floor like teeth. Dozens of folded papers spilled, some partially opened, exposing fragments of horrors. Words like *floorboards*, *basement*, *numb*, *ruined*.

"I thought you were different," he said. "I thought we had something,"

"We do," she said, stepping closer. "We have truth."

He backed away until his legs hit the edge of the couch and he sat hard, breath shallow.

"Why now?" he whispered.

"Because you let me in," she said. "And now you'll feel it. All of it."

He shook his head violently. "I didn't know. I didn't—" His voice cracked. "I was just a kid."

"You were *old enough to know better*," she said, her eyes sharp as broken glass. "And now you'll know what it's like to beg for air inside a memory that won't stop replaying."

She crouched beside him, gently placing her hand on his chest.

He tried to move.

He couldn't. His eyes widened. Andie whispered, "This is mercy."

His body tensed beneath her hand, as if something had gripped him from the inside. His limbs were still, not paralyzed but heavy, dulled. His eyes darted wildly, pupils dilating with panic. He tried to speak, but only a rasp came out—half breath, half question.

Andie remained crouched beside him, calm, steady. Her fingers lightly pressed against his sternum. She wasn't restraining him. Not physically. This was deeper. She had entered the places of him that even he didn't visit. The shadows behind his memories. The rooms behind the locked doors in his mind.

"I'm not going to break your bones," she said softly. "I'm not going to slice your throat or blind your eyes."

He gasped. A tear slid down his cheek.

"I'm going to show you what you did."

William blinked once—hard—and suddenly the room around them shifted. Not physically, not to the eye. But the air *changed*. The light took on a reddish hue, and the walls pulsed faintly, like something breathing.

His breathing quickened. His mouth moved but formed no words.

Andie stood and stepped back, watching him carefully as the first illusion bled in.

The couch he sat on warped into a grimy mattress. The lighting dimmed until only a hanging bulb swung gently overhead. The air reeked of mold, cheap liquor, and sweat. The room was a re-creation—not perfect, but close enough to stir the bile in his throat.

"No," he whimpered. "No, this isn't real..."

He tried to stand, but his knees buckled beneath him. He landed hard on the ground, palms scraping the old, yellowing carpet—except they didn't. Not really. The room hadn't changed. But *he* was no longer in his own body. He was inside hers.

Inside her memory.

"Welcome back," she said. Her voice echoed from all corners of the room.

He spun around. The television played static. The music thumped from nowhere. A bottle rolled off the nightstand and shattered.

In the far corner, shadows took shape—four of them.

One laughed.

One adjusted his belt.

One zipped up his pants.

And one—his face—*his own face*—stood frozen in the doorway, smirking.

"No, no, no—" William fell back, arms shielding his head as the shadows stepped closer.

"You're not watching this time," her voice said. "You're *feeling* it."

One of the shadows reached out and touched his shoulder.

Andie stood at the edge of the illusion, untouched by the storm of memory.

“You’ll live inside this moment until you understand it,” she said, “and you’ll beg to forget.”

William screamed, but no one outside would hear him.

Because to the rest of the world, he was simply a man sitting silently in his apartment, eyes wide, body still, while inside his own mind...

The walls were bleeding.

It started to loop.

The laughter. The hands. The heat of breath and the sting of shame. The mattress springs. The sting of a bruise blooming across skin. The way the ceiling tiles became a grid of escape routes none of them opened. The sound of her voice breaking—cracking, pleading, dissolving.

William felt it *all.*

He gasped, chest heaving in the real world, though his limbs remained unresponsive. Sweat rolled down his forehead. His pupils danced erratically, trying to blink away a vision that wouldn’t end.

He was on the floor now—both in memory and reality.

The apartment around him flickered, like a glitching projection. The couch, the coffee table, the framed photo of his mother on the shelf—all pulsed like dying stars, overlaid by the rot and rot and rot of that room. Her room. The room they made unholy.

The loop restarted.

The joke.

The breath.

The *smile*.

"No—" he croaked, voice breaking like glass. "Stop—*stop it!*"

But Andie was already kneeling beside him again, her face close to his, her presence still as death.

"You always had a choice," she said. "You could've left the room. You could've pulled them off me. But you laughed, Billy."

"I didn't know—" he sobbed.

"You *knew enough* to grin."

Her fingers brushed his temple, gentle and ice cold. The memory surged again, deeper this time. Now he could feel it in his skin—not just as an observer, but as the victim. As her. The weight of hands. The burn of restraint. The way the world narrowed into a tunnel of heat, pain, and silence.

"I can't breathe," he choked.

"I couldn't either," she said. "But no one stopped to ask me."

William tried to move his arms. They didn't respond. He tried to cry harder, but his throat was raw. All that came out was a shallow wheeze.

The shadows whispered in his ear. They called him a hero. A man. A king. Then laughed again. The same laugh he used to carry in the back of his throat like a badge of approval.

"I'm sorry," he whispered. "I didn't know—I was just—"

"You were *old enough to know what 'no' sounds like,*" she said.

The apartment groaned.

The walls bent inward like a collapsing lung.

Andie stood again, towering over him now, calm, composed. Her eyes shimmered with something unnatural. Not anger. Not even vengeance.

Purpose.

“You’re not dead yet,” she said.

He whimpered.

“But you will be,” she added. “Not by fire. Not by blade. By the weight of your own memory.”

Then she turned her back to him.

And William—once Billy—screamed into a darkness that only he could see. Time unraveled.

To William, the loop had no beginning anymore. No end. The memory no longer felt like something being shown to him—it *was* him. He existed in it now. It coated the inside of his lungs, made his skin ache. The cold tiles beneath his back. The stale breath of boys who called themselves men. The weight of shame too large to hold, and yet Andie had carried it for years.

Now it was his turn.

He writhed on the floor, his muscles stiffening, his joints locking and unlocking in uneven rhythm. His jaw opened wide in a silent scream. His throat had given out long ago.

And still, he remained *alive*.

Andie stood by the window, arms crossed, eyes distant. She didn’t need to watch him anymore. The trap had been sprung. Her words had settled in his bloodstream. Her memory had taken root in his spine.

She closed her eyes.

Inside, she felt quiet.

Not peace.

Not satisfaction.

Just stillness.

His pain was not a balm. His terror was not a feast. It was simply a requirement—an accounting.

Behind her, William gasped and sputtered. He wept now in strange, broken patterns. He clawed at his skin like something inside it had turned against him. Tears, snot, sweat—his body collapsed into primal disarray.

"Make it stop," he groaned. "Please... *please*... I can't—"

She opened her eyes slowly.

"I know."

He tried to crawl toward her, dragging his limbs in grotesque rhythm, like a puppet missing its strings.

"I'll say it," he moaned. "I'll admit it—I remember—I *did it!* Just—please..."

His voice cracked again. He coughed hard, a wet, rattling noise. A thin trickle of blood spilled from his nose. His body shuddered.

Andie turned.

She didn't smile.

She didn't cry.

She simply watched as his body continued to fail—bit by bit.

The illusion still wrapped around him, even now. The ceiling flickered between his apartment and that room. The shadows danced on the edges of his vision. He tried to focus on her, but all he could see was the girl. The girl he'd laughed at. The girl they left behind.

But she wasn't a girl anymore.

She was something else now.

He collapsed again fully, body twitching once, then stilling for a moment.

Then a sharp inhale.

Then a tremor.

"I'm sorry," he whispered again. "I didn't mean to—I didn't know—"

But the words didn't sound like absolution.

They sounded like survival.

Andie stepped closer, crouched down beside him.

Her hand reached out and touched his face—gently, like a mother calming a fevered child.

"I know," she whispered.

Then she leaned in close, her lips brushing his ear.

"That's why it hurts."

He didn't know who he was anymore.

The room—the real room, his apartment—flickered in and out of his vision like a dying signal. One moment he saw the peeling posters on his wall, the guitar in the corner, the dirty bowl in the sink. Then it would twist, distort, and bleed into that other place. The place he'd buried deep. The room with the mattress. The ceiling tiles. The girls whose names he'd never cared to learn.

Now, one of them had a name.

And she stood over him, motionless, emotionless, while he came apart.

His hands shook. He kept looking at them like they belonged to someone else. The same hands that had zipped a fly, clutched a red solo cup, high-fived a friend in drunken celebration.

He saw it now—like a memory forced into slow motion.

The girl crawling to the wall. Her silence mistaken for weakness. Her blood. Her terror.

And his *smile*.

"No," he whispered. "I'm not that person."

Andie crouched in front of him again, her face level with his.

"Then who are you?"

He looked up at her, wild-eyed, desperate for an answer.

"I'm—" His breath hitched. "I'm trying to be better."

"Too late," she said simply.

"I was just a kid."

"So was I."

He broke. Fully. His hands covered his face, fingers pressing into his skin as if he could squeeze the memory out. "I didn't *know*. I was drunk. We were all—"

“You weren’t too drunk to smile,” she said. “You weren’t too drunk to stay afterward. You were sober enough to laugh. Sober enough to remember.”

He pulled at his hair, the pain now completely internal. His sense of self cracked in half, then quarters, then splinters.

“I didn’t *mean* to ruin you,” he cried.

“You didn’t ruin me,” she said, rising slowly. “You just changed the shape of what I became.”

He looked up at her.

“Please,” he whimpered. “What do you want from me?”

Andie stared at him, silent for a long moment. Then she whispered, “I wanted you to *see*. That’s all.”

He blinked.

She nodded slowly. “You’ve seen now.”

William—*Billy*—sank further into the carpet. His legs gave out beneath him. His head hung low. His body trembled with every breath.

“I’m scared,” he said, barely audible.

“I know.”

“Is it over?”

She didn’t answer right away.

Then, finally, she leaned close and said:

“Almost.”

His shoulders sagged. A flicker of relief passed through him—but it was the kind that came right before a blade. He didn't understand it, not yet.

Andie turned away, crossing the room once more.

Behind her, he sobbed.

Not just for what he'd done.

But because he finally understood who she was—and what that meant for him.

She stood in the kitchen again, facing the darkened window above the sink.

The apartment was silent now, save for William's whimpering behind her. The once-crisp lines of the room had blurred, the corners smudged by fear and memory. The air no longer felt breathable. It clung to the skin like damp cotton, thick and suffocating.

She looked out at the street, but the glass offered no view—only a reflection.

Her reflection.

But not the girl she once was. Not even the girl who walked through rain and trauma and silence to get here.

This reflection had *glowing eyes*.

Faint at first. Then pulsing. A steady, otherworldly glow that shimmered like deep embers under her skin. There was no warmth in them. No light born of salvation. It was the glow of something awakened.

Something elemental.

Something that had *waited*.

She stared at herself for a long time. Not in horror. Not in awe.

In acknowledgment.

This was her now. Not a victim reborn.

A reckoner.

A consequence.

Behind her, William coughed again, sharp and shallow. His body slumped half against the wall, legs tangled beneath him. He had stopped calling her name. Had stopped pleading. His voice was gone. But his eyes watched her, glassy and wide.

Andie turned slowly, the glowing from her reflection now radiating in the real world—faint, but present. Like fire behind fog.

She walked back into the living room.

Each step was quiet.

Final.

William tried to sit upright but lacked the strength. His body had begun to betray him. His motor control flickered—hands twitching, mouth slightly parted, breath coming in strained gasps.

He looked at her like a man watching a storm drift toward him. Not fast. Not chaotic. Just *certain*.

"You said it was almost over," he rasped.

She nodded.

"It is."

He tried to say more. Maybe another apology. Maybe a prayer. But his mouth barely moved. A tear slid down his cheek.

Andie knelt beside him again, brushing the hair from his face. The gesture could have been mistaken for compassion.

“You wanted love,” she whispered. “But you never learned how to ask for forgiveness.”

His eyes filled.

“You wanted to be saved,” she continued. “But you never looked back to see who you buried.”

She placed her hand against his chest again.

The heartbeat was still there—barely.

“One more night,” she said. “That’s all you get.”

His lips moved, but no sound came.

Andie leaned down and kissed his forehead.

As she stood again, the reflection in the window shimmered once more—eyes burning like coals, face no longer hers, or anyone’s.

The light in the room dimmed.

The clock on the wall stopped.

And William slipped fully into the darkness inside his own mind.

Andie didn’t leave.

Not yet.

She stood in the center of the room, arms folded, watching William’s body like a woman keeping vigil over something already gone. He lay twisted on the floor, not unconscious but trapped somewhere between reality and memory—a space carved out by her will, not time.

His eyes were still open, staring into nothing.

His chest rose and fell in short, stuttering patterns.

The room had grown cold. Not the kind of cold that seeped in through windows, but the kind that whispered through walls—subtle and unnatural. The breath that left his lips formed faint clouds that vanished too fast. The lights no longer flickered. They had simply dimmed and remained that way, as though mourning.

Andie walked slowly to the bookshelf and ran her fingers over the spines of his books—titles about the modern man, art films, psychology, masculinity. She pulled one out absently and flipped it open. Inside the margin of the first page was a note in his handwriting:

"Don't let the past define who you become."

She read it once.

Then closed the book and set it on the floor.

Behind her, William's head twitched. A soft moan escaped his throat. Not a plea. Just a fragment of someone unraveling.

"I gave you a chance," she said aloud. "You could've come clean. You could've remembered on your own. But you didn't."

Her voice didn't carry rage—it carried *weight*.

"You moved on. Changed your name. Changed your tone. You taught yourself how to be good, but you never *became* it."

She turned toward him again, watching the way his hand twitched against the carpet.

"You wanted me to love you. You wanted me to save you from what you were."

She stepped closer, kneeling beside him once more.

“And for a second,” she whispered, “I wanted that too.”

His lips parted. His eyes blinked, unfocused.

“But all I found inside you,” she said, “was the same silence you left me in.”

A single tear trailed down his cheek.

Andie reached out and caught it on her fingertip, holding it up as if studying a rare specimen.

“So fragile,” she said. “And yet, this is what broke me once.”

She stood again, walking to the far end of the room. Her glowing reflection in the glass returned—less human now, her form blurred by the flickering of something *other*. Her eyes glowed steadily. Not fire. Not fury.

Finality.

Behind her, William stirred once more, his breath catching. His legs twitched violently. His hand scraped at the air, as if reaching for something—*someone*.

But there was no one left to reach.

Andie looked toward the door.

Not yet.

She would stay until the last thread of what he was came loose.

Then—when all that remained was the echo of the boy who laughed—*then* she would end it.

She hadn’t always planned to find him.

In the early months—after the screams had gone quiet, after the blood dried, after the hospital lights and courtroom silences had chewed her into pieces—there had been no vengeance in her heart. Only survival. Only breath and hunger and waking up one more day.

But vengeance is patient.

It waits in the hollow spaces, grows like mold in unclean corners.

The first time she saw his face again, it wasn't in person. It was in a friend's phone photo, passed casually between people who had no idea what they were showing her. A college party. A dim room. Billy—now *William*—holding a red cup and grinning, arm slung around a girl who looked like Andie used to look.

The sickness hit her first.

Then the silence.

Then the decision.

She'd followed him online at first. Watched his transformation in curated squares. "Reformed." "Empathetic." "Deep." He quoted Rilke. He took black-and-white photos of trees. He started a podcast about "accountability and culture."

But never once—not in a post, a caption, a joke—did he *mention her.*

Or what he did.

And so she began walking in the same circles. Submitting college applications with a different name. Moving through the same town, the same campus, wearing a face sculpted from pain and purpose. And when they finally met—at the bookstore, by the coffee shop, under the trees—he didn't see her.

Not the real her.

Only the mystery he could pursue.

And now?

Now, he was barely a person at all. Just a tremor on the floor, breath thin, body twitching under invisible pressure. Her spell—her will—kept him alive in that in-between space.

Just long enough.

She crouched beside him again, resting one hand lightly on his shoulder. His skin was cold now, slick with sweat. His eyes opened briefly. Bloodshot. Lost.

"I saw you before you saw me," she whispered. "And I waited. I waited to see if you'd change. If you'd remember. If you'd feel *anything*."

She tilted her head, studying his face the way a sculptor studies cracked marble.

"But you never did. You just smiled."

He twitched violently again—shoulders locking, fingers curling into claws. His breath came in short gasps, like he was drowning in air. The memory loop still played behind his eyes, the phantom echoes of that night infecting every cell.

Andie leaned in close.

Her lips brushed his temple.

"Now you'll never forget."

She stood again and walked to the hallway mirror just outside the bathroom.

She looked.

And there it was.

Not a girl.

Not a victim.

A creature cloaked in flesh, lit from within by something ancient and merciless. The eyes glowed back—constant. Unblinking.

Andie stared into them. And did not look away.

She stared into the mirror for a long time.

The girl who once cried herself to sleep was gone. Not buried. Not hidden. *Gone.* Andie could remember her—the softness of her voice, the flicker of hope that someone might come to help, the way she'd clung to the lie that love was redemptive.

That girl had died the night Billy laughed.

And what had risen from the ashes wasn't a resurrection.

It was an answer.

Andie leaned in closer to the mirror, letting the dim light above the bathroom buzz faintly over her shoulders. Her breath didn't fog the glass. Her pupils did not adjust. The glow behind her eyes remained steady, unnatural.

"You were right to die," she whispered.

She didn't say it with hatred.

She said it with finality.

"You couldn't survive what came next. You weren't built for it. I was."

The silence in the hallway was complete. Behind her, William hadn't moved. The only sound was the soft hum of something—*not electricity,* something *older*—circulating in the walls, like a heartbeat running through the bones of the house.

Andie touched the mirror, her fingertip cold against the surface.

"I'm not here to mourn you," she said. "I'm here to finish what you couldn't."

She stepped back. For a moment, her reflection lagged—just a split second, but enough to show that whatever was watching her through the glass... wasn't only her.

She didn't flinch.

She turned from the mirror and walked down the hallway, pausing at the doorway to William's room.

He lay where she left him, arms slack now, one hand curled like a child's. His eyes stared upward, locked in a vision only he could see.

She knew what he was witnessing now.

Not the event itself.

But the fallout.

The hospital lights. The whispered doubts. The lawyer who said there wasn't enough evidence. The mother who couldn't look her in the eye. The way people stopped saying her name—started saying things like "that girl" or "the case."

That was the part no one saw.

Not just the act.

The *after.*

She stood over him and whispered, "You're almost done."

A spasm ran through his leg. His lips moved again—mumbling sounds that resembled prayers, regrets, fragments of confession. They didn't matter anymore. They were seeds cast into dead soil.

Andie knelt beside him, gently placing two fingers on his forehead.

"There's nothing left for you here," she said softly. "This world won't miss you. But *I* will remember. And so will she."

She closed his eyes with her thumb, though he wasn't dead yet.

Not yet.

That would come soon.

She rose again, casting one last glance over her shoulder at the man who'd once been a laughing boy in a basement.

His name was Billy.

And he was already gone.

She stepped into the living room once more, and the air shifted.

It wasn't just the cold now. It was *weight.* A slow, atmospheric pressure pressing in from all sides, as though something vast and invisible had entered the space with her—something ancient, with breath that moved between dimensions.

Andie exhaled quietly and reached for the glass of water left on the counter. It hadn't been hers, but it didn't matter. The water rippled slightly in the cup as she touched it, though her fingers made no motion.

The ripple came from *within.*

She looked down at her hands.

They were hers—but they weren't. The lines in her palms seemed deeper, like old riverbeds carved by time. Her skin was pale, too pale, not bloodless but... *drained.* As if her body had learned to survive on something else.

The thing inside her—whatever it was that found her that night, or maybe had been *waiting* for her all along—was no longer silent.

It stirred.

It approved.

Andie felt it moving not through her veins, but through her memory. Through her purpose. Through her *truth*.

She wasn't becoming something new.

She was finally becoming *honest*.

Behind her, William made a soft choking noise. It didn't disturb her.

She looked toward the ceiling, past it even, into some hidden layer of night just outside the fabric of reality.

"Not yet," she whispered, to herself... or to it.

Her eyes fluttered closed.

And in that moment, she remembered the river. The dark waters after Liz and Billy had died. The whispers in the shadows. The reflection that spoke back. The *offer*.

It hadn't been a pact.

It had been *permission*.

And now, standing on the other side of a boy's dying breath, she knew: this was the shape of retribution. Not loud. Not violent. *Inevitable*.

She turned toward the window again.

Her reflection was gone.

In its place, shadows swirled—vague impressions of form, hollow eyes, smiles that weren't smiles at all. The darkness didn't threaten her. It recognized her.

It welcomed her.

Andie stepped forward and reached out, her hand brushing the cool glass. The swirls coalesced, just for a second, into the image of her younger self—bloody, broken, eyes wide with horror. Then the image melted away.

She didn't flinch.

She simply whispered, "Thank you for dying."

And turned back to the man on the floor.

William's breath had grown slower now.

Shallow.

He was slipping.

She walked to him and crouched beside his form for the last time that night.

"You'll die in your sleep," she said softly. "But you'll die remembering."

His fingers twitched once, weakly. His lips parted.

And then... nothing. But it wasn't the end. *Not yet.*

The final breath left his body with no sound.

No gasp, no twitch, no scream.

Just the hush of surrender. The quiet exhale of something ceasing to be. William—*Billy*—was no longer a name, no longer a face, no longer a vessel of denial and reinvention. He was gone.

Andie watched the stillness settle like dust on a long-abandoned room. His chest no longer rose. His eyes, which had been shut by her hand earlier, remained closed—thankfully. She didn't want to see them glaze over. She didn't want to grant him that humanity.

Not now.

She reached out and placed two fingers on his neck.

No pulse.

She waited five full seconds.

Still nothing.

Final.

She stood slowly, not triumphant, not burdened—just *there*, in the stillness. The walls didn't shift. The lights didn't surge. There were no heavenly choruses or hellish roars. The world continued as it had before, uncaring of his exit.

And yet, something *had* changed.

Inside her, a seam that had been sewn shut through rage and resolve was finally coming undone. Not unraveling—but evolving.

She moved to the window again, now able to see the street beyond. A couple walked under a streetlamp, laughing gently, arms around each other. Somewhere, far off, a dog barked. The world was still breathing.

She was still *in* it.

But she didn't feel *of* it.

Her gaze returned to William's body.

"Why did you exist?" she whispered aloud.

The question hung in the air, more to herself than to him.

"To hurt me?" she asked, stepping closer again. "To mark me? Was that all?"

She crouched next to his body, studying the stillness with an almost academic detachment. "Or were you the beginning of something? A catalyst?"

She searched his face, searching for some final answer that wouldn't come.

"Did fate put you in my path again so I'd finish this... or begin something else?"

The glow in her eyes dimmed, not from loss of power, but from deep thought. The hatred she once wielded had served its purpose. Now it began to reshape itself—into philosophy. Into purpose. Into legacy.

She rose once more.

A strange stillness followed her up from the floor. The room felt less haunted now. The cold was lifting. The pressure gone. As if the entity within her had been satisfied.

But she hadn't.

Not entirely.

Because she still didn't know *why.*

Why she had survived. Why she had changed. Why the universe had chosen *her* to carry the weight—and the wrath.

William was dead.

And yet the story hadn't ended.

Andie looked down at him one final time.

"I don't forgive you," she said. "But I understand you."

Then she turned and walked into the night.

The hallway seemed longer than before.

Andie walked it slowly, her footsteps silent, her silhouette gliding beneath the cold ceiling lights like a shadow unmoored from time. She passed the photos on William's walls—childhood smiles, adolescent triumphs, manufactured joy. All of them meaningless now. Every captured moment a lie told in still frames.

She paused only once, standing before a picture of William and two other boys.

Mark.

Sean.

The others.

Her eyes narrowed slightly.

Still breathing, she thought.

She reached out, touched the glass frame with one finger, and felt it hum under her skin. Not from emotion. From the strange, unnamed current that had lived inside her since Charon's invitation.

The photograph cracked.

A thin, perfect split down the center.

She didn't smile.

She just moved on.

Outside, the city had begun its quiet descent into dawn. The world slept in layers—college students curled in beds they didn't own, joggers rising early to outrun the weight of their own thoughts, parents preparing school lunches. None of them knew what had just happened. What had *ended.*

Or what had been *set in motion.*

Andie walked slowly down the steps and into the street, no longer bothering to obscure her face. The person she'd pretended to be for William's sake had no purpose now. Her eyes, though no longer glowing, held something deeper—an intensity that didn't belong to a girl at all.

Something watched from inside her.

Something that had *waited.*

She wasn't afraid of it anymore.

As she passed beneath a streetlamp, the bulb above her flickered once... then stayed dead.

The others remained lit.

A car drove past and slowed briefly, the driver staring at her through the window. She didn't turn her head, but the man behind the wheel felt something chill crawl over him—a memory he'd never had. He looked away.

Andie walked on.

The wind picked up.

She welcomed it.

Her legs carried her through familiar streets she barely recognized anymore. This had once been a city of choices. Of dreams. Of escape. But now she saw it for what it truly was—*a feeding ground.* Not for her. For pain. For power. For silence.

She stepped over a dead crow at the edge of the sidewalk.

Its wings were outstretched. Its body untouched by blood. Eyes wide open.

She didn't pause.

By the time she turned the corner, the streetlight above it shorted out.

She exhaled through her nose, steady, as if she'd finally removed a weight from her chest. But it wasn't relief. It was *clarity.*

William was dead.

But what he represented still lived—in others.

And those others were not beyond her reach.

She didn't know where the next name would come from.

But she would find it. She always did. By midday, the sky had soured to a colorless gray, the kind that pressed against the earth like a lid. The world beneath it moved in stuttered rhythm—cars inching through traffic, people sipping lukewarm coffee, unaware that something had shifted beneath their feet.

Andie had vanished.

Not into smoke, not into shadow—just into *motion.*

She moved with the practiced invisibility of someone who had learned the seams of the city by instinct. Buses, alleyways, convenience store restrooms—each a passage, each a place to shed another layer of her old identity.

She didn't change her appearance drastically. She didn't need to. The Andie she had shown William had been a mask layered over her truth. But the mask had melted. And now what walked through the streets wasn't pretending to be human anymore.

She was simply passing among them.

As she walked past a newsstand, she heard murmurs—idle, distracted chatter from two college students flipping through their phones.

"You hear about that guy on Halloway Lane?" one asked.

“Which one?”

“Some freak seizure or something. Cops won’t release the name, but they found him half-naked in his living room. No sign of drugs. Just... *gone*. Like his brain broke.”

Andie didn’t pause, didn’t slow.

But she felt it.

The ripple.

Whispers were spreading.

Not fast. Not loud.

But they were growing.

She made her way through an underpass, the metal of the support beams above groaning faintly in the wind. There, she ducked into a forgotten stairwell behind a shuttered laundry mart. She’d found it weeks ago. It had no surveillance, no scent of habitation. Just darkness and cold tile.

Home, for now.

Inside, she sat cross-legged on the floor and pulled out a small notepad from her jacket. It wasn’t a kill list. Not exactly. It was a *ledger*. Names she’d heard. Faces she’d remembered. Things Billy had laughed about while drunk with friends. Mark. Sean. A few others. Still shadows. Still *living*.

She drew a line through one name.

William B.

One name gone.

The silence afterward wasn’t satisfying. It was simply *quiet*.

She clicked her pen shut and slipped it back into her coat. Then she sat still, letting the dark wrap around her. Not hiding. *Becoming*.

Outside, the police were already trying to explain the death away.

Inside, Andie had no interest in their conclusions.

She hadn't come to create mystery.

She had come to restore memory.

And if the world didn't recognize what it had done to her, then it would remember her in pieces—one shattered life at a time.

They found William's body two days later.

His landlord, an elderly woman named Mavis, had called the police after a strong odor began wafting into the hallway and flies gathered at the apartment's peephole. She hadn't heard from him. No music. No podcasts. No deliveries or packages left on his door.

When officers forced entry, what greeted them was not gore, nor chaos, but an overwhelming *wrongness*.

William lay in the center of his living room, on his back, eyes shut, limbs oddly positioned as though in mid-recoil. His mouth was slightly parted. There were no wounds, no bruises, no blood. Not a scratch on his skin. But something was *off*.

His expression, they would say later, didn't look peaceful. It didn't even look pained.

It looked *haunted*.

The apartment was cold—unnaturally so. The thermostat was broken, despite being brand new. The lights in the living room didn't work. The digital clock on his wall had stopped at 3:11 a.m. and would not restart, even after being unplugged and tested elsewhere.

One officer said he felt nauseous the moment he crossed the threshold.

Another reported hearing something faint behind the walls—like whispers, or water running through dead pipes.

Detectives canvassed the apartment for signs of drug use, trauma, external force—*anything*—but found none. No signs of forced entry. No fingerprints but his own. Security footage showed William entering the building on the night in question... and no one else.

Toxicology found nothing. No poisons. No stimulants. No alcohol.

The coroner couldn't even confidently name the cause of death.

They marked it down, reluctantly, as a "neurological event of unknown origin." The medical examiner called it *neurogenic shock with atypical presentation.*

The detectives called it something else:

Unnatural.

And so, protocol kicked in.

When death comes without reason—when physical evidence fails but *everything* screams that something is wrong—it triggers the clause that allows the case to elevate.

The file made its way up the ladder.

Until it landed on the desk of Special Agent Damian Nash.

The official request from the local precinct was dry:

Unexplained death of young male, age 21.
Victim found under unusual environmental conditions.
No trauma. No drugs. No prior health concerns.
Prior sealed juvenile record indicates potential connection to a

historical sexual assault case.
Victim recently changed his name from William T. B. to William S. Ellison.
Behavioral pattern suggests potential false identity or motive to hide past.

Damian Nash read the summary once. Then again.

Then he folded the file closed and stared out the window of his Washington field office.

There was something about the details—the absence of answers wrapped in the language of science—that prickled his instincts. He had worked enough homicides to know when death was a *message*.

This one wasn't random.

It was *designed*.

Damian Nash didn't believe in monsters.

Not the kind hiding under beds or lurking in forests.

He believed in *patterns*.

He believed in silence that didn't make sense.

And this case reeked of it.

He sat alone in the archive room beneath the FBI's regional headquarters, the hum of fluorescent lights above him buzzing in the quiet like nervous energy. The physical file lay open in front of him—a thick manila folder labeled only with initials and a redacted case number. The juvenile court had sealed it tight, but he had clearance, and more importantly, *instinct*.

The documents inside were sparse, almost insultingly so.

Andrea Montgomery.

Assaulted at sixteen.

Hospital intake showed extensive trauma—physical, emotional, psychological. Multiple contusions. Signs of struggle. Sexual trauma confirmed.

Police statements were vague.

Three boys named in her initial statement.

Then nothing.

No charges filed.

No trial.

Andie's name disappeared from the system two months later when her family abruptly relocated out of county. The school district logged her as a transfer—no follow-up.

And the boys?

Each one "admonished" in private hearings. Records sealed. Identities protected.

No restitution.

No consequences.

No justice.

Until now.

Damian leaned back in his chair and tapped the side of the folder, his mind connecting dots between that file and the lifeless body found in that cold apartment two days prior.

William Ellison.

Born William T. B.

Initials matched.

Birthdate matched.

One of the boys from the sealed case.

Now dead.

Damian didn't believe in monsters—but he had seen what trauma could forge in the crucible of abandonment. And there was something *uncanny* about the lack of evidence in William's death. Like the universe had closed in on him with surgical silence.

Damian scribbled a name into his notebook.

"Montgomery, Andrea."

He circled it once.

Then again.

And sat still.

He didn't alert his superiors—not yet. Something about this didn't feel procedural. It felt *personal.*

He opened his laptop, bypassed internal protocols, and began tracing data across jurisdictions—school records, social media remnants, public licenses.

Andrea Montgomery had vanished two years ago.

No high school diploma.

No digital footprint beyond age 17.

No job history.

No bank account.

No *residence.*

As if she had been wiped clean from the map.

But someone—someone who *knew*—had visited William Ellison the night he died.

Damian felt the air in the archive room shift.

Not from ghosts.

From truth.

It was circling him now.

And whatever killed William wasn't finished.

Damian stood in the precinct's evidence room, arms folded across his chest, eyes narrowed at the single grainy photo he'd been able to extract from an old social media post. Four boys at a party. One red cup held aloft. One camera flash too bright. The caption was stupid and cocky: *"Kings of the night."*

But it wasn't the pose that unsettled him.

It was the girl, barely visible in the background.

Andrea Montgomery.

Half-turned. Distant. Out of focus. But unmistakably *there.*

Damian tapped his pen against the photo.

William. Mark. Sean. Jacob.

Four names. Four smiles.

He didn't need a signed confession. His instincts were already whispering: *something was buried.*

He stepped out of the evidence room and returned to his desk, pulling up the archived report on Andrea again. She'd only spoken to police once. Her interview had been redacted, but fragments remained in summary form.

Pain. Shame. Fear. And silence.

The kind of silence that didn't just stem from trauma.

The kind that was *imposed.*

He picked up the phone and dialed a contact in juvenile records.

"I need everything you can get me on Andrea Montgomery," he said. "All sealed files. Witnesses. School reports. I don't care how deep you have to dig."

The voice on the other end hesitated. "Nash, are we talking about a live investigation?"

"Not yet," he replied. "But it's about to be."

He hung up without another word.

Miles away, Andie stood barefoot on the cold concrete of a rooftop, her arms folded tightly across her chest. The wind played through her hair, but she didn't feel it. Her body barely registered the cold now. The entity inside her had grown quiet—not absent, but *watchful.*

She opened her eyes slowly.

The city stretched below her like a puzzle waiting to be solved.

Then she whispered a name.

"Sean."

The sound didn't echo. It sank—like a stone through deep water.

She held out her hand, palm up, and let her breath slow.

From somewhere in the city's veins—through power lines, sewer pipes, gutters, and dust—the faintest ripple began to move. The air darkened slightly around her, not with cloud or storm, but with *intent.*

She didn't need a GPS.

She didn't need to ask questions.

She simply *felt.*

Felt the direction her vengeance wanted to flow next.

Felt the pulse of a man living under the false belief that the past couldn't catch him.

Felt the cold grin of something ancient waiting inside her, nodding in quiet approval.

Andie opened her eyes fully.

They glowed.

Found him, she thought.

Then she stepped off the rooftop and disappeared into the shadows, the next chapter of vengeance already unfurling beneath her feet.

Chapter 7

Damian Nash was a man who believed that some answers lived between the lines—not in what was said, but in what people *didn't* say. That quiet space between a shrug and a smirk, between a nervous laugh and a pause too long. That was where truth lived, raw and waiting.

He stirred his coffee absently as he leaned on the railing of his second-floor apartment in D.C.'s Petworth district. His view wasn't glamorous—a cracked sidewalk, two parked squad cars, a bakery that opened late and closed early—but he liked it. It was *honest.*

He took a slow sip, watching the sunrise drag orange across the rooftops. In his hand was a manila folder, worn at the edges, held together by a metal clasp. He hadn't opened it yet this morning. He didn't need to—not before letting the quiet talk to him.

Inside were photos.

Notes.

Names.

Three of them now.

William.

Mark.

Sean.

He rubbed his thumb along the edge of the folder, then looked down at the ceramic mug in his other hand. The inscription was almost faded completely: *"Morehouse College – Class of 2008."*

His mother had given it to him.

Flashback.

Damian, age twenty-one, sat in the small library of his childhood home in Richmond, surrounded by open textbooks and yellow highlighters. His mother, Janice Nash, a public-school teacher with an iron spine and gospel soul, leaned on the doorframe.

"Boy, you read like you're gonna argue with the devil," she'd said, smiling.

"Maybe I will," he replied without looking up.

He did later. Only the devil didn't wear horns. He wore neckties and signed warrants.

Back in the present, Damian set the mug down on the patio railing and finally opened the folder.

His handwriting was clean, all-caps, deliberate:

Andrea Montgomery – PRIMARY VICTIM
William T. B. (Deceased)
Mark H. (Alias: M. Carter, located)
Sean J. (Occupation: Building Maintenance – Still Local)
Jacob L. (Unknown – final point of contact redacted)

He traced a line from William to Sean, circling Sean's name.

Then he stared.

The lines weren't just names. They were echoes. What had been done to Andie wasn't a single act—it was a *system of permission,* of boys laughing and walking away while she crumbled.

Now someone was reversing that system.

With violence.

He didn't know if he wanted to stop it yet. That disturbed him.

Inside his apartment, Damian rolled up his sleeves and spread the files across a plain oak desk, the same desk he'd used since his Quantico days. He never replaced it. Scratches on the surface reminded him that some scars were worth keeping.

The apartment itself was bare—function over form. No family photos. No decorations. Just the essentials: coffee, case files, and quiet. That's how he lived. Not because he couldn't afford more, but because *he couldn't trust permanence.*

People came and went. Only *patterns* stayed.

He clicked on a voice recorder and spoke into it.

"Subject: Andrea Montgomery. High school student. Raped at sixteen. Four suspects named. No convictions. Victim disappears. Years later, suspect one—William—dies mysteriously. No physical trauma. Subject two—Sean—is still local. Subject three—Mark—relocated. Subject four—Jacob—unaccounted for. All four changed their lives after the event. Name changes, relocations, sealed records."

He paused.

Then added:

"Someone is hunting them. One down."

He clicked the recorder off and leaned back in his chair, allowing his gaze to settle on a grainy photograph of Andrea from years ago—taken from a high school yearbook. She looked small, uncertain, but there was a sharpness behind her eyes. The kind you see in survivors. The kind that either broke… or *transformed*.

He hadn't figured out which she'd become yet.

But something about the William Ellison death told him she hadn't just *survived.*

She'd *evolved.*

Flashback.

At Quantico, Nash was one of the few recruits who volunteered for the psychological forensics program. Not because it was easy—it wasn't—but because that's where the *weird* went. The ones who killed without logic. The ones who left no fingerprints, no trail. The ones the Bureau didn't like to talk about.

"Why are you here, Agent Nash?" his instructor had asked on the first day.

"Because I don't think monsters are myths," he answered.

The room had gone silent.

He'd been given *all* the strange ones ever since.

Damian returned to the present and opened his laptop. Sean's file was already loaded. Custodian at a downtown office building. Night shift. Two complaints for inappropriate comments made to female tenants—settled quietly. No charges filed.

That was the pattern again.

Always just short of punishment.

He closed the laptop and jotted a note.

Visit Sean's building.
Review camera logs.
Ask tenants about recent behavior.

Establish proximity risk.

But he already knew.

It was too late.

Whatever had found William... was likely circling Sean already.

And he couldn't shake the feeling that Andie—if that was still her name—wasn't simply *reacting*. She was *orchestrating*.

There had been a case years ago—Damian's first as lead.

The file was thin, the body count one, but the scar it left never healed. A teenage girl in Roanoke had jumped from her high school's gym roof after months of silent bullying. Her name was Camille Reece. No journal, no suicide note—just a long silence broken by a single fall.

He remembered standing in her room, staring at the dozens of sticky notes on the wall. Bible verses, chemical formulas, song lyrics. None of them in any particular order, but all written in the same neat, looping handwriting.

Camille had loved *systems*. That's what Damian learned first. And people had broken hers.

The investigation revealed that she had been harassed by three classmates—girls, not boys. Names that surfaced in rumor, in whispers, never in official complaints. Camille never reported it. Not once. She just folded inward like a dying star.

The system had failed her because it had *never seen her.*

And Damian had vowed never to let that happen again.

Back in the present, he thumbed through a small folder of personal notes he kept apart from the official case files—thoughts, questions, hunches. At the top of the page was one simple scribble:

What if she never wanted justice?
What if she wanted him to suffer the way she did?
What if the pain didn't kill her—but rebuilt her into something that delivers it back?

He had no evidence that Andrea Montgomery was behind William's death.

But he didn't need evidence to feel it.

Something inside her had survived what happened.

And it had *grown teeth.*

He stood up from his desk and retrieved a worn leather satchel—inside was his field kit: gloves, forensics swabs, a UV pen, a blacklight, backup charger, and his badge, tucked behind a clear ID panel.

Damian had always prepared for things others never thought of.

That's why the bureau called him for the *quiet* crimes. The ones with no forced entry. No bruises. No mess.

The ones where people just... *died*, without explanation.

He locked up his apartment, walked out onto the street, and glanced up as a crow passed overhead. A single feather dropped into his path. He stepped over it.

Some would call it superstition.

Damian called it pattern recognition.

And this case was starting to hum. Damian drove in silence.

No radio. No podcasts. Just the low hum of the tires and the city's subtle breath beyond the windshield.

Washington, D.C., at night always felt like it was holding something in. Something unspoken, maybe even ashamed. A city full of people keeping secrets, and buildings that heard everything.

As he turned off North Capitol and merged onto a quieter street lined with worn office towers, he thought about a phrase his old unit chief had once told him: *"Nash gets the deathwatch cases."*

The term wasn't official, of course.

It was slang for the files no one wanted. The deaths that didn't belong anywhere. No weapon. No prints. Sometimes, no body. Just... *absence.*

He had never complained.

It was in those voids that he felt most *useful.*

He pulled into a narrow parking garage beneath the 14-story administrative building where Sean James worked night maintenance. A scan of the personnel database showed Sean clocked in two hours earlier. He'd be making rounds now—probably alone.

Damian shut off the engine but didn't exit the car immediately.

Instead, he sat still.

Listening.

His mind replayed the cold-case details of William's death.

No signs of forced trauma. Eyes wide open. No cardiac history, yet the heart had simply... stopped.

If there was something else—if Andrea Montgomery had anything to do with it—then it meant she'd developed an *ability* far beyond anything rational.

Or...

Maybe it wasn't *her* doing it at all.

Maybe it was something *with her.*

The car's cabin light blinked off on its own.

He raised an eyebrow.

Electrical interference wasn't unusual in old parking structures, but the timing was odd.

Too clean.

He got out of the vehicle, grabbed his satchel, and approached the elevator.

The keypad blinked, flickered... then returned to normal.

Damian narrowed his eyes, hit the button for the lobby, and stepped inside.

As the doors closed, he whispered to himself:

"She's already been here."

Back in the stairwell above, in the same building, a shadow passed along the wall—no footsteps, no sound. Just a flicker where Andie had stood moments earlier, surveying the upper floor.

Sean was close.

She could hear him humming, badly off-key.

The elevator behind her rumbled.

The gears strained.

The building exhaled tension like a living thing ready to snap.

Sean James had no idea he was being hunted.

He was pushing a janitor's cart down the sixth-floor hallway, earbuds in, nodding to a beat that didn't match the music. The overhead fluorescents buzzed in staggered pulses, blinking off and on like Morse code trying to send a warning he couldn't understand.

He stopped to check a locked office, jingling the keyring clumsily, muttering something about how no one ever said thanks anymore. His breath fogged slightly, though the building's heat was on. He didn't notice.

Behind him, the corridor stretched like a tunnel.

Empty.

Too empty.

He glanced once over his shoulder.

Nothing there.

But Andie had already passed.

Two floors below, Damian stepped off the elevator into the building's security suite. A tired-looking guard in his mid-fifties glanced up from a half-eaten sandwich.

"FBI?" he said, startled.

Damian flashed his badge. "Agent Nash. Following up on an active case. I need access to live security feeds. Sixth and seventh floors."

The guard shrugged. "No problem. We got some cameras—couple blind spots. Motion sensor's been acting up lately, though."

Damian stepped behind the desk and eyed the monitor array.

Something about the elevator schematics caught his attention—four lifts in total, one of them logged for maintenance.

“Which elevator is that?” he asked, pointing.

“Back one,” the guard said. “Only goes from the lobby to top floors. Acting funny lately. Door sensors are slow.”

Damian didn’t answer. His gaze lingered on the flickering floor tracker.

The elevator was rising.

Fast.

On the sixth floor, Sean wiped a smudge off a glass panel and dropped the rag. As he bent to retrieve it, the light above him went out. Not flickered. *Went out.*

He stood slowly, squinting into the dim hallway.

“Damn breakers,” he muttered, shaking his head.

Then he turned—and stopped.

There was a figure down the hall.

Still.

Silent.

Just standing there, in the half-light, framed between two flickering panels like an unholy portrait.

“Hello?” he called, his voice catching.

The figure didn’t move.

He took a step forward.

The panel lights died behind him.

Then ahead of him.

Darkness came rushing forward like a wave.

Downstairs, Damian stared at the screens. “We’re losing feed,” he said sharply.

The guard frowned. “That doesn’t usually—wait...”

From one of the monitors, static cracked and cleared—just long enough for a single frame:

Sean turning. Eyes wide.

A blur behind him.

A shape, feminine, draped in shadow.

Then the feed went dead.

Damian’s jaw tightened.

He reached for his satchel, already sprinting for the stairs.

“She’s here,” he said.

Sean James staggered backward as the lights blinked above him, casting the hallway in a stuttering pulse of white and shadow. The building’s power surged violently, sending a low, teeth-rattling hum through the walls. He stumbled over a mop bucket and landed hard against the elevator doors, knocking the wind from his lungs. His keys clattered to the floor, but he didn’t reach for them. His wide eyes weren’t on the tools or the exit.

They were on *her.*

She stepped forward slowly—no footsteps, just the soft brush of presence, like something unearthly gliding just above the floor. Her face emerged from the strobing light and gloom, pale, composed, framed by that black hair pulled behind her ears.

Sean's mouth fell open.

He knew that face.

"You... no. No, it can't be."

Andie didn't speak.

Sean's voice cracked as he tried to laugh, though it came out strangled and sickly. "You—Jesus, you— Andie Montgomery? That you?" He tried to straighten up, puffing out his chest like the coward he'd always been. "Girl, we thought you were dead. Or locked up somewhere."

Her expression didn't change.

"I mean... you *liked* it," he said, voice rising defensively. "Don't act like you didn't. You wanted it. You were into it. I saw it in your face."

That's when she stepped forward—just once, one slow shift of her bare foot on the floor—and everything in the hallway went *still*.

The humming deepened.

The lights pulsed blood-red, then white again.

Sean's grin faltered.

He tried the elevator button behind him, slapping it repeatedly. "You're crazy," he spat, hands trembling. "I didn't do nothin' you didn't *ask* for! You didn't say no!"

He was shouting now, not because he believed it, but because some small voice inside him was beginning to scream.

"You ain't right in the head! You were always messed up!"

Andie blinked slowly.

When she finally spoke, her voice wasn't loud. It was calm. Icy. "I never said yes."

Sean flinched.

A low, deep groan echoed from above. The elevator cables creaked violently, as if under some unbearable pressure. Dust sifted from the ceiling tiles. The buttons beside the doors flickered erratically.

Sean spun around in panic. "What the hell's happening?!"

From far above, something heavy began to descend—metal scraping against metal, growing louder with every floor. The hallway shook with it.

Andie raised her gaze.

Sean did too.

A rush of cold air swept through the corridor like the last breath before a scream. Every fluorescent tube blew in sequence, darkening the hallway in a violent wave of sparks and shattered glass.

Sean screamed and bolted, feet slipping on wet tile.

Behind him, Andie followed without hurry.

The elevator was still coming down. And it wasn't stopping.

Sean rounded the corner at full sprint, breath hitching in his throat, the hallway blurring as tears formed in his eyes. He slipped once, crashing into a wall, but scrambled upright. Behind him, he could hear nothing—no running feet, no gasps—but he *felt* her. Like gravity had shifted to follow her steps.

The elevator shaft roared above him, the sound no longer mechanical. It was predatory—alive.

Sean flung himself at the double doors of the secondary elevator, smashing the call button in a frenzy. The panel blinked. *DING.*

His chest heaved as the light over the doors glowed a sickly yellow. The mechanical moan above sharpened into a shriek of metal on metal. Sparks rained from the ceiling grid. A pipe burst, drenching him in a freezing mist. The building itself seemed to be suffocating.

Then—

CLANG.

The elevator doors buckled inward slightly.

He tried to backpedal, but his soaked shoes slid on the floor.

"Fuckin' Bitch! How are you doin' this? No, no—please, please!" he sobbed.

Andie came into view from the corridor behind him, face still calm, untouched by the chaos. Her eyes glowed faintly—white-blue, like frozen stars.

She didn't speak.

She only watched.

Sean turned away from her and grabbed at the doors as they began to creak open. "Help me!" he screamed into the darkness beyond.

Then something inside the shaft *jerked downward* with incredible force.

The elevator wasn't stopping.

It wasn't *slowing.*

It was *hungry.*

Damian Nash reached the floor at that instant, flashlight sweeping the corridor.

Then he heard it—

The *wet crunch* of sudden impact.

The building seemed to groan with it, a shudder that rolled up through the walls like an aftershock.

He turned the corner and saw the doors to the elevator easing open, steam curling out.

Inside—

Blood.

Not splattered. Not spattered.

Soaked.

The metal walls were painted red from floor to ceiling, the scent metallic and thick. In the center lay what remained of Sean James—his lower torso twisted grotesquely, the body severed cleanly at the waist as though drawn and quartered in a machine made for something else entirely.

Broken mop handles lay in the corners like discarded bones.

The floor of the car was flooded.

And there was no sign of the girl.

No evidence.

No fingerprints.

Just a single handprint across the steel door, faintly glowing in blue light before fading as if it had never been there.

Damian crouched low, his gloved hand hovering just over the slick floor outside the elevator. The heat from the blood hadn't fully dissipated, which meant Sean had died within the last sixty seconds. Maybe less. A dozen sensory impressions hit him at once—burnt metal, copper, ozone, and something *faintly floral*, unnaturally out of place.

He stood and stepped away from the threshold, careful not to disturb any trace evidence.

A second figure approached from the stairwell—building security, his eyes wide, face pale.

"I... I think I saw her," the man said, breathless.

Damian turned sharply. "What?"

The guard swallowed hard and nodded. "On the camera feed. Right before it cut out. Looked like a girl... barefoot, real still. Just standing at the end of the hallway."

"Where'd she go?"

"I—I'm not sure. After the lights blew, I ran for the emergency phone. When I looked out the front lobby window, I think... I think I saw her walking away. Just calmly. Down the steps. Like she wasn't even in a hurry."

Damian stared at him. "Did you recognize her?"

"No. She had her hair up. Face was hard to see. But... she didn't look right. Not scared. Not panicked. Just *quiet.*"

He nodded slowly and looked back at the elevator.

Another corpse.

Another vanishing act.

Another *absence* that defied rational explanation.

He walked to the maintenance office and accessed the main system log. The building's elevator had recorded a rapid override—an unauthorized manual acceleration from Floor 12 straight down to 6, skipping all braking protocols. No human operator could've done that from outside the shaft.

Not unless they were wired into the machine itself.

Damian stepped back from the screen, his thoughts racing. The pattern was familiar now. Unseen entry. Psychological disruption. Anatomical precision. Emotional targeting.

This wasn't random.

And if his instincts were right—if this was tied to Andrea Montgomery—then the girl wasn't just acting out of vengeance.

She was *hunting*.

Outside, in the cool air of the city, Andie walked beneath flickering streetlamps, head low, eyes vacant. No blood touched her skin. No emotion colored her features. The wind rustled her clothes like they weren't part of her anymore.

As she passed a darkened storefront, she glanced once at the glass.

Her reflection paused.

The eyes in the mirror glowed faintly.

Then faded.

Flashing red and blue lights bounced off the glass lobby as two more patrol units arrived, parking at sharp angles across the street. Uniformed officers ducked under the yellow tape, shielding their eyes against the elevator's open gore.

“Jesus Christ,” one muttered. “Looks like he got fed through a damn woodchipper.”

Damian didn’t look up from the elevator schematic he’d pulled from the maintenance office’s control station. He could already feel the tension building behind him as the site transformed from a private horror into a public *event*.

A uniformed sergeant approached, nodding politely. “Agent Nash, right? Sergeant Ruiz, Third Precinct.”

Damian gave a nod. “You’re the responding officer?”

“First on scene, yeah. Dispatch said you were already en route.”

“William Haywood—two days ago,” Damian replied. “Same pattern. No witnesses. No trace. Now Sean James. I’m seeing a progression.”

Ruiz shifted uncomfortably. “Both were maintenance guys. No gang ties. No priors beyond some dumb kid stuff. But this?” He gestured toward the elevator. “We don’t have crimes like this, Agent. Not... *surgical executions.*”

Damian’s eyes flicked toward the blood-soaked interior. “That wasn’t surgery.”

He stepped aside as two techs wheeled in a portable scanner and a forensic kit. “This was punishment.”

Outside, the crowd had already started to form—bystanders, off-duty office workers, two TikTokers holding up phones like crucifixes to ward off boredom. Behind them came the first news van, parking fast and crooked, its satellite dish rising like a predator’s dorsal fin.

A reporter stepped out, already mid-call with her station.

"Confirming—male body found, possibly dismembered, federal agents on-site. I'm telling you, Rami, this has serial case written all over it. We've got to go live—"

Inside, the elevator shaft creaked again as the cleanup team secured the area. A tarp was unfolded. Cameras weren't far behind.

Ruiz eyed the press gathering beyond the doors. "You want us to hold them back?"

"For now," Damian said, not looking up. "But they're going to find out. When they do, this gets big. Fast."

Ruiz nodded grimly. "You think we've got a serial on our hands?"

Damian didn't answer immediately. He tapped a finger against the schematic.

"There's a name," he said softly. "Andrea Montgomery. Disappeared. Victim in a sealed-case sexual assault. Father died under... unnatural circumstances."

"You think she's the one doing this?"

"I think she's not the same girl who went missing."

Just then, an officer stepped in from the front doors. "Sir. One of the reporters is asking about 'the glowing handprint.' Did we confirm that?"

Damian's jaw tightened.

"No comment. Not yet."

But the story was already slipping out of their grasp. The lobby's glass doors rattled from the pressure of the press outside.

It was no longer just one van.

Now there were five, each with their masts stretching skyward, competing for signal dominance. Reporters with powder-caked faces and wind-shielded microphones jostled for position against the yellow tape, demanding statements with voices that bordered on frenzy.

“Agent Nash! Was this a ritual killing?”

“Any comment on the connection to William Haywood’s death?”

“Are you investigating a cult or a serial offender?”

“Is it true the FBI is suppressing evidence of supernatural involvement?”

Nash remained inside, arms folded, watching the chaotic ballet of lights and half-truths unfold. Every minute spent here tightened the net around whoever—or *whatever*—was responsible. And yet, as he listened to the babble, a cold understanding dawned:

The media wouldn’t help him solve this.

They would help hide it.

Behind fear. Behind sensationalism. Behind carefully edited headlines that fed on tragedy but never *understood* it.

“Keep them out of the building,” he told Ruiz. “No cameras, no statements. If they catch wind of her name, they’ll turn her into either a victim or a monster before I can do my job.”

“Understood,” Ruiz said. “You think she’s still local?”

Damian shook his head slowly. “Not for long. She’s got a plan.”

An hour later, in the field command van parked behind the building, Damian sat in front of a terminal.

The Bureau had begun quietly pulling sealed juvenile records from the town where Andrea Montgomery once lived. Her case file was thin—intentionally so—but the names *around* it weren't.

A social circle.

A football team.

A locker room.

Four boys.

Two dead.

The third...

Damian leaned forward as the search engine returned a hit.

Mark Joseph Langley. Age 22. Now residing in Sandoval County, New Mexico. No criminal record. No recent arrests. But a civil complaint had been filed against him six months ago—by a young woman. No charges pursued. File sealed.

"Coward's learned how to hide in plain sight," Damian muttered.

Attached to the record was a photo—Mark, now slightly bulkier, sun-scorched skin, standing with a girl who couldn't be older than nineteen. Her posture was stiff. Her smile didn't reach her eyes.

Nash stared at the image.

It wasn't just about revenge.

It was about *patterns*.

Mark had fled across the country, but his sickness had traveled with him.

And if the pattern held...

She was coming.

The sun beat down on Sandoval County like a punishment.

Dust curled up in little flares with each passing car, and the highway stretched out in cracked, endless lines—one long, dry artery winding through desert scrub and faded towns. A rusting sign welcomed travelers to a place that time didn't bother to visit.

Andie stood at the edge of a gas station parking lot, her hoodie zipped high, the sleeves too long for the heat. Her face was half-shadowed by the brim of a borrowed ball cap. She sipped from a lukewarm water bottle, her eyes fixed on a single tan pickup parked beside a shuttered diner.

Inside the truck: *Mark.*

He was laughing, the kind of easy, barking laugh that always sounded too loud for its surroundings. In the passenger seat sat a girl with fair skin, wearing a denim skirt and trembling hands. She smiled every time he spoke—but it was the smile of someone who didn't want to be corrected later.

Andie didn't blink.

She recognized that smile.

Recognized the way Mark leaned too close, tapped the dashboard too hard, controlled even in casual gestures.

It wasn't new. It wasn't unique.

It was *textbook.*

Andie watched as Mark stepped out of the truck, adjusting his belt. He smacked the side of the vehicle and muttered something to the girl—who nodded, quickly, before staring down at her lap.

He entered the diner alone.

Andie waited. One minute. Two. Then slowly crossed the road.

Meanwhile, in the FBI mobile field unit, Nash was already on the phone with New Mexico state law enforcement.

“I need your cooperation on a potential third victim,” he said, eyes on the screen still showing Mark’s file. “Name’s Mark Langley. He’s on record in a sealed case tied to a series of violent crimes now under federal review.”

“Federal review?” the voice on the other end asked. “That sounds above my pay grade, Agent.”

“It is,” Nash replied flatly. “That’s why I’m calling you.”

He sent over the photo package—Mark’s ID, a map of his last known address, and the recent complaint from the girl. It didn’t take long for the officer to recognize the name.

“We’ve had disturbances at that residence,” the officer admitted. “Nothing we could nail him for, but the neighbors talk. Yelling. Screaming. A girl afraid to open the door. Sounds like your guy.”

“I want eyes on him now,” Nash said. “And I want the girl safe.”

“We’ll dispatch a unit—”

“No lights. No sirens. He’s not a threat to us. But someone’s coming who *is*.”

Andie circled behind the diner, eyes narrowed against the sun.

She could smell it—something in the air. Not just heat. Not just decay.

Something *familiar.*

Fear.

The house was small, sun-bleached and warped from years of heat. A sagging porch, a dust-choked front yard, and aluminum blinds that never opened. From her position across the street, half-hidden behind a leaning mesquite tree, Andie studied every detail. She had already counted the footsteps. Mark came home around five. The girl—his wife—barely left. Groceries were delivered. The trash was never full. When they spoke, the windows were closed. When they fought, the walls still leaked sound.

Tonight was no different.

The pickup truck pulled in. Mark got out, slammed the door harder than needed. From the other side, the girl climbed down quietly, head low. She reached for the bags in the backseat, but Mark barked something and grabbed them himself. She flinched—not from the words, but from the *tone*.

Andie didn't move.

She only watched, the heat around her rising in little gusts of dry wind. Her eyes followed the woman's shoulders. Too stiff. Too submissive. She recognized the telltale signs of someone always preparing for pain.

Then came the voice in her mind—her own mother's voice.

"Just be quiet, baby. Just don't move. He'll calm down."

Memory surged like a blow to the chest.

Suddenly, she was ten again, crouched in the hallway of that old trailer, holding little Billy as he whimpered. The television was still on, casting a blue flicker down the hallway like a warning beacon. From the living room came the sound of Patrick's rage—bottles clinking, furniture scraped, their mother crying but trying not to let it sound like sobs.

She could still hear it.

"Don't talk back to me, woman! You're lucky I come home at all!"

Her mother had never looked smaller than in those moments—bruises hidden beneath long sleeves, teeth clenched as she pretended the bleeding lip wasn't there.

Andie remembered thinking: *One day, I'll make him afraid.*

Across the street, Mark slammed the front door.

Inside, the lights flickered for a moment. A shadow passed behind the blinds. Then silence.

Andie breathed in slowly, the air tasting faintly of rust.

Her hands weren't shaking. But her chest ached.

She didn't know if it was rage or grief. Or both.

Was that humanity? Or just residue?

She touched the pendant she wore beneath her shirt—the one piece of the past she'd kept. Not for Patrick. Not for herself.

For Billy.

He'd never cried to sleep again after that night.

Because he never got another one.

Behind the blinds, Mark yelled again. Something thumped. Something broke. Then nothing.

Andie's jaw clenched.

She hadn't come here to save anyone.

But *this*—this was too familiar to ignore. She hadn't meant to stay this long.

It was supposed to be simple—watch, confirm, strike.

But every time Mark raised his voice, every time that girl disappeared behind the curtains with bruised posture and trembling arms, something old twisted inside Andie's chest. Something too close to memory. Too close to *herself.*

A streetlamp above her head buzzed sharply, then flickered out.

The tree branch beside her trembled, shedding its dry leaves all at once, as if recoiling from her presence. The air rippled faintly. The world held its breath.

Andie inhaled slowly, trying to calm it down—*whatever it was*. The thing inside her that responded not only to hatred, but to grief. To injustice. To history.

To pain.

She stepped back into shadow, forcing her breathing to stillness.

In the house across the street, Mark's silhouette moved from room to room, pacing like a restless animal. He shouted again—muffled, but clear. A crash followed, and the porch light flared on.

Andie stiffened. The front door slammed open.

The girl stumbled out.

She wore shorts and a faded T-shirt. No shoes. Her hair was tangled. One arm clutched her ribs.

Mark followed behind her, his voice tight with venom.

"Go on! Run, then! Let the coyotes have you, see if I care!"

The girl paused at the end of the porch. She didn't cry. She didn't beg. She just stood there, shaking, looking at the sand like it might swallow her whole.

Mark spat into the dirt and stormed back inside, muttering, "Ungrateful bitch," before slamming the door.

Andie watched it all.

She felt her fingers curl into fists. The wind picked up again—sharper this time, swirling dust around her ankles.

Her reflection in the corner of a darkened store window caught her eye.

For a moment—just a flash—her face looked like her mother's. Hollowed by exhaustion. Barely held together.

The vision passed.

But the ache stayed.

Back in the house, Mark's shadow moved through the window again.

The girl sat on the edge of the porch, still trembling. But she didn't leave.

Because that's what they *do*, Andie thought.

They stay. Because they hope it'll get better.

Because they believe the next bruise will be the last.

Because somewhere deep down, they still think it's *their* fault.

Andie stepped forward slightly, just enough for the wind to carry her breath across the street.

The porch light flickered.

Inside, Mark looked toward the window, frowning.

Andie didn't smile.

But the thing inside her did.

Damian Nash stood in front of a whiteboard in the temporary FBI field office, arms folded, eyes scanning over a web of names and red-threaded timelines.

Three confirmed dead: Patrick Montgomery. William Haywood. Sean James.

One missing: Andrea Montgomery.

Three suspected targets: Sean, Mark, Jacob.

The problem was evidence—or the lack of it.

"Every scene's been wiped clean," he muttered. "No DNA. No prints. No witnesses who can remember a damn thing that makes sense."

He flipped through photos. Sean's body, or what was left of it, splayed across the elevator floor. William's contorted corpse, eyes wide in terror, mouth open in a silent scream. Patrick's death, the first in the chain, labeled a bizarre and tragic accident.

All unsolvable by traditional means.

Each more brutal than the last.

And still... no tangible trace of her.

Just fear. Just whispers. Just shadows.

"Ritualistic staging," said the young agent behind him. "But with no sigils, no altars. Just... carnage."

"She's not performing for gods," Nash replied coldly. "This isn't summoning. It's *sentencing.*"

He tapped a finger on the printed copy of Andie's high school photo.

"If it's her, she's not a person anymore. She's something else. But she remembers who they are. And she's choosing each target with intent. She's not erratic."

"But how?" the agent asked. "How's she doing it?"

Nash shook his head.

"I think she *became* it."

Across the country, the desert sky deepened into shades of purple and rust. Andie crouched in the sand behind a low fence bordering Mark's backyard, her eyes fixed on the shifting patterns of light and shadow spilling from the kitchen windows.

Laughter echoed out—loud, slurred, *familiar.*

Four men inside. All drunk. Their voices rang with arrogance, misogyny, and threat. She didn't need to hear the words to know the language. The cadence. The violence underneath.

She knew this music.

She'd heard it every weekend for years.

Patrick's friends—men who laughed too hard, drank too deep, hit too quickly. Men who smiled at her too long. Who always had something to say about how she walked, how she looked.

One of them had once said to Liz, "You're lucky he still comes home at all."

She felt the old bitterness rise in her throat like bile.

Mark wasn't just a rapist.

He was a *host.*

He'd built his own den of monsters.

Andie pressed a hand to the dirt. Felt the hum of the world tremble against her palm. The warmth of the earth curdled beneath her fingertips.

She could feel the pulse of the house.

She didn't need to rush.

Mark was hers.

But *they* could go first. One. At. A. Time.

The house buzzed with drunken noise.

One of the men—a broad, loud-mouthed guy with a red baseball cap turned backward—stumbled out to the back porch to relieve himself, cursing at the heat and the lack of beer. The screen door slammed behind him. The porch light flickered twice before holding steady.

Andie was already moving.

She didn't make a sound. Just a shift in the wind. A change in the silence.

The man stepped down into the dirt, whistling tunelessly as he unzipped. His voice echoed in the dark like a stupid, hollow birdcall. When he finished, he turned, blinking.

The yard looked wrong.

The swing on the old frame was rocking.

The beer can he'd left on the porch railing was crushed flat.

The light above his head buzzed again. Then died.

"Mark?" he called. "Yo, man. You out here?"

No answer.

He pulled out his phone. The screen refused to light.

That's when he saw it—movement behind the mesquite tree. Not fast. Not aggressive.

Just... standing there.

He stepped forward.

"You someone's kid? The hell are you doin' out—?"

The shape vanished.

The wind picked up hard. Something brushed his neck. Cold.

He spun around.

No one.

Inside the house, Mark laughed over a cruel story from high school—something about a girl and a dare. Another man leaned against the kitchen counter, eyes bleary, knuckles bloodied from a recent bar fight. The third fiddled with the stereo.

They didn't hear the back door creak.

They didn't notice one of them was missing.

Not yet.

Meanwhile, back in the New Mexico field office, Damian Nash leaned over a federal terminal as data streamed across the screen. The Bureau had just unsealed the forensic evaluations from Patrick Montgomery's scene—and they were disturbing.

Blood coagulation was off. Cell deterioration was accelerated. The coroner had noted an inexplicable state of cellular dehydration—as if the body had been drained of vitality *before* death.

It wasn't consistent with any known chemical or biological process.

Nash compared it to Sean's and William's records.

The pattern held.

And now, one chilling commonality stood out:

Each victim had shown signs of severe psychological trauma—*immediately preceding death.*

Not historic trauma. Not childhood. *Immediate.*

"Fear beyond threshold," Nash muttered. "As if they saw something... unnatural."

The tech beside him looked nervous. "You thinking it's paranormal?"

Nash didn't answer.

Instead, he pulled up Andrea Montgomery's sealed trauma report—the one filed years ago, detailing the rape that never made it to prosecution. The one that showed every sign of a shattered psyche, but no justice.

"They broke her," he said quietly. "And now she's putting herself back together... in pieces."

The second man died without ever screaming.

They found him folded into the crawlspace beneath the porch—his neck twisted at an angle that suggested he had crawled there, panicked, before something snapped his spine like a twig. No footprints led in. No blood on the ground. Just wide gouges in the wooden frame, as though he'd tried to claw his way through the floor.

Andie watched from the distance, crouched behind the slats of a half-collapsed storage shed. Her eyes didn't blink. Her heart didn't race.

She felt *nothing*.

Except a distant vibration under her skin—the *entity,* perhaps. Or the memory of what she once was.

Inside the house, the mood had shifted.

Mark was now agitated. Two beers in each hand, barking at the last man left—his buddy Joey—to "check the back" while he locked up the windows.

Joey went out reluctantly.

The screen door slammed.

Andie followed.

She didn't walk—she *moved*. One blink, one breath, and she was behind him.

Joey felt the air turn.

He looked up, confused. "H-hello?"

Then he froze.

Standing before him, just outside the porch light's reach, was the girl.

The girl who should've been older. The girl they never saw again.

"...a broad?"

Her expression didn't change.

Joey's breath caught. He backed up, nearly tripping on the porch steps. The light above him popped, exploding in sparks.

She took a step forward.

He yelled something profane, bolted for the gate—slipped—and never saw the coil of hose that wrapped around his ankles like a snake. He fell hard, hit his temple on the concrete edge, and crumpled.

She leaned down close to him.

The entity inside her whispered something.

Joey heard it. Eyes wide. Begging with his last conscious breath.

Andie didn't speak.

She placed one cold fingertip to his forehead.

And then he was still.

Mark, now alone inside, paced the living room.

He slammed a cabinet. Loaded a pistol. Turned off the music.

Silence fell.

He looked toward the back window—and for the first time, thought he saw a figure in the reflection.

His own? Or hers?

He turned around.

Nothing.

But the lights flickered.

The air dropped ten degrees.

And somewhere behind him... came a single, hollow knock.

Meanwhile, at the field office, Nash spoke into a recorder, voice even.

"Subject: Andrea Montgomery. Current psychological hypothesis: blend of dissociative identity fracture, supernatural possession, and strategic retribution. Not driven by impulse, but by orchestration. Subject selects targets with precision, and executes with both ritualistic absence and poetic violence. Subject is not operating in human time. She's executing judgment."

He paused, eyes on a map. Three pins already marked.

The fourth... hovered.

New Mexico.

He picked up a black marker. And pressed.

Mark stood in the center of his living room, the .45 in his hand trembling slightly despite his best effort to look composed. The lights in the house flickered again. He spun toward the hallway, back to the kitchen, and then froze at the sliding glass door.

She was there.

Andie.

No longer the quiet, invisible figure from a decade ago. She stood straight-backed and composed, eyes dark and unreadable. Her hair, longer now, draped down one shoulder. She wore black jeans and a simple top, dusty from the desert wind. She didn't look like a ghost.

She looked like a *verdict*.

Mark raised the pistol instinctively, chest tight with panic. "You stay the hell back!"

She didn't move.

"You think this is funny?" he barked. "You're dead. You're not real."

Still, she didn't speak. Just tilted her head slightly.

That's when he fired.

The first shot cracked through the room—shattering the silence and one of the side lamps.

The second hit her chest. She jolted backward slightly but did not fall.

He fired again.

And again.

Six rounds.

Seven.

The last one clicked empty.

Andie stood, a faint dark stain spreading beneath her ribs, but her posture was unchanged. Her expression never faltered.

Then she turned.

Walked toward the front door.

Calmly.

Casually.

Like it had never happened.

"Hey! What the Fu…" Mark screamed. "You bitch, I *shot* you!"

She didn't look back.

He didn't sleep that night.

Instead, he drank.

Paced.

Stared at the bloodstain on the carpet where Joey had fallen before being dragged outside—*somehow*. Tried to convince himself that this was a setup. A prank. A breakdown.

But he couldn't explain the bodies.

Or the crushed ribcage of the man beneath the porch.

Or the way Andie didn't die.

By morning, the house was surrounded by cruisers.

The sheriff came in first, followed by two deputies, guns drawn.

Mark didn't fight.

He sat on the couch, shirt stained with sweat and bourbon, the .45 lying useless beside him.

"She came back," he muttered. "I shot her. You don't understand. It was Andrea. She was here. She killed them."

"You're saying you shot someone," the deputy asked, trying to stay calm.

"I unloaded into her. But she walked away. I swear to God, she just walked away."

A sergeant came in from the backyard, pale.

"You need to see this."

Within twenty minutes, the press was at the perimeter. The coroner was wheeling out three bodies, all twisted in unnatural ways. One wrapped in a hose. One missing part of his jaw. One with pupils dilated and frozen in terror.

Mark was cuffed and placed in the back of the squad car, screaming.

"You think I did this? You think *I* did this?! She's the one! She's the one you should be afraid of!"

The cell was cold and dimly lit, painted in the same washed-out beige used in every rural lockup across the country. Mark sat on the metal bench, elbows on his knees, hands knotted together like a man trying to keep his bones from shaking. He was coming down hard—no booze, no noise, no bluster. Just silence.

And memory.

But which one?

He'd seen her. He *had*. He was sure of it when they first brought him in. The voice, the stare, the way she didn't bleed like a person should. That had been Andie Montgomery. No doubt.

But now?

Now the liquor had drained from his system, and all that was left was the churning pit of fear in his gut... and the second vision forming in its place.

His wife.

Maybe *she* had snapped.

She'd been acting strange lately—quiet, withdrawn, twitchy. Maybe she'd had enough of his friends, enough of *him*. Maybe she'd waited until the right moment, then gone berserk. That would explain the strength. The blood. The look in her eyes.

Maybe it *wasn't* Andie.

Maybe it was his miserable little wife finally doing what she'd always been too weak to do.

He clung to that idea like a lifeline.

He even chuckled.

"Heh... yeah. That makes more sense," he muttered aloud to the walls. "She did it. Had to. She's got that temper. Always thought she might do somethin' crazy one day."

A shadow shifted outside the cell window, but no one was there.

He leaned back, forcing himself to breathe, to relax.

"I ain't crazy," he told the ceiling. "I didn't kill nobody. They were just drunk. They started fightin'. Things got outta hand. She—my wife—she lost it."

The narrative took shape like plaster molding around a rotting frame.

In the adjoining hallway, Damian Nash stood watching through the two-way mirror, arms crossed.

"This is what guilt looks like when it refuses to speak plainly," he said, his voice low and unimpressed. "He's not just lying. He's reshaping reality to survive it."

The sheriff stepped beside him. "So what do you think? Was it really the girl? Andrea?"

Nash didn't answer right away.

He stared at Mark, who was now pacing his cell like a man trapped inside a story of his own design.

"I think... she *was* there," Nash said slowly. "I think he saw her. And then he saw something he couldn't process. Something that *looked* like her—but wasn't."

The sheriff rubbed the back of his neck. "You mean like a ghost?"

"No," Nash replied. "Worse."

Outside the station, a figure stood across the road, just beyond the reach of the streetlamp. Wind pushed strands of her dark red hair across her face. She didn't smile. Didn't blink.

Andie just *watched*.

They found her three blocks away at a bus stop, barefoot and shaking, her nightgown torn near the hem. Mark's wife—her name was *Eva*, though most people didn't know that—had run without looking back the moment she heard the gunshots. Her phone had been left behind. So had her shoes, wallet, and sense of safety.

When the cruiser pulled up beside her, she flinched. The officer approached slowly, hands open, calm voice.

"Ma'am? Are you hurt?"

She didn't answer. Just blinked, wide-eyed, lips slightly parted.

"We need to ask you about what happened at your home. Your husband's been taken into custody."

At the word "husband," she flinched again.

That was all they needed.

At the station, she sat in a thin hoodie and borrowed jeans in a side room, gripping a Styrofoam cup of water she hadn't touched. A female officer sat across from her with a clipboard and a quiet, non-threatening tone.

"We're not accusing you of anything, Eva. But we need to understand what happened tonight."

Eva looked down. Her voice, when it came, was barely audible.

"I heard the shots. I thought he was gonna kill me."

"Why?"

"He... he's been drinking more. Since we moved. And he's been meaner."

"Mean how?"

Eva pulled up her sleeve. Dark purple fingerprints marred her bicep.

Another bruise, older and green-yellow, peeked from under the collar of her shirt.

The officer gently set the clipboard down and looked her in the eye.

"Did he hurt you tonight?"

Eva shook her head, unsure. "I don't think he meant to. He was yelling at someone. Or something. I thought it was me. I just ran."

"Did you see who he was yelling at?"

She paused.

"No. I didn't see anyone. Just the back door swinging open. I didn't look. I just ran."

Nash stood on the other side of the glass, watching again.

"She's not lying," he said.

"No," the sheriff replied. "But she doesn't know what she saw. Couldn't help if she wanted to."

"She *is* helping," Nash said. "She's the ghost of the next victim. Andrea saw her. That's why she didn't hurt her. That's why she let her live."

The sheriff looked confused. "Why?"

"Because this woman already carries the scars," Nash said. "Andie doesn't kill to make a point. She kills to *end the cycle*. Mark's wife isn't the guilty one. She's the mirror."

Outside, the desert wind picked up, hurling dust across the road.

Andie was already gone.

But her shadow lingered—in the bruises, in the silence, and in the words Eva had never been brave enough to say until now.

The motel room was silent, lit only by the flickering glow of a muted television she hadn't turned on. Andie stood in front of the cracked mirror above the bathroom sink, shirt lifted. The entry holes were still there—round, black-rimmed tears just beneath her collarbone, lower ribs, and side.

No blood.

No pain.

She touched the skin around the wounds, watching how it didn't respond like human flesh should. There was no inflammation. No bruising. Only something *beneath*—something that had caught the bullets like teeth snapping shut around a fly.

She pressed harder.

Her fingertip came away dry.

The mirror caught her eye then, and for a moment she didn't see herself. Not entirely. The face that stared back wore her features, but the pupils glowed faintly, pulsing like embers beneath water. She didn't gasp. She didn't recoil.

She just looked.

And wondered.

“Why are you still here?” she asked aloud, voice flat.

There was no answer.

But the hum behind her ribs—the *thing* that had whispered to her since that night in the woods—shivered like a coiled wire. Not loud. Not violent. Just... present.

Like a companion.

Or a parasite.

She left before dawn.

No trace. No footprint. No DNA.

The Arizona desert stretched in every direction, and for now, she let it have Mark and his ghosts. The police would be chasing paperwork. Nash would be dissecting the psychology. But she had a new direction.

Jacob.

The last.

The worst.

The one who had smiled afterward.

She’d found him weeks ago, a name buried in an old class roster, traced to an outdated cell plan, and then through a half-deleted social media profile. He was in Chicago now, working along the lakeshore as a longshoreman. Harder to reach. Surrounded by people. A city too big for ghosts.

But she wasn’t a ghost.

Not anymore.

Meanwhile, in a cluttered office deep inside the county station, Nash sat with a printout of Andie's high school transcript beside the photos from two crime scenes. He wasn't speaking into a recorder this time. Just studying. Mapping her logic.

"She doesn't kill like a monster," he murmured. "She kills like a philosopher."

He marked something on a notepad: **Pattern: escalation followed by withdrawal. Precision followed by vanishing.**

Then, at the top of the page, he circled one word: *Jacob.*

Andie boarded the train that night.

It was cold in the cabin. Not winter cold—*other* cold. A stillness that made strangers turn their collars up and check the reflection in the window twice before settling in.

She sat by herself. No luggage. No phone.

Just the sound of steel grinding against steel as the train pulled north.

Chicago awaited. And so did *he.*

The city greeted her with wind and shadows.

Chicago in early fall was a gray cathedral of noise—horns, steel, the grit of boots on concrete. Andie moved through it like a phantom, unnoticed but deliberate. The rail yards bustled with longshoremen and cargo lifts, voices shouting over wind and engine rumble.

She saw him immediately.

Jacob.

Taller than before. Heavier, broader in the shoulders. The swagger hadn't changed. He wore reflective gear and barked orders like he owned the pier. A shaved jaw now, no boyish softness—just the rigid edge of a man who thought the past had forgotten him.

He hadn't seen her.

Not yet.

From the edge of the loading dock, Andie leaned against a post. She let the distance blur her vision, watching not just Jacob but how others reacted to him. There were snickers when his back turned, flinches when he barked too close. Even now, he enjoyed small power over others. The same tone. The same pride.

She could taste it in the air like rust.

The entity within her stirred.

But she didn't approach.

Not yet.

She hadn't come to kill him today.

That night, she stayed in a low-rent motel near the red line. Her window faced the alley. Inside, she lit no lights. She sat cross-legged on the bed, knees to her chest, the Chicago skyline barely reaching her through cracked blinds.

She thought of Mark.

He was still alive.

Still breathing.

Still blaming.

And that couldn't stand.

Somewhere, Nash was connecting threads. She could feel him—not his presence, but the drag of his logic. He'd built a sequence in his mind: William, Sean, Mark... Jacob. He thought she moved forward like a clock. Rational. Predictable.

But clocks can lie.

And Andie was not running on time.

She stood, grabbed her coat, and turned back toward the shadows that had never let her go.

She would return to Mark.

She would finish what she'd begun.

Back in New Mexico, Mark had been moved from the local station to county holding after multiple fits of screaming in his cell and one failed attempt at self-harm. He now sat in a padded room under suicide watch, muttering different versions of the same story to every officer who'd listen.

"It wasn't me," he'd say. "It wasn't her either. It was something *wearing* her. She's not alive. She's not."

And when they asked *who* he meant, the answer changed.

"My wife. No, the girl. Both. Maybe both."

Nash arrived late that evening and read the new psychological evaluations with a tightening jaw.

"She's coming back," he said softly, more to himself than the room.

Andie was always two steps ahead. Mark hadn't slept in two days.

Not really.

He'd closed his eyes—sure. He'd curled into the corner of his padded cell, knees to chest, waiting for the dreamless dark. But each time his eyes shut, something moved in the shadows. Not footsteps. *Shifting*. Like pressure building in the walls. A breath beneath the foam.

The fluorescent lights above flickered—always in pairs.

buzz—click—buzz

Then silence.

Too much silence.

He'd started talking to the mirror.

There wasn't a mirror, not anymore—not after he shattered the one in county intake and tried to swallow the shards—but the memory of one still hung on the opposite wall like a framed threat. Mark stared at the blank vinyl, sweating, eyes rimmed red.

"I know you're not real," he whispered.

No reply.

"But if you're gonna come, come now. Just—just make it quick this time."

The air turned cold.

A whisper of static crept through the ceiling vent. His eyes flicked upward. The noise sounded like a voice—but all vowels, no consonants, like something trying to *remember* how human speech worked.

Then it was gone.

A nurse passed by with a clipboard.

"Patient is uncooperative... verbal... distressed," she murmured, marking notes. She didn't linger.

In the adjacent wing, Nash stood watching Mark through a reinforced glass panel.

The deputy beside him looked uneasy. "He's cracked."

"No," Nash said. "He's preparing."

"For what?"

"For her. She's not done with him."

The deputy shifted. "You still think this is one person?"

Nash tapped the file in his hand, flipping through the reports. "You ever see someone survive two bullets to the lung and walk away without so much as a limp?"

"No."

"Exactly."

Back inside the cell, Mark stood slowly. The walls seemed closer than before. His breath fogged faintly, and for the first time he noticed the temperature—unnatural for this kind of facility.

The opposite wall shimmered for just a second.

And there—just there—he saw her.

Not in full.

Just her reflection.

A faint outline behind a memory.

Andie. Watching him. Face calm. Eyes glowing. Hands still.

She didn't blink.

She didn't move.

And then the light returned, and she was gone.

He dropped to his knees. Started sobbing. Started laughing.

"Please," he murmured. "Please, just finish it. Just finish it this time."

But the silence offered no promises.

Only time.

The coroner's office was tucked behind the main hospital—sterile tile floors, humming freezers, and the chemical sting of formaldehyde baked into the walls. Damian Nash stood in front of a display monitor as Dr. Halperin—gray-bearded, exacting, and a bit too old for digital forensics—scrolled through Sean's autopsy files.

"What you're looking at," the doctor said, "shouldn't exist."

The screen showed cross-sections of Sean's upper body: spine crushed, major arteries severed, pelvis nearly sheared in half by the elevator's descent. But none of that held Nash's attention.

It was the pattern scorched across the remains.

"What is that?" Nash asked.

"Subdermal burn," Halperin said. "Shape of a spiral. Irregular. Organic. Almost like a... fingerprint or branding. But we found no accelerant. No flame. And here's the real kicker—"

He pulled up a thermal scan taken post-mortem.

"This part of the tissue? Still holding heat thirty-six hours later. Internal core temp higher than the ambient room. No plausible cause."

Nash frowned. "You saying he was cooked from the inside?"

"I'm saying he *stayed hot*, long after he should've cooled. It's like something marked him. And that mark is still *active.*"

Nash turned from the screen and stared at the steel doors that led to the morgue drawers.

"William was like this too. Cells breaking down unnaturally. Sean was crushed, but the signs are consistent. Something metaphysical."

Halperin raised an eyebrow. "You think it's one person doing this?"

Nash nodded.

"Not a person," he said. "Not anymore."

Back at the county detention center, just before dawn, the officer on duty made his final rounds before shift change. He paused outside Mark's cell, checked the clipboard, then peered inside.

And yelled.

The report would note later: no security breach. No cell tampering. All cameras malfunctioned between 3:11 and 3:13 a.m.

When the medics arrived, they found Mark's body suspended midair—his chest impaled by two warped steel bars torn from the overhead ventilation grate. The force had driven the bars downward through his shoulders and rib cage, splitting him open in the shape of a crucifix. Blood soaked the padding and pooled across the floor in an almost *symmetrical* fashion.

His eyes were open.

Mouth agape.

As if he had died looking at something he could neither understand nor escape.

Nash arrived less than an hour later, trench coat catching the wind as he ducked under the perimeter tape. The sight stopped him cold.

"This wasn't rage," he said. "This was ritual."

He stepped closer, face tightening.

"She doesn't just kill. She performs."

And in doing so, she leaves no evidence... only meaning.

Eva sat on a bench outside the women's shelter, clutching a paper cup of coffee with both hands, though it had long since gone cold. Her body was still in shock. The bruises that marked her skin were healing faster than the bruises inside—those seemed to be burrowing deeper.

She didn't cry.

She just... stared at the street.

Andie approached from the side—quiet, slow, no sudden movement. Hood up, posture small, hands empty. She took the bench beside her without asking.

Eva turned.

Andie met her eyes.

Recognition flickered—but not full comprehension. Somewhere inside, Eva *knew*. But the grief and exhaustion dulled the impact.

"I'm sorry," Eva said automatically. "Do I know you?"

"No," Andie said gently. "But I know *you.*"

They sat for a moment in silence.

"I know what it's like to love a man who breaks things," Andie said, voice soft and without judgment. "And to believe—somewhere deep down—that if you stay, maybe that's how you fix it."

Eva didn't respond. Her eyes welled with unshed tears.

Andie continued.

"You didn't deserve what he did to you. None of it. And you're not weak for surviving. That part's the lie they feed you."

Eva looked down at the coffee. "I don't feel strong."

"You don't have to," Andie replied. "That comes later. For now, just breathe. Every breath is proof he didn't win."

A breeze carried dust along the sidewalk. The traffic light changed and back again. Somewhere in the distance, a dog barked.

Eva looked at her again, brow furrowing slightly. "You look familiar."

"I shouldn't," Andie said, standing. "I just wanted to tell you one thing."

Eva waited.

Andie met her eyes again.

"He can't hurt you anymore."

She turned and walked away.

No flames. No whisper of vengeance. Just the hollow echo of boots on concrete and the quiet strength of a woman who had once been shattered—and now shattered others in return.

Eva sat still for several minutes.

Then, finally, for the first time in days, she exhaled.

A breath that did not tremble.

Flashes from cameras lit up the gray morning like distant lightning. Outside the detention center, a wall of reporters shouted questions over each other, their microphones pointed at the podium where Damian Nash stood.

He hated press briefings.

They forced him to say too much—or not enough—and this one was worse than most. The crime scene behind him defied explanation, logic, or precedent.

“Agent Nash, can you confirm the identity of the deceased?”

“Was this a suicide or a homicide?”

“Is there any link between this and the elevator death from last week?”

He leaned into the mic, calm but precise. “The deceased is Mark D____, who had been in county custody on unrelated domestic charges. We are currently treating his death as suspicious. No further details are available at this time.”

A hand shot up from the middle row. “Do you believe there’s a serial killer targeting abusers?”

Nash's expression didn’t flicker, but his pause said everything.

“We are exploring all leads,” he replied.

That answer satisfied no one.

In the back of the crowd, unnoticed in the swirl of questions and microphones, Andie stood with her hood drawn low. No one saw her. No one *felt* her. She’d become practiced at that now—*non-presence* was her cloak.

She watched Nash closely.

There was intelligence in his eyes. Controlled emotion. The kind of man who didn't scare easily. And yet, she saw the way his fingers tightened on the podium edge.

He knew she was real.

He just didn't know where she'd strike next.

By the time the press conference ended, Andie was already walking toward the train station. Her boots clicked over uneven sidewalk. Her wounds from Mark's shooting had long since closed—skin smooth, but not quite *right*. A new kind of tissue. Stronger. Colder.

She didn't limp.

She didn't breathe heavily.

Her body had adapted.

What once would've made her scream now barely registered as discomfort.

Still, something stirred beneath her ribs. Not hunger. Not rage. A slow, creeping *expectation*.

Jacob.

The last of them.

The one who smiled when the others laughed.

He had always been the worst.

She boarded the outbound train to Chicago without speaking. The conductor didn't notice her boarding. The other passengers looked away. No one sat beside her.

She pulled her hood lower and leaned back into the hard vinyl seat, letting the hum of steel wheels lull her into stillness.

This wasn't about catharsis anymore.

This was about balance.

Nash sat alone in the makeshift field office, the only light coming from the desk lamp casting long shadows across stacks of printed case files and photos. The room smelled of dry paper and stale coffee. Three crime scene photos lay in front of him: William, Sean, Mark. Different manners of death. Different locations.

But the signature?

It was there.

Not physical. Not forensic.

Symbolic.

Each death had echoed something. Something psychological. Philosophical. He scribbled into his notepad:

- William: suffocation without force. Prolonged closeness.
- Sean: mechanical execution. Swift, industrial.
- Mark: impalement. Displayed. Judgment.

And behind each—a whisper of ritual, a performance executed by someone who understood pain on a molecular level.

Someone who didn't just *kill*, but *delivered verdicts.*

Nash flipped to the last page in the growing file: **Andrea Montgomery – Missing**. The high school photo was faded. Her expression unreadable, lips just beginning a smile that never reached the eyes.

He exhaled through his nose.

"Are you even the same person anymore?" he asked the page.

Thousands of miles away, in Chicago, Jacob pushed a heavy dolly across the concrete dock floor. Steel containers lined up in rows, ready to be offloaded. He was laughing with two coworkers, hands calloused, uniform dusted with rust stains.

Nothing unusual.

Nothing out of place.

Until the dolly's wheels caught on something.

A dead bird.

Mangled, feathers twisted in unnatural spirals. No sign of trauma. Just... wrong. Jacob blinked at it. Frowned.

He kicked it aside.

Later that afternoon, the loading crane jammed mid-lift. A shriek of metal rang out overhead, sending workers scattering. The foreman cursed, shouting about overworked machinery.

Jacob looked up.

Something flickered in the glass window of the control booth. A shape. A *shadow*.

Gone in an instant.

His hand tightened on the crate lever.

"Get it together," he muttered.

By nightfall, Jacob sat alone in his truck, engine idling, parked beside the warehouse.

A bottle of warm beer balanced between his thighs. His fingers twitched against the steering wheel. He hadn't touched a woman in over a year—not since the last one ran crying from his apartment after he got too rough.

"You're too sensitive," he'd told her.

But even now, in the dark, he felt something else pressing in.

A presence.

Not visible.

Not loud.

But watching.

The night settled over the Chicago docks like a thick wool blanket—muting sound, smothering color, softening every hard edge with creeping fog. The loading cranes had gone still. The forklifts parked. The workers gone.

Jacob remained.

He leaned against the open door of his truck, smoking a cigarette and staring at the water. The last shift had ended two hours ago, but he didn't want to go home. Something about the quiet unsettled him more than the work ever did.

The sound of footsteps made him jolt.

He turned fast—too fast—but the voice that followed was calm. Familiar.

"You still come here alone."

Andie stood ten feet from him. Same voice. Same eyes. But changed. Older. Colder. Like time had carved her out of granite.

Jacob's cigarette fell from his lips.

He blinked twice. Swallowed.

"An—Andrea?"

She didn't answer. She simply looked at him.

He laughed nervously, stepping back. "You—you look... I mean... what are you doing here?"

"I wanted to see you again," she said.

Jacob looked at the shadows, as if expecting others to appear. "You... what for? I haven't seen you since—God, since high school. I thought you moved or something."

"I did," she said quietly. "Then life moved through me. Then past me."

He didn't understand. That was okay.

"You're not afraid?" he asked, surprised at her stillness.

"No," she said. "Not of you."

He rubbed the back of his neck. "I—I've thought about you. Sometimes. I mean... not like that. Just, I wondered if you were okay."

Andie tilted her head slightly. "Did you?"

Jacob sighed, his bravado slipping. "Yeah. I mean... I know I should've said something back then. But I didn't know what to say. I—I was just a stupid kid—peer pressure, ya know? I wasn't... I didn't think—"

"You didn't stop them," she said, softly. Not angry. Just truth.

His shoulders sagged. "No. I didn't."

There was silence between them.

The fog crept in tighter around their legs. Lights from the distant ferry shimmered like candles on water.

"I used to like you," Andie said, finally. "Back then. You were the only one who made me feel seen. I'd wait for you to come in the café. You'd smile. Say something clever. I used to think about what it'd be like to kiss you."

Jacob's throat caught.

"And then," she continued, "you came with them that night. And you laughed."

"I didn't touch you," Jacob said quickly. "I—I didn't... I swear."

"But you *were there*. You *watched*. And you didn't leave. You didn't call anyone. You didn't stop it."

He opened his mouth.

And closed it.

Andie took a slow step forward. "So now, I'm here."

He didn't run. Not yet. Some part of him—the wounded, guilty part—wanted to hear her out.

Jacob sat slowly on the edge of the loading dock, elbows on his knees, face cast in shadow by the flickering yellow bulb above. The fog had settled behind them like a curtain, leaving the two in a strange, isolated stage of memory and consequence.

"I didn't know they were gonna do that," he muttered, avoiding her eyes. "I swear, Andie... I thought they were just drunk. I mean, Mark always talked trash, but I didn't think— I didn't *know.*"

Andie stood a few feet from him, arms at her sides, body unreadable.

"You could've pulled one of them off me," she said. "You could've dragged me out. Called someone. Anything."

Jacob nodded. His hands trembled.

"I should've. I *should've* done something. But I froze. And then Billy—he egged me on. Said if I bailed, they'd come after me next. Called me a bitch." He scoffed at himself. "So I stood there. Watching you cry. Watching you scream."

He finally looked up.

"I think about it every fucking night."

Andie's voice was low. "And what do you tell yourself to sleep?"

"That I was scared," he said, bitter. "That I didn't have a choice. That it wasn't me who did it."

He laughed again, hollow this time.

"But it *was* me. I might not have touched you, but I didn't stop it. And I let them. All of them. Because I didn't want to look weak."

She took a slow step forward, face still blank.

"Do you remember what I looked like afterward?"

Jacob swallowed. "Yeah."

"I wore that look for *months*," she said. "It followed me home. Into my bed. Into my dreams. I wore it like a skin."

His voice cracked. "I'm sorry."

"I believe you," she said. "But that doesn't change what you did. Or what I became because of it."

Meanwhile, back at the field office, Nash stood before a corkboard now covered in red string and photos. He circled the final face—Jacob.

Andrea Montgomery's case file lay open on the desk. The interview transcripts from her school counselor. The nurse's report. The note scribbled in her yearbook, from *Jacob*.

You're the only one who ever looks like she gets it.

Nash pressed his knuckles into the desk, eyes narrowing.

"She's not killing randomly. She's delivering judgment."

He circled the last victim's name in red ink. The pattern was nearly complete.

"She's not done," he whispered.

He didn't know where she was yet—but he knew *who* was next.

Jacob wiped his palms on his jeans, though they weren't sweating—just shaking. Andie stood across from him like a silent stormcloud, a figure from a past he thought had been buried, now risen, staring him down not with fury... but with something colder. Something surgical.

"I wanted to talk to you after," he said, voice thin. "I even wrote down what I was gonna say... but I never got the guts to call."

Andie's expression didn't change. "Say it now."

He took a breath. Eyes lowered.

"I was gonna say... that I never stopped thinking about you. That I was sick over what happened. That I didn't sleep right after it. That I—I liked you. I really did. I just..."

"Caved," she supplied.

He nodded. "Yeah. I caved. I let my fear win. I let what people thought of me control me. I didn't just fail *you*, I failed myself. Every day since... I've wondered what would've happened if I'd pulled you out of there."

Andie tilted her head slightly, scrutinizing him. “And what do you think would’ve happened?”

“I don’t know,” he admitted. “Maybe you’d be okay. Maybe we’d talk more. Maybe you’d still hate me anyway. But maybe I’d be able to look at myself in the mirror without wondering if I’m the kind of guy who lets a girl get hurt because he wants to be liked.”

She stepped closer.

He tensed but didn’t move.

“You liked me?” she asked, softly.

He nodded, mouth dry. “A lot.”

A flicker passed through her eyes. Regret? Memory? Or just the mimicry of human emotion?

“You were different,” she said. “You didn’t leer like the others. You asked questions. You listened.”

Jacob swallowed. “I meant every word. I just didn’t know how to be brave when it counted.”

“That’s not courage,” Andie said, stepping even closer, her voice calm. “That’s just convenience. Cowardice is knowing what’s right and choosing to keep your hands clean anyway.”

He flinched. But didn’t run.

“Do you hate me?” he asked.

She studied him for a long, long moment. The silence felt surgical.

“No,” she said finally.

His shoulders sank—relief mixing with confusion.

"But I don't feel *anything* either," she added. "Not anymore."

That shook him. "Nothing?"

"I don't even know if I *can* feel anymore," she said. "The only thing that stays with me is what was done—and who did nothing."

Jacob stared at her, searching for something—remorse, hope, even contempt.

But she offered him nothing.

Only silence.

Damian Nash stood before the glow of three monitors, each showing snippets of security footage—bus terminals, train platforms, subway stations. He sipped lukewarm coffee, fingers tapping the desk in a syncopated rhythm.

There she was.

Twice.

Once in Albuquerque. Then again outside a Greyhound terminal in Kansas City. A blurred, hooded figure boarding without hesitation.

He narrowed his eyes.

"She's not hiding," he muttered. "She wants us to *watch*."

He pulled up an overlay of travel routes, triangulating a line between the three deaths and this new lead. Chicago burned red on the map.

"Jacob," he said aloud.

He tapped a pen against his lips, then opened a search on the dockyard's employee database. Jacob R. B____—longshoreman, no criminal record. Moved from Ohio. Three minor citations for disorderly conduct, one dismissed assault report.

Just enough to stay invisible.

But not enough to *deserve* invisibility.

Nash reached for the phone and dialed.

"This is Special Agent Nash. Get me the Chicago field office. We need a soft approach. One operative. No sirens. I think she's already there."

Jacob shoved his hands into his coat pockets as he walked beside Andie through the mist-thickened streets. Neither spoke for the first block. The silence wasn't awkward—it was heavy. Weighted. As if both were trying to breathe through history.

"You still live close?" he asked, mostly just to say something.

"No," she replied. "I don't live anywhere, really."

He tried to laugh. "That some kind of poetic thing, or..."

She glanced at him. "You ever try sleeping without dreams?"

Jacob paused. "Sure. I mean, when I'm exhausted, yeah."

"No," she said. "I mean *never* dream. Just... silence. Black. Like your soul has nowhere left to visit."

He stopped walking.

Andie kept moving forward a step, then looked back over her shoulder. "That's what it's like now. For me."

Jacob caught up, steps slower. "Jesus, Andrea..."

"I go by just Andie now," she said.

He nodded. "Andie."

They walked another block in silence. Neon signs flickered overhead. A rusted fence groaned in the wind.

"I still can't believe you're here," he said.

"I never really left," she murmured. "Pieces of me always stayed in that town. In that moment. Everything else... kept moving without me."

He glanced sideways. "Is that why you came? For closure?"

Andie didn't answer right away. Then she smiled—but it didn't reach her eyes.

"Something like that."

He slowed again, this time without knowing why.

"Would you—do you want to get coffee? Or something? Just... talk more?"

She looked at him carefully.

"I'm not ready to sleep yet," she said.

His heart thudded once—hopeful. Stupid.

She turned the corner. He followed.

Jacob's apartment was a third-floor walk-up tucked above an aging bakery that closed at 6 p.m. sharp. The stairwell reeked of yeast and bleach, but Andie barely noticed. Her senses were attuned elsewhere—Jacob's gait, the rhythm of his breath, the keys jangling from his nervous fingers.

He unlocked the door and pushed it open, stepping aside like a gentleman. "Sorry it's a mess. I wasn't really expecting company."

Andie stepped in, her gaze sweeping over the cluttered studio. It wasn't filthy, just lived-in—grease-stained pizza boxes, a laundry basket full of wrinkled shirts, an unused bookshelf stacked with old gym trophies and broken video game cases.

“Nice place,” she said, though the words carried no weight.

He tossed his keys on the counter. “Can I get you something? Water? I’ve got some soda, I think...”

She shook her head. “I’m fine.”

He hesitated, then sat down on the edge of the couch. She didn’t move at first—just stood near the window, watching the neon light pulse on the street below.

“You ever think about going back?” he asked.

“To where?”

“Home. Your mom. Your... anyone.”

She turned slowly. “My mother’s dead. So is my little brother.”

His face fell. “Jesus. I—I didn’t know. I’m sorry.”

Andie sat in the chair across from him. “You keep apologizing. You think it helps?”

“I don’t know,” he admitted. “I just don’t know what else to say.”

“Then don’t say anything,” she said gently. “Sometimes silence is more honest.”

Jacob leaned back, rubbing his face with both hands. “It’s not just guilt. I really did like you. That wasn’t fake.”

“I know,” she said. “That’s what made it worse.”

He blinked.

“You weren’t some stranger,” she went on. “You were someone I... hoped for. And then you became part of the worst night of my life. That kind of betrayal leaves a mark deeper than bruises.”

Jacob didn’t speak. His eyes glistened faintly under the apartment’s lone lamp.

“You ever think about what you’ve become?” she asked.

“All the time,” he said.

Andie looked at him carefully. “Then why haven’t you changed?”

He opened his mouth, but no answer came. Only breath.

She rose and walked past him, slow and deliberate, trailing her fingers across the top of his kitchen counter. The air grew still. Not hostile—*expectant.*

He watched her with something between confusion and awe. He didn’t realize he was leaning forward.

“You’re not the same girl I used to know,” he said.

“No,” she agreed. “I’m not.”

Andie leaned against the counter, watching Jacob like someone studying a painting they once loved—no longer moved by it, but still curious why it ever held power.

He hadn’t moved from the couch, but his posture had shifted—shoulders drawn slightly inward, hands clasped between his knees. Not defensive. Not quite afraid. Just unsure. Off-balance.

“I used to think about your hands,” Andie said, quietly.

Jacob looked up.

"When you ordered coffee... when you counted bills... I wondered what your hands would feel like on mine. What it'd be like if you kissed me."

He opened his mouth, unsure if he should speak. So he didn't.

Andie stepped forward slowly. The floor didn't creak beneath her. She stopped just in front of him, close enough for him to see the unnatural stillness behind her eyes.

She held out her hand.

"Touch me."

His brows knit. "What?"

"Take my hand."

He reached, hesitating, then gently wrapped his fingers around hers. They were cool. Not cold. Smooth, but firm—like glass that remembered heat.

For a moment, neither moved.

Jacob looked into her face, searching for something—connection, maybe. The past. Redemption.

Andie didn't blink.

"I don't feel anything," she said, almost to herself.

Jacob began to withdraw, but she held his hand a moment longer. "It's not you," she whispered. "It's me. Whatever was in here... it's gone now."

She let go. The distance between them felt cavernous.

He sat back, visibly shaken. "Then why come here?"

"To see if there was anything left," she said. "Of me. Of you. Of that girl who thought you were kind."

Jacob stared at the floor. "I wanted to be."

Andie turned from him, walking back toward the door. "But you weren't."

He didn't argue.

Across town, Damian Nash sat in the back seat of a black SUV parked on a side street near the waterfront. A thin stream of steam from his thermos fogged the window beside him as he reviewed the latest digital trace.

"She's here," he told the agent in the front. "She's circling him. Slowly."

"You want backup?"

"No," Nash said. "She's not reckless. She doesn't strike in panic. She takes her time. Makes it personal."

He closed the file on Jacob, then looked out at the city skyline.

"She's deciding."

The agent raised an eyebrow. "On what?"

"On whether she still wants revenge," Nash said. "Or if there's any part of her that can be spared."

Andie's hand rested on the doorknob, her body angled toward the exit, her presence already beginning to evaporate from the room like mist.

"Do you have to go?" Jacob asked softly, still on the couch.

She paused. Not dramatically—just long enough for the weight of the question to press into her spine.

He stood, taking a careful step forward. "I didn't mean like... you have to *stay* or anything. Just... maybe talk a little more. I won't ask questions. I won't push."

Her hand slipped from the knob.

She turned back slowly. "Why?"

He gave a weak smile. "Because for the first time in a long time... I don't feel like pretending."

Andie tilted her head slightly.

"Most people want something when they ask you to stay," she said. "Comfort. Sex. Forgiveness. What do *you* want?"

"I don't know," he said honestly. "Maybe just a little peace. And maybe to give you some too. If that's possible."

The air between them settled—less tense, but not quite warm.

"I'll sit," she said. "Nothing more."

He nodded quickly and gestured to the couch again. She crossed the room with a slow grace and lowered herself beside him, leaving just enough space to feel intentional.

He didn't speak at first. Neither did she. The television flickered muted images of a local news broadcast. A bar fight. Weather pattern shifts. A carjacking.

Noise.

Andie turned slightly, glancing at the photo on the end table. It was Jacob as a boy—maybe fourteen. Baseball uniform. Braces. A crooked smile trying hard to look confident.

"Do you ever think about who you used to be?" she asked.

Jacob followed her gaze. “That kid had it all figured out. Thought being good meant not getting in trouble.”

She looked back at him. “Being good means standing between others and the trouble.”

“I wish someone had told me that.”

Andie nodded. “Me too.”

He shifted slightly, careful not to let their knees touch. “You can stay here, if you want. For the night. No strings.”

She didn’t answer right away. Then:

“I won’t sleep.”

“That’s okay.”

They sat like that for a long moment, surrounded by the hush of unresolved things. The past. The almosts. The never-weres.

Across the city, Nash pressed a pair of binoculars to his eyes, observing Jacob’s apartment from the rooftop of a derelict parking garage. A faint buzz of static hummed from his earpiece.

“No movement,” came the agent’s voice on the other end. “No lights turned off. Looks calm.”

Nash lowered the binoculars. His jaw flexed.

“She’s in there. Watching him.”

He looked toward the horizon.

“And she’s not finished.”

Jacob poured her a glass of water and one for himself. The clink of the ice cubes was the loudest sound in the apartment. The city beyond the window had softened into that strange quiet that only arrives at 3 a.m.—when the world seems to hold its breath.

They sat again, side by side. Still apart. Still tethered.

"You ever think about redemption?" she asked.

Jacob blinked. "Redemption?"

"You know. Making up for something you can't undo."

He exhaled slowly. "I think about it every day."

She sipped from her glass, never taking her eyes off him.

"I mean, what would that even look like?" he asked, almost laughing. "Me doing charity work? Handing out soup to the homeless?"

Andie didn't smile.

"No," she said. "I think it looks like telling the truth. Even when it costs you everything."

Jacob stared down at his hands. "To who? My parents? A priest? God?"

"To yourself," she said, voice flat but not unkind. "And to the people you damaged."

"I don't know if I'm brave enough for that," he admitted.

Andie turned her gaze back to the window. "Then you're not sorry enough."

He flinched but nodded. "You're probably right."

The silence returned, not awkward but full. She could feel him unraveling—layers of armor sloughing off with every truth he allowed himself to say. It was not forgiveness she sought. It was *clarity*.

“Why didn’t you stop them?” she asked.

His voice cracked. “Because I was afraid.”

“Of what?”

“Losing them. Losing status. Looking weak.”

“Looking human.”

He looked up sharply.

“You could’ve pulled me out,” she said. “I saw it in your eyes. You *knew* it was wrong. You wanted to help.”

“I did,” he whispered. “I just...”

“You chose comfort,” she said. “You chose fear. And I paid the price.”

Jacob’s head dropped into his hands. “I know. I’ll never stop knowing.”

Andie didn’t reach out. She didn’t cry. She just sat there and watched him unravel. Her calm was terrifying, even to herself.

On a rooftop three blocks away, Damian Nash leaned against a steel girder, the breeze tugging at his jacket. His eyes were red from hours without sleep, but his mind remained sharp.

He scrolled through the notes from his past cases—cult killings in Vermont, a string of ritual suicides in Utah, the abandoned asylum in Georgia with its mutilated caretakers.

None of them had *this*. This silence. This lack of evidence. This *focus*.

“Who the hell are you, Andrea Montgomery?” he murmured.

Behind him, a pigeon fluttered noisily across the rooftop edge. Nash didn't flinch. He stared out at the apartment building, where two lights still burned—two figures still awake.

He pulled out his phone, opened a secure folder, and added a single note:

Subject appears to form psychological rapport with male targets prior to fatal event. Delayed execution suggests emotional probing, not spontaneous rage.

He exhaled and tucked the phone away.

"She's waiting," he said. "But not for long."

The bathroom door creaked softly as Andie pushed it open. A single overhead light buzzed faintly, casting a jaundiced pall over the chipped sink and fog-streaked mirror. The air was still, thick with the scent of old tile cleaner and faint mildew. Jacob hadn't followed—he remained on the couch, hunched in silent guilt, sipping the water she hadn't touched.

Andie closed the door behind her.

She stared at herself in the mirror. Her face was still. Beautiful, but pale—like marble warmed under moonlight. She leaned forward slowly, her breath not fogging the glass.

The eyes.

They glowed.

Not a harsh light. Not fire. Just the faintest gleam of something unnatural. Something *awake*.

She didn't look surprised.

She raised her hand and touched her cheek, dragging a finger beneath her lower lid. The glow remained, steady. Not even human blood vessels disrupted its cold hue. She turned her face slightly, inspecting herself from different angles—this was not the face of the girl who had once felt giddy when Jacob smiled at her across a café counter.

It was something else.

Something evolved.

The memory came unbidden—her mother's bruised arms. Billy's shattered toy beneath Patrick's boot. The night Jacob first touched her hand and made her believe, even for a few days, that something kind might bloom in her poisoned world.

She felt nothing now.

Nothing but a distant hum—like static wrapped in smoke—coiling beneath her skin. Not rage. Not sorrow. Just purpose. The purity of it. The inevitability.

She pressed both palms against the cold ceramic sink.

"Why am I still talking to him?" she whispered aloud, her voice barely a sound.

The mirror gave no answer. But the eyes did.

They pulsed, faintly—like an answer from the void.

A message in her blood.

She straightened her spine. The girl she once was had asked for affection. The creature she'd become needed only finality.

And yet...

She looked at the small towel hanging limp on the wall. It had Jacob's name embroidered in sloppy navy thread—something probably stitched by a mom or aunt. It was *human*.

So was the photo. So was the tremble in his voice. So were the things she could not forget no matter how deep the entity buried them.

She closed her eyes.

When she opened them again, the glow had receded. Not gone. Just tucked behind the veil once more.

Andie turned off the light and exited the bathroom.

Jacob looked up, his eyes searching hers for something—perhaps forgiveness, perhaps judgment.

"I'll sleep here," she said.

He nodded, uncertain.

Andie curled up in the armchair across from the couch. She kept her eyes open as he closed his.

Her gaze did not blink.

Jacob stirred to the distant echo of traffic. Pale sunlight bled through the blinds, casting uneven shadows across the floor. The clock on the wall ticked faintly—too faintly, like it was trying not to be noticed.

He blinked against the crust of sleep and turned his head.

She was still there.

Andie sat curled in the armchair, motionless, her eyes open and staring at the door. Her arms were folded beneath a gray throw blanket he barely remembered having. Her expression was unreadable.

He sat up slowly.

"Did you sleep?" he asked.

"No," she replied without looking at him.

He rubbed the back of his neck. "You... want coffee?"

"No."

The answer was soft but firm. Not hostile. Just final.

He stood and moved into the kitchen anyway, as if routine might erase the strangeness pressing in around them. He poured water into the machine, measuring out grounds with shaking fingers. He didn't know why her presence made him feel like a child—maybe because deep down he knew he'd never been a man.

"I meant what I said last night," he called over his shoulder.

"I know," she said.

He faced her. "Does that matter?"

Andie turned her head slightly toward him. "Not to me."

He swallowed and looked away.

Across the city, Damian Nash sat in the sterile hum of a mobile forensics van, the fluorescent lights overhead buzzing like angry insects. A technician handed him a tablet loaded with new data.

"EM spectrum anomalies," the woman said. "Same as the other sites."

Nash scrolled through the report. "Give me plain English."

"Localized electromagnetic surges. At the exact times of death. Not enough to trip the grid, but enough to scramble nearby devices. Phones glitch. Clocks freeze. Even cameras blink out for two to three seconds."

“Consistent?”

“Perfectly,” she said. “It’s like someone hits the pause button on reality just long enough to do what they came to do.”

Nash tapped the screen. “Any other explanation?”

“None we can prove.”

He handed back the tablet. “We’re not dealing with a serial killer.”

The technician frowned. “Then what are we dealing with?”

Nash looked toward the van door, the city sprawled beyond it like an endless puzzle.

“I don’t know yet,” he said. “But she’s not hiding. Not really. She’s *showing* us. Piece by piece.”

Back in the apartment, Andie rose from the chair as Jacob handed her a mug of coffee. She took it, held it, but didn’t sip.

He watched her like a man watching a wave just before it breaks—beautiful, terrifying, unstoppable.

“You staying another night?” he asked.

Andie met his eyes.

“We’ll see.”

The water lapped gently against the cracked stones of the lakefront promenade. Gulls circled overhead, their shrill cries folding into the rush of wind off the water. Andie walked slowly along the edge, her coat drawn tight, hood up despite the clear sky. The cold didn’t bother her. It rarely did anymore.

She passed joggers, a couple holding hands, an old man feeding breadcrumbs to birds. No one looked twice at her. She moved like a shadow against the light, absorbed rather than seen.

A memory bubbled up without warning: Jacob standing outside the café, waiting for her shift to end. A simple moment. He'd laughed about something she couldn't remember. The wind had lifted her hair and he'd tucked it behind her ear. She had felt... fluttery.

She stopped walking.

The water ahead shimmered with the morning sun. It reminded her of a time when beauty had struck her, when the world had still felt like it *might* be enough.

She closed her eyes.

The image shattered.

In its place came the rough press of Jacob's fingers against her shoulder that night. His hesitation. Then his failure. The way he turned his face away when she screamed.

The lake offered no comfort. Just reflection.

She opened her eyes and looked down into the water. For a moment, the ripple of her hooded form warped into something else—something darker beneath the surface.

She stepped back.

The entity didn't speak. But she felt it—like a pulse beneath her own, waiting. Watching. Approving.

She exhaled slowly and walked away from the edge.

Across the city, inside a quiet field office built into a brownstone's basement, Damian Nash sat at a metal desk strewn with notes, sketches, and crime scene photos. The air smelled of printer ink and coffee gone cold.

An agent stepped in with a sheet of paper.

"Anonymous tip came in this morning. Name used on a local food co-op membership: Andrea L. Morris."

Nash raised an eyebrow. "Morris?"

"Signed up two weeks ago. Same building as Jacob's apartment complex."

Nash took the page and stared at it. "She's getting sloppy."

"Or confident," the agent offered.

Nash tapped the paper. "Let's pull the apartment logs. Elevator footage. Payment records. Anything connected to that name."

"You think it's her?"

"I know it is."

The agent left.

Nash leaned back in his chair and stared at the name again. The handwriting was neat. Precise. Too deliberate.

He murmured aloud, "Why would she want to be seen now?"

There was no answer. Only the quiet tick of the old wall clock, counting down toward something inevitable.

The scent hit her before she reached the door—garlic, seared onions, something simmering low and slow. Jacob's voice carried faintly through the hallway, singing off-key to a forgotten 90s song playing from his phone. The kind of domestic noise that once would have brought her warmth. Now it simply announced *location*.

She knocked, gently.

The door opened a moment later, Jacob's face lighting up—not bright with joy, but with an unspoken hope. He wore a black hoodie dusted with flour and had a wooden spoon tucked into his back pocket like a holstered weapon.

"I was hoping you'd come back."

"I said I might," she replied.

"True," he said, stepping aside to let her in. "I just didn't expect you to knock."

"I didn't want to startle you."

He gave a faint smile. "You could walk through walls and I wouldn't be surprised."

She said nothing.

Inside, the apartment looked cozier than it had the night before. A single candle flickered on the coffee table. The couch had been straightened. Plates were already set on the counter. Jacob moved back to the stove and stirred the contents of a pan.

"I made pasta," he said. "Nothing fancy. Just... a thing I used to do when I felt like someone was worth cooking for."

She approached slowly, every motion deliberate. Her eyes swept the space—noting exits, proximity of utensils, the scent of cheap wine opened and breathing beside the dishes.

"Do you miss being liked?" she asked suddenly.

He blinked. "What do you mean?"

"You were the popular one, weren't you? The guy who coasted through on charm. The guy others followed."

Jacob stirred in silence for a few seconds.

"Yeah. I miss that. But I miss *deserving* it more."

She watched him. "What do you deserve now?"

He looked up, meeting her gaze. "A clean slate. Not forgiveness. Just... understanding."

Andie's lips parted slightly. The faintest twitch. Not a smile.

"You think you've earned that?"

"I think I'm trying."

The wine was already poured. She took the glass, swirled it, then set it down untouched.

"I remember when you used to come into the café," she said. "I'd start smiling before you even got to the counter."

He looked stunned. "Really?"

"I didn't understand it then. But I used to hope you'd ask me out."

He laughed softly—sadly. "If I'd known..."

"You wouldn't have," she interrupted, voice neutral. "Because that version of me is dead."

The silence between them pressed in, tighter now, almost mournful.

Jacob stepped forward. "You're still here."

"Not for long," she replied.

The grainy footage looped again and again.

There she was—hood drawn low, steps precise, body language calm. The camera above the co-op caught her walking past the loading dock just thirty minutes before William's death. No rush. No attempt to hide. Her face only half-lit, but unmistakable to Damian Nash.

He hit pause.

There.

Not the Andrea Montgomery in the missing person's database, but the woman she had become—leaner, colder, more refined. He studied her eyes in the still frame. Even distorted by pixels and shadow, they seemed to glow.

"You left a trace," he whispered.

An agent stood beside him, expression tense. "Facial recognition confirms a match to the driver's license photo of Andrea L. Morris. Purchased a six-month food co-op membership. She's in the system now."

Nash didn't smile. He didn't blink.

"Good," he said. "Now run her recent purchases. See what she eats, when she shops. Build her rhythm. If she's anchoring herself with routine, that's a weakness."

The agent nodded and stepped out.

Nash stared a few moments longer, then added the still frame to a growing board of images and notes. His mind pieced together the puzzle not just of her kills, but of her motives, the pacing, the *pauses* between violence.

"She hesitates," he murmured to himself. "That means there's still something human in her."

But even as he said it, the doubt crept in.

Jacob lay sprawled across the bed, one arm over his eyes, the rise and fall of his chest slow and steady. An empty bowl and wine glass sat forgotten on the nightstand. A faint trace of garlic hung in the air.

Andie stood at the foot of the bed, barefoot, watching him.

She tilted her head slightly.

He slept like a man at peace—at least for now. No nightmares. No flinches. She had lulled him with memories, softened him with confessions.

And yet...

Her hands remained still at her sides, her face unreadable. She thought of the others—of William's final breath, Sean's panicked crawl, Mark's drunken rage and crucified corpse. But Jacob was none of those. He hadn't struck her. He hadn't laughed.

He'd only *looked away*.

Sometimes, that was worse.

She moved closer.

The wooden floor creaked under her step. Jacob stirred, murmuring incoherently and shifting to his side. His face fell into the pillow, vulnerable and oddly innocent.

Andie reached out... and gently touched his hair.

No feeling stirred inside her. No flicker of doubt. Just the quiet tension of waiting.

She turned away, walking to the window.

Outside, sirens wailed in the distance—unrelated, for now.

But that would change.

Behind her, Jacob slept on, unaware that judgment stood in his doorway, rehearsing the mercy of patience.

Chapter 8

Jacob's Apartment. Night.

The walls were quiet, but Jacob's thoughts weren't. He paced from the kitchen to the sofa, restless, clutching a sweating glass of water that hadn't touched his lips. The curtains were shut. The lights, dim. Every time he blinked, he saw her face—Andie Montgomery—older now, but unmistakable. The café girl. The ghost of that night.

She stood in his doorway before he could hear the knock.

Jacob froze.

She stepped inside without permission, not in anger, not in haste. Just a soft, chilling presence like the cold wind after the sun dies.

"Andie—"

"No," she cut in quietly. "Don't say my name like you have the right."

He looked away, swallowing hard.

She stepped closer, letting the silence burn.

"You remember the night. Don't pretend you don't."

His lips parted. "I didn't... I didn't do it like the others did. I swear to God—"

"I was there, Jacob," she said, emotionless. "I saw you standing by the wall. Laughing. Watching. Not stopping it."

"I didn't laugh!"

Her voice dropped to a whisper. "But you didn't stop it."

Jacob collapsed into the armchair, rubbing his face. “I was scared, alright? I thought—I thought they’d turn on me too. Mark was out of control. Billy just followed him like a dog. Sean—he recorded it—”

“I know,” she said.

His eyes met hers. Wide. Pale.

“I have the video,” she added. “The texts. Even the ones you deleted. And I’m not here for revenge—not yet. I’m here for the truth.”

Jacob shook his head. “Why haven’t you killed me?”

“Because,” she said, taking a seat across from him, “I want you to understand what you really are. Not just what you did—but what it made you.”

He trembled. “I don’t know who I am anymore.”

“You’re a coward,” she replied. “And cowards don’t get to die easy. They get to live long enough to feel everything they buried.”

He started to cry then—deep, ugly sobs.

She let him.

When he could speak again, he looked up at her through wet eyes. “What do you want me to do?”

“Confess. Name them. Turn in the video. Admit it all to the police. The judge. Your parents. The world.”

“And then?”

“Then I leave you alone. You get to rot behind bars instead of bleeding in a gutter.”

Jacob hesitated. “I’ll do it.”

"You will."

She stood and walked toward the door. Before leaving, she turned back.

"Jacob..."

He looked up, broken.

"You're the only one who'll get a second chance."

She was gone before he could respond.

County Courthouse – Holding Room

Jacob sat in a gray jumpsuit under fluorescent lights that buzzed like wasps in his ears. His hands were cuffed. A public defender sat across from him, eyes darting between a notepad and the file folder containing the flash drive he had submitted.

"You understand what's on here is damning," the attorney said. "Full admission. Names. A recording you took of the event. You didn't just witness the crime—you were complicit by omission."

"I know," Jacob said softly.

The attorney sighed. "The prosecution is likely to push for ten to fifteen years minimum. Sexual assault cases with video evidence and a confession don't get leniency."

"I'm not asking for leniency," Jacob murmured. "I'm asking for peace."

The attorney blinked. "What do you mean?"

"I can't live with it anymore," Jacob replied. "Not after seeing her again. Not after what we did."

He leaned forward, voice cracking. “She could’ve killed me. And I would’ve deserved it.”

Location: News Broadcast – Local Evening Segment

The story broke wide within forty-eight hours.

“Former High School Student Confesses to Role in Shocking Sexual Assault Case”

Anchorwoman’s voice: “Authorities have confirmed that Jacob Reid, 22, has confessed to withholding evidence and being present during the 2019 assault of then-teenager Andrea Montgomery. The case, thought closed due to lack of cooperation and no available footage, is now being reopened following Reid’s confession and the release of a damning video.”

Clips roll: A pixelated silhouette of Jacob. Courtroom sketch. Protesters holding signs. Social media reaction.

#JusticeForAndrea trends within hours.

FBI Regional Office – Agent Nash’s Desk

Special Agent Damian Nash leaned back in his chair, fingers steepled, as he played the confession video again.

He studied the broken boy on screen. His tone. His words. His guilt.

“Why now?” Nash muttered.

Another agent dropped a file on his desk. “We’ve got a match on the other names—two out of three still in state. One’s enrolled at Eastlake University. The other never left town.”

"And Andrea Montgomery?" Nash asked.

The agent shook his head. "Still presumed missing. But now we know she's not dead."

Nash's jaw tensed. "No. She's something else now."

He clicked back through the drive. Paused on a blurry frame—shadow in the background. A woman watching. Silent. Still.

Not a ghost.

A reckoning.

Jacob's Jail Cell – Late Night

Jacob lay on his cot, staring at the ceiling. His eyes were bloodshot. His lips trembled silently with unspoken words.

He hadn't seen her since that night. But he felt her.

Every shadow in the corner. Every gust of wind through the tiny window. Every dream turned nightmare.

Andie.

She hadn't killed him.

But he'd never be free of her.

Somewhere Else – Andie's Reflection

Andie stood in a motel bathroom, watching herself in the mirror. Her face calm. Still. Her eyes darker than they used to be.

She whispered to her reflection, "One complete."

She turned off the light.

And disappeared into the night.

Fort Polk Army Base, Louisiana – Mail Room

Sergeant Jarrod Montgomery flipped through his stack of mail with one hand, balancing a half-eaten protein bar in the other. Junk. Recruitment memos. His sister Kayan's latest wedding photos, with a note scribbled in her slanted French-English mix. Then—a plain white envelope. No return address. No stamps. Hand-delivered?

He frowned and opened it.

The letter was printed on crisp paper in block-style font. Clean. Unemotional.

To Sergeant Jarrod Montgomery,
Andrea Montgomery is dead.
She did not die of wounds that bled, or a sickness that could be named. She died the night her innocence was stolen, the night justice failed her, and the night silence made cowards of men.
There will be no funeral. No vigil. No body to bury. A symbolic grave has been arranged in Willow Grove Cemetery, under her name. That is where she lies now, and where she remains among the living no more. You may visit, but she cannot hear you.
There is no comfort in remembering the dead when you were not present to protect them.

Jarrod read it twice. Then again. His knuckles whitened. The paper shook in his hand. A sergeant passing by glanced at him, then kept walking.

Paris, France – Kayan's Apartment

The buzz of Kayan Montgomery's intercom broke the quiet morning. A courier's voice announced a special delivery.

She padded down to the lobby in her robe and accepted the envelope. Again, no stamp. Just her name written by hand: *Kayan Montgomery.*

Inside was the same letter Jarrod received. Only hers had a final line added in French:

"Il n'y a pas de retour pour les âmes mortes."
There is no return for dead souls.

She stood motionless in the hall, letter trembling in her fingers. A neighbor's dog barked distantly as the city outside carried on. Unaware. Unmoved.

She pressed the page to her chest. And sobbed.

Willow Grove Cemetery – Two Days Later

The small grave sat beneath a birch tree. The stone was simple:

Andrea Montgomery
Beloved Daughter and Sister
She lies here and remains among the living no more.

Fresh earth. No flowers. No visitors—yet.

Kayan arrived first, a black shawl wrapped tightly around her. She knelt and placed a bouquet of white lilies at the base of the stone.

Jarrod arrived hours later. In uniform. Jaw clenched. He stood in silence for what felt like an hour. Then he asked no one in particular, "Who buried my sister while I was fighting a war?"

Intercut – Two Siblings, Same Thought

In different parts of the world, brother and sister stared at the same letter. They both said it aloud to no one:

"Andrea is dead?"

But they both knew—deep down—*she wasn't*. Not really.

And whatever she had become now...
She wasn't coming back.

Willow Grove Cemetery – Early Morning

The gravel crunched under Jarrod's boots as he approached the grave again. His uniform still bore desert dust from base drills, his jawline shaded by a few days' worth of anger-fueled neglect. He crouched in front of the tombstone, staring at the name etched in quiet granite.

Andrea Montgomery.

He didn't believe it. Couldn't. There was no obituary. No death certificate. No flag-folded coffin like he'd seen too many of in the Army.

Just a grave that looked real and felt wrong.

"She wouldn't just die and have the world forget her," he muttered.

He stood, determined. Someone out there knew something. Someone buried a box. Someone mailed the letters.

And someone would answer for it.

Outside the Cemetery – Minutes Later

A black SUV waited at the edge of the gravel road. Engine idle. Tinted windows.

Jarrod spotted it immediately. Military instincts flared. He approached, cautious, hand resting on the back of his belt—not on a weapon, but ready for one.

The passenger window rolled down.

A tall, composed Black man in a dark gray suit looked back at him. His FBI badge hung from his breast pocket like a silent challenge.

"Sergeant Montgomery," the man said. "I was hoping we'd meet."

Jarrod narrowed his eyes. "You been following me?"

"No," Nash said calmly. "I've been following someone else. You're just close enough to get in the way."

Jarrod stepped forward. "Who the hell are you?"

"Special Agent Damian Nash. FBI—Violent Crimes and Behavioral Analysis Unit. I'm investigating a series of incidents connected to a cold case you're already familiar with."

He handed Jarrod a document—a sealed copy of Jacob Reid's confession, the video summary, the case number. Jarrod scanned it quickly. His mouth hardened.

"That bastard," he said. "They all walked free back then. Now one confesses? What changed?"

"She came back," Nash answered.

Jarrod looked up, heart punching his ribs. "Andrea?"

Nash nodded once. "Not the Andrea you knew. Someone else. Someone... remade."

Jarrod's fists clenched. "If she's alive, why the letter? Why the grave?"

“Because the Andrea Montgomery you remember is dead,” Nash replied. “Whatever’s walking around now isn’t asking for help. She’s delivering justice.”

Jarrod’s military mind clicked into place. “So what—you’re hunting her?”

“I’m trying to stop a spree before it escalates. She’s already left a trail. Reid is just the first.”

Jarrod leaned in, voice low. “If she’s alive, I’m not going to stand by. She’s my sister.”

Nash didn’t blink. “Then don’t get her killed. Or worse—make her kill you.”

The silence between them was cold and thick.

“You’re angry,” Nash added. “I get that. But whatever road she’s on—it doesn’t lead home.”

Jarrod stared at the grave again, then back at Nash.

“Maybe not,” he said. “But I’m still walking it.”

Nash put the SUV in gear.

“Then keep your eyes open, Sergeant. You may not like who you find at the end.”

He drove off, gravel spitting beneath the tires.

Andie sat alone on a worn bench beneath a canopy of skeletal trees, their bare limbs clattering gently in the wind like bones brushing together. The sky above was overcast, a pale sheet of gray that matched the silence of the park. A rusted swing creaked back and forth nearby, moved not by children but by the discontented breeze that stirred the dead leaves at her boots.

She held a folded newspaper in her lap, picked up from a corner box two towns back. The headline was nothing new. *“Local Girl Claims Assault—DA Declines to Prosecute.”* Below it, another: *“Repeat Offender Released Early, Attacks Again.”* And a third: *“Family Mourns Daughter After Lenient Sentencing.”*

She flipped pages with a slow, deliberate rhythm. Each article spilled its ink like fresh wounds—details of unpunished cruelty, of systems that failed the vulnerable, of monsters smiling as they walked free. Victims who looked like her. Girls with trembling voices, bruised spirits, and nowhere to turn.

Her grip on the paper tightened.

She read about a woman stalked by her ex for months. Police ignored the warnings. She was found in pieces.
She read about a judge who dismissed a case because the victim "wasn’t dressed appropriately."
She read about a fifteen-year-old boy who filmed an attack—smiled in court—and got six months’ probation.

Her breathing changed. Slower. Deeper. Like the sound of an oncoming storm.

Her eyes locked on the final column. A mother begging for justice after her daughter vanished without a trace. The only evidence: a bloodstained notebook and a whisper in the town that "she had it coming."

Andie didn’t blink.

The paper in her hands trembled. Then curled.

The temperature around her dropped. A frost formed at the edges of the bench, drawing thin crystalline webs like veins. The newspaper began to blacken, its corners glowing faint orange as if gripped by an invisible ember. Flame slithered outward from the center, tracing the inked names of the guilty—marking them.

The pages ignited, not fast but deliberate, consuming each article one at a time as if judging them word by word.

Andie did not move. She watched it burn, her face expressionless. Her pupils narrowed into pinpricks. The whites of her eyes seemed to dim, while from within them, a subtle light stirred—deep gold at first, then red around the rim like a smoldering coal.

When the last of the flame reached her fingertips, it licked upward toward her palms. Her skin did not blister. She felt nothing.

The newspaper turned to ash and scattered on the wind like black snow.

She closed her hands slowly.

Her jaw clenched once.

And then she stood.

Andie Montgomery no longer carried grief.

No longer bore the name of a victim.

What rose from that park bench was something reborn in fury, baptized in silence, and armored in every scar the world forgot.

Her eyes glowed faintly as she walked away, vanishing into the gray horizon.

Retribution... had a pulse again.

EPILOGUE

Time: Unknown. Place: Everywhere and nowhere.

They say revenge is a fire—that it consumes the vessel before it scorches the enemy.
But they were wrong.
It didn't consume Andie.
It reshaped her.

Andrea Montgomery, once a shy girl with too much heart and too little voice, was no more.
She died in a forgotten hospital room, crying in silence. She died on the courtroom steps, unheard.
She died the night her soul screamed and no one answered.

What walks now is not Andrea.
What walks now is the echo of every girl who was told, *"It's your fault."*
The consequence of every smirk in a courtroom, every predator protected by money, by silence, by law.
She walks unseen by the innocent, but known by the guilty.
The hunted.
The ones who laugh at the pain they cause.

She doesn't come with sirens.
She doesn't knock on doors.

She waits until you think you're safe—
Until you think she never existed.
And then she shows you she was there all along.

A shadow behind the curtain.
A whisper in the vent.
A cold breath on your neck in a locked room.

They never find a murder weapon.
They never find fingerprints.
Only one thing is ever left behind:

A mark.
A scar.
A name.
Burned into the wall.
Written in ash, or blood, or bone:

"I remember."

And so does she.

ACKNOWLEDGMENTS

This story would not exist without the voices that helped shape it.

To the survivors, advocates, and tireless allies: thank you for your courage and truth. To the readers who demand accountability and empathy from the stories they embrace—your hunger for justice fuels fiction with purpose.

Special thanks to Mentors, Editors, Beta Readers, and Family for unwavering support, fierce feedback, and belief in dark stories told honestly.

Special thanks to **Victoria 'Tori' Shropshire** who helped birthed Andie and to **James 'The Flash' Phillips** who christened her. When we worked those long nights, you two, I was listening.

And to those silenced by trauma—your silence echoes. May this story carry it forward.

GLOSSARY

Andrea (Andie) Montgomery – The protagonist; a once-victim turned agent of supernatural vengeance.

Charon – A mysterious, otherworldly entity that merges with Andie, enabling her transformation.

Agent Damian Nash – FBI profiler pursuing the truth behind a series of killings connected to Andie.

Jacob Reid – A former classmate who stood by during Andie's assault. His arc turns on guilt and confession.

Jarrod Montgomery – Andie's older brother, active-duty Army Sergeant.

Kayan Montgomery – Andie's older sister, a professional living in France.

Willow Grove Cemetery – The symbolic burial site of "Andrea Montgomery," marking Andie's rebirth.

REFERENCES & RESOURCES

While *Angry Andie: Spoils of Vengeance* is a work of fiction, it is rooted in real and difficult truths about trauma, abuse, and the justice system. The following resources offer help, information, and deeper insight for survivors, families, and anyone seeking to understand or combat sexual violence and its aftermath.

Support for Survivors of Sexual Assault

- RAINN (Rape, Abuse & Incest National Network)
  24/7 Confidential Hotline: 1-800-656-HOPE (4673)
  Website: ***https://www.rainn.org***
  The largest U.S. organization supporting survivors of sexual violence. Offers crisis support, counseling resources, and legal information.

- NSVRC (National Sexual Violence Resource Center)
  Website: ***https://www.nsvrc.org***
  Resources for survivors, educators, and advocates, including research, prevention materials, and community programs.

- End Rape on Campus (EROC)
  Website: ***https://endrapeoncampus.org***
  Advocacy for students and survivors in educational institutions. Provides resources for Title IX support, reporting, and survivor empowerment.

Legal Advocacy and Justice Reform

- The Innocence Project
  Website: ***https://www.innocenceproject.org***
  While focused on wrongful convictions, their resources often

touch on the gaps in victim protection, criminal justice reform, and legal ethics.

- Victim Connect Resource Center
  Website: ***https://victimconnect.org***
  Offers a confidential helpline and access to legal, medical, and safety planning resources for victims of crime.

Understanding Trauma & Psychological Recovery

- ***The Body Keeps the Score by Dr. Bessel van der Kolk***
  Groundbreaking book on how trauma reshapes the brain and body, and the paths to healing.
- National Child Traumatic Stress Network (NCTSN)
  Website: ***https://www.nctsn.org***
  Resources for families, survivors, and professionals dealing with trauma-informed care and recovery for youth and young adults.
- Psychology Today – Find a Therapist
  Website: ***https://www.psychologytoday.com/us/therapists***
  Searchable database for licensed therapists and counselors by location and specialty.

Recommended Reading

- ***Know My Name* by Chanel Miller** – A raw and powerful memoir from the survivor in the Stanford sexual assault case.
- ***Missoula: Rape and the Justice System in a College Town by Jon Krakauer*** – A harrowing look at campus assault and legal failure.
- ***What We Talk About When We Talk About Rape* by Sohaila Abdulali** – A global, survivor-centered reflection on justice, silence, and healing.

READER'S GUIDE

Discussion Questions and Prompts

About the Guide:
This reader's guide is designed to help individuals and reading groups reflect on the themes, characters, and emotional journey within *Angry Andie: Spoils of Vengeance*. It includes discussion questions, writing prompts, and ideas for further exploration.

Discussion Questions

1. What does vengeance mean to Andie—and how does that differ from justice?
   Where do you think the line is drawn, and does Andie ever cross it?

2. How did Andie's transformation affect your perception of right and wrong?
   Did your sympathy for her increase, decrease, or shift throughout the novel?

3. Consider the role of silence in the story.
   Who stays silent, and why? How does that silence shape the outcome for each character?

4. What impact does Jacob's confession have?
   Is it enough? How does Andie's decision to spare him redefine her power?

5. How does the novel depict institutions like the police, the legal system, and the media?
   Are they portrayed as complicit, broken, or redeemable?

6. How do Andie's severed ties with Jarrod and Kayan reflect her internal state?

What does her symbolic burial of Andrea Montgomery represent?

7. Damian Nash serves as a foil to Andie.
   In what ways do they reflect opposite sides of a shared moral pursuit?

8. How did the supernatural elements (like Charon's influence) enhance or shift the story's realism?
   Do you believe the horror is more psychological or paranormal in nature?

Further Exploration

- Research restorative justice and how it's used in real-world cases of trauma and abuse.
- Read survivor memoirs (*Know My Name*, *The Unspeakable*) and compare their tone to Andie's fictional journey.
- Discuss the portrayal of trauma in media—how does *Angry Andie* align with or differ from typical revenge narratives?

A Note to Readers;

If ***Angry Andie*** resonated with you emotionally or personally, please know you are not alone. Your story matters. Your voice matters. Whether you're a survivor, an ally, or a seeker of truth—there is power in facing the dark and choosing to speak.--------- ***Megaverse City.***

ABOUT THE AUTHOR

E.S. Bennett is a novelist, screenwriter, and creator of bold, genre-blending fiction. Known for weaving real-world trauma into mythic, cinematic narratives, Bennett's stories often place emotionally complex characters against sprawling backdrops of corruption, justice, and transformation. With a focus on trauma, justice, and mythic transformation, Bennett crafts stories that disturb, resonate, and challenge the limits of morality.

E.S. Bennett writes stories for the forgotten, the silenced, and the defiant. Whether exploring courtroom chaos, mythological epics, or psychological horror, Mr. Bennett believes in building characters who wrestle with truth and transformation. ***Angry Andie*** is their rawest work yet—a book born from darkness, but lit with the flame of reckoning.

When not writing, Mr. Bennett can be found developing projects across genres—from fantasy to horror to courtroom drama—each grounded in deeply human truths.

To learn more or explore other works, visit:
www,TheMegaverseCity.com

Andie will Be Back.